# SIX YEARS OF ABSENCE

## An Endless Confinement

# SIX YEARS OF ABSENCE

*An Endless Confinement*

**A novel inspired by true events**

**Alain Rolland**

For permission requests, contact the author at
www.alain-rolland.com

First Edition 2024

ISBN 979-8-9906010-1-7 (Paperback)
ISBN 979-8-9906010-0-0 (eBook)
Library of Congress Control Number: 2024908596

Cover by Fiverr Cover Designer
Published by Alain Rolland
San Diego, CA 92131

Visit the author's website at www.alain-rolland.com

*For Olivia, Devyn, Julian and Penelope*

# Acknowledgments

First and foremost, thank you to my wife, Corine, who supported me during the writing of my first fictional novel and provided constructive criticism of the early drafts. This historical novel would have not come to life without her encouragement.

My sincere thanks to Marguerite Rolland, who improved several sections of the book with interesting ideas; Nathalie Debry, who proofread the French version; Christophe Rouault, who checked the accuracy of historical facts; and all the readers of the French version published at Éditions Spinelle, Paris.

To Benjamin Rolland, thanks for showing an interest in your grandfather's odyssey and for your help in editing the English version.

A special mention to Alan Engbring for his masterful proofreading of the manuscript and his attention to details.

To my dad, Alexandre Rolland, for succinctly committing his journey through World War II to a few pages that inspired me to write this novel that is true to the dates and locations of his adventures. May the sacrifices of those brave men and women to save an ideal, a threatened freedom, without worrying about their own wellbeing, stay in the collective memory and serve as an example for future generations.

# Alexandre's Odyssey

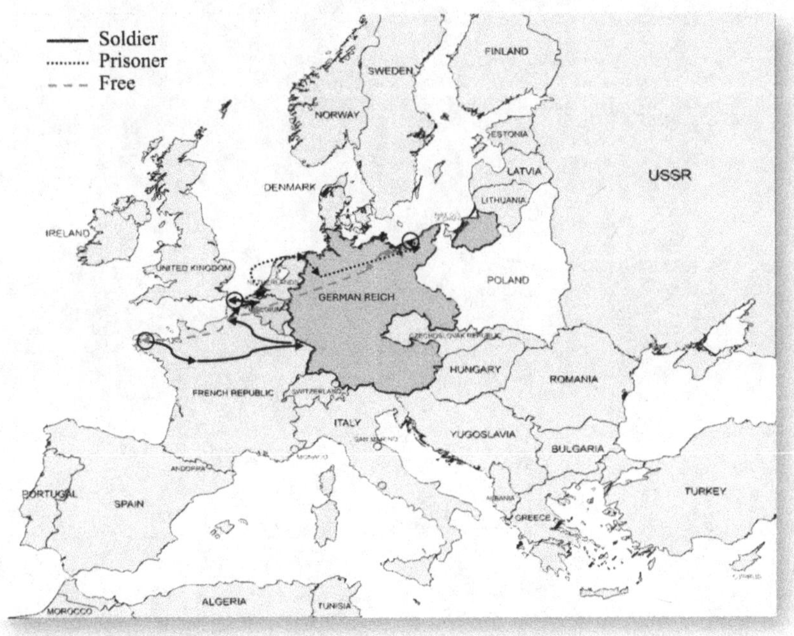

# "Soldier"

*The war! It is too serious to entrust it to the military.*
Georges Clémenceau (1841-1929)

*We don't make war: war makes us.*
Jean-Paul Sartre (1905-1980)

# Chapter 1

## *From Arrival to Departure*

The day was barely breaking when I got on my Mercier bike that day in May 1939 to go to work in a bluish morning mist. Like every day, I was going to the carpentry workshop where, with my brother François, we built wooden doors, windows, cupboards, and stairs. I loved so much to breathe in the intense smell of sawdust, to hear the harmonious purring of saws, and to see the result of our labor which would then furnish many homes in the four corners of Brittany.

But today would not be a day like any other.

Around eleven o'clock in the morning, one of our neighbors arrived, panting, in the warehouse, "Alexandre, come quickly, your wife broke her water! We have asked for the doctor."

I grabbed my cap and my jacket and, faster than Gino Bartali who had won the *Tour de France* the past year, I rode down an alley lined with poplars which seemed to bow in my path as if to encourage me. As I pedaled harder, I thought about how lucky I was to have married Gabrielle two years earlier when I was turning twenty-seven.

Arrived home, I climbed the stairs four by four and discovered a major commotion: Doctor Jaouen, the village doctor, a short and plump *bon vivant* was in our bedroom, sleeves rolled up, small round glasses perched on the tip of his nose; he was as frantic as a toreador before entering the arena, ready for the deliverance. A neighbor had volunteered to play the role of the nurse, although her only qualification in the medical field was limited to distinguishing between the cod liver oil she used for her osteoporosis and a good sip of absinthe, which she abused regularly! Dressed in the same blue and white checkered apron that she wore year-round, she was constantly walking back and forth between the kitchen and the bedroom to bring clean hot towels and basins filled with boiled water.

The minutes passed slowly, long, so long, interminable ...

The hours elapsed sluggishly, heavy, so heavy, unbearable ...

All of a sudden, while I was pacing in the hallway, cries of a newborn resounded throughout the household, louder than the sound of bombard on Saint John's Eve!

I rushed into the bedroom and hugged my exhausted but smiling wife, Gabrielle. After being congratulated by Gabrielle's stepmother who had meanwhile joined the neighbor assisting Dr. Jaouen – and now deserved as many sips of a tonic pick-me-up as she wanted – I took in my arms my baby boy whom we had already agreed to name Jean-Pierre. I looked tenderly at this miniature being, his face lit by the glow of this new world he had finally discovered. Reassured, snuggled against me, he slowly fell asleep, and I savored this magical moment of happiness while addressing a fulfilled smile at Gabrielle.

Jean-Pierre was welcomed to the world by a select committee but far more excited than the crowd at the election of the President of the 3$^{rd}$ Republic, Albert Lebrun, seven years earlier following the assassination of President Doumer, or even after his recent re-election a few months earlier.

Spring gave way to summer.

I took advantage of the two weeks of paid vacation, officialized three years earlier, by spending precious and memorable family time with Gabrielle and Jean-Pierre.

We spent happy moments in our garden, stretched out on the lawn strewn with daisies, rocked by the songs of the nightingale and the wagtail, while cuddling our newborn baby nestled between us for his nap. Sometimes, with our grey Simca 8, we took the road to spend the day at the sea. It felt like going on an adventure, exploring the depths of an unknown land that we rediscovered time and time again. On high tide days, I let Jean-Pierre and my wife doze off under our parasol extolling the merits of the *Perrier de la source* – the champagne of table water – and I went fishing for rock, spider, and velvet crabs, as well as periwinkles. Sometimes, I was lucky enough to even harvest a few flat oysters which we feasted on that very evening at home.

The days drifted like clouds in the wind.

We were happy!

Summer passed very quickly. Our baby was growing day by day, smiling and stammering always more, awakening to the world, carefree.

But on Friday, August 25, 1939, our life was once again going to be turned upside down.

In the kitchen, Jean-Pierre was hanging on his mother's breast, like a barnacle firmly anchored to its granite rock. During the feeding time, Gabrielle listened to the *Radio-Journal de Paris PTT*, the state radio station that, since the end of July, was now directly controlled by the President of the Council, Édouard Dalladier. A year earlier, the same Dalladier had been the first to sign the Munich Pact, thus encouraging the conquest of the world initiated by Nazi Germany.

I was in the garden trimming the hedges with a pair of shears worthy of the antiques from our cousin Arthur's second-hand store when Ernest, the postman, arrived on his bicycle, his cap askew as usual, a Gauloise butt at the corner of his lips.

"*Bonjour* Alexandre, here is your mail. How are your wife and the little one?"

"They are both fine, Ernest, and it's time for the baby's feed."

"Well, me too, I'd like to have a nip, because it is such a hot day, *vingt-dieux!* I can't wait for autumn to come!"

"We were at the beach yesterday and the heat was much more bearable. But today, what a heat wave! I am trying to put the garden in order because I am unfortunately going back to work on Monday after a vacation that was far too short."

Ernest slowly wiped his sweaty brow with the back of his sleeve and asked me, lowering his voice, "Did you read the newspaper? Our commies have approved this damned German-Soviet Pact. Are they nuts? They don't even realize that with the partial mobilization we are fast approaching war. *Vingt-dieux!* I was at the Chemin des Dames in 1914 and it was not a pretty sight. That damned mustard gas was suffocating us! Now I keep having a bad cough," said Ernest, religiously relighting his cigarette.

"Thanks, Ernest, for the mail. I have to go because I must join Gaby who surely needs my help. *Kenavo.*"

I went back inside and meticulously stored my gardening tools in the cellar, near the washtub and the hand wringer. I told myself that one day we should concrete the dirt floor. After removing my wooden garden clogs, I went upstairs in my slippers, observing the elegant curves of the wooden staircase that my brother François had built with his hands and, after freshening up, I entered the kitchen. Jean-Pierre painstakingly raised an eyelid but, full of milk, immediately fell back asleep in my wife's arms.

"I heard the mailman," Gabrielle said to me. "Is there any interesting mail?"

"Ah, I forgot it downstairs on the washtub. I'll be right back."

A few minutes later, I came back up, sweat dripping down my clammy forehead.

"You're all out of breath and dripping with sweat. You should get some rest from the heat before you go back to work next week," she instructed me, with a sulky pout of slight annoyance.

Surprised that I wasn't answering her but instead kept staring at the mail in my shaking hands, Gabrielle asked me, "You don't look quite yourself, maybe you got heat stroke? I prepared a large glass of chilled grenadine for you."

As I still kept silent, stunned by the cursed mail sitting in the hollow of my callused hands, she added, "Do you hear me, Alexandre? What is going on?"

Like an automaton at the Foire du Trône, I walked up to her mechanically and handed her a beige card, without an envelope. She took it, read it intensely and stammered, "No, not you, this can't be happening. Not with a newly born son."

She handed me back this piece of paper that would change our lives for so many years to come. A simple missive, with my name elegantly written in cursive with a fountain pen.

An enlistment order in the French Army!

I had to join without any delay the garrison of 6th Engineer Regiment in Angers.

That same day, thousands of kilometers from our home, a non-aggression pact was being signed between Germany and the USSR in Moscow, by the German Foreign Minister, Joachim von Ribbentrop, and that of Russia, Viatcheslav Molotov, in the presence of Stalin. The path to the conquest of Western Europe was now wide open for the German Chancellor, Adolf Hitler, an artist at heart who unfortunately had decided rather to join a military career in The Great War – where he was ironically decorated with the Iron Cross on the recommendations of his Jewish lieutenant! He had then turned towards politics by integrating the *Nationalsozialistische Deutsche Arbeiterpartei* – the National Socialist Party of German Workers or the Nazi Party – for which he proposed a symbol that would become infamous until the end of time: a swastika – a black bent cross, in a white circle on a red background.

After receiving this cursed card, the next day was extremely gloomy. We spent time visiting my brother, some of our relatives, and our best friends before my departure for the unknown. Sadness and fear were clearly visible on all the tense and somber faces. These visits were a brief escape, attempting to forget that the shadow of war was slowly looming upon us.

On Sunday, August 27, 1939, after a long sleepless night, constantly turning over in our bed, I got up and quietly left the bedroom where Gabrielle and Jean-Pierre were both still sound asleep. From the house, I went for a walk in the garden. I thought back about those last few months of happiness and insouciance, enjoying each day the wonder of starting a family. I wondered how many days, maybe months, I might be away from them, without receiving or giving any news. My heart sank at the thought that I may never return from this war.

The specter of war was already hovering dangerously all over Europe.

I tried to convince myself that a war would probably be short-lived and that I would rapidly be back, safe and sound. I closed my eyes and breathed in the mixed fragrances of damp earth, multi-colored roses, and bluish irises that Gabrielle so loved to brighten up our table. I anchored deep in my memory those earthy scents. Who would take care of my vegetable garden? Who would trim the hedges, remove the weeds, prune our sparse fruit trees, and take care of the few rabbits residing in our hutches? All these questions swirled in my head, and I had the sensation that the earth was wavering under my wooden clogs. How could one part me from my wife and my newborn baby? I thought of all those bureaucrats, snug in their cozy beds or perhaps already putting on their Sunday best, oblivious to the effect of their decisions, but who certainly would never hold a rifle, except to go hunting game in full safety in the fall.

At least, with the help of my brother François, who had been declared unfit for service due to heart problems, there would be someone to harvest the potatoes, salads, carrots, turnips, and cabbages that would help feed my family during the long months to come.

The garden was calm, silent, nature holding its breath as if to accompany me in my departure and my dismay.

I had to be strong, hide my pain, and enjoy these last hours with my family.

I went back inside. In the meantime, Gabrielle had woken up and was waiting for me in the kitchen.

"I made you a *café au lait* with three sugars and I toasted a few slices of bread for you. The good Lord will not hold it against you for this one and only transgression of not fasting before Communion."

"Thank you, Gaby," I replied, kissing her tenderly on her forehead. "You're right. The good Lord seems very distracted these days to let this damned Hitler set up his invasion plans with impunity."

Then, I confided my thoughts during my walk in the garden to her.

"You know, if war does break out, it will surely be short-lived, and I will be back home before you know it. Meanwhile, François will be able to come and help you maintain the garden, and I know that our neighbors will be there for you too if you need any help with Jean-Pierre or at home. I promise to be extremely careful and to be back before winter."

In her emerald-blue gaze, I clearly saw the doubts she was unwillingly trying to hide. Words were becoming futile in the face of such an uncertain future.

After breakfast, it was high time to get ready for mass, which the bells were already announcing vehemently. Gaby had put on her prettiest beige cotton dress and was getting Jean-Pierre ready. I put on a white linen shirt, charcoal black dress pants supported by wide suspenders attached to buttons of my pants, cachou-colored socks, and I grabbed my grey Sunday cap.

All set, we left for high Mass, crossing a large fairground where horse dealers and brokers did their business at the monthly fair with buyers from all over Europe. It is true that the Breton horse was somewhat the second religion of our village of Landivisiau: a proud and robust horse, ready to defy bad weather and hard work. The Champ de Foire was a fairground surrounded without interruption by multiple bistros and bars, where various transactions were concluded around a Chartreuse, a Pastis or other alcoholic plant extracts which, without a doubt, helped tremendously in finalizing the deals. In this year 1939, nearly eighteen thousand horses would be dispatched by cattle wagons from the village train station, the same station where this very afternoon I would sadly have to say goodbye to my family.

We walked down the Pasteur Avenue, an unpretentious street, but nevertheless the main street of the village, lined with various shops. The crowd was already streaming towards the church, a flow of blood cells converging rapidly and continuously towards a beating heart, the vital center of the bourg.

We took our place in the front rows, arriving as usual at least a quarter of an hour early. Jean-Pierre was dozing, and the crowd continued to gather in the pews while the glorious organ was already starting a rhythmic hymn.

Mass began at last.

The parish priest, Louis Favé, in his immaculate cassock, officiated today, flanked by two altar boys in lace cassocks. The mass proceeded peacefully, but a heavy anguish hovered in the glances and the tremolos intoning in Breton, *"Me Zo Ganet E Kreiz Ar Mor."* I would soon be far away from this land in the middle of the sea where I was born almost thirty years ago. At Communion, although having made an exceptional transgression at breakfast by not fasting, I nevertheless accepted the Host that Father Favé placed on the tip of my tongue, while watching me with a profound sadness. Indeed, the cleric was a regular at Gaby's delicious meals; he also frequently stopped at home to get some coffee and ask for news of the family. His furtive but emotionally charged gaze clearly revealed his feelings.

At the end of the mass, many were those who had teary eyes. A cloud of pain and anguish enveloped the crowd which could not disperse, as if this congregation formed a single organism, less vulnerable, more reassuring, almost invincible. Many of us would unfortunately find ourselves in a few hours on a train that would take us to the unknown.

On our way home, we stopped at the pastry shop to buy a *Kouign Amann*. Lunch was eerily silent and gloomy, interrupted only by the prattles of Jean-Pierre, who was far from understanding what was happening. After devouring the *Kouign Amann* accompanied by a *café au lait*, I hastily prepared a bag with my personal belongings. I then joined Gaby for a short nap in our bedroom where Jean-Pierre had already fallen asleep in his wooden cradle.

"Promise me to come back soon, safe and sound," Gaby said, tearfully.

"Don't worry. I won't take any chances and will be back very soon. The German troops are still far away; they will never dare to invade France and risk confronting us and the Brits. They learned their lesson thirty years ago. Don't worry. I will think of you every day and I have already put in my wallet a photo of you two, taken in the garden."

Gabrielle was looking at me with teary eyes, filled with worry.

"Don't be reckless. I'll be thinking of you too, all the time."

As soon as Jean-Pierre woke up I got ready and, shortly thereafter, François arrived at the wheel of his black Citroën Traction Avant to accompany us to the train station. When we arrived at the station, there was already a large gathering, some couples kissing tenderly, others trying to anchor in their memory a look, a face, the curves of a body, a perfume.

We then went to the only platform where I took Jean-Pierre in my arms, kissing and promising him to be back as soon as possible. After handing him to François, I hugged Gabrielle and our embrace seemed to last forever. I felt her heart race against mine and I breathed her whole being. I prayed that this moment would become eternal and that I would wake up realizing that it had all been only a bad dream. But already we could hear in the distance the shrill whistle of a train approaching from the west. I kissed Gabrielle passionately, promising her one last time to get back before long, and I got on the train. I found a seat by one of the windows, dropped my bag in the overhead luggage net and, as the train started to move off, I blew Gabrielle and Jean-Pierre an ultimate kiss. With a heavy heart, I saw her wet gaze slowly fade away. It became a tearful face, then a crumbling silhouette that finally disappeared from my line of sight.

The train, crowded with men having been ordered to join their regiments, was carrying us towards our destiny; we feared that war was imminent. The mechanical hum of the train barely covered the muffled sobs and sniffles of those men torn from their families, separated from their daily lives, and suddenly slashed from their origins.

It was with great sorrow that I left my wife and my three-month-old son.

# Chapter 2

## *From Preparation to Declaration*

The hours spent in this crowded train, which progressively took us away from our civilian lives, had gradually increased our anxiety and sorrow. The train entered the station in Angers around seven o'clock on Sunday evening. The faces were grave and worried amongst the small groups already forming on the platform between friends and acquaintances. Before going to the barracks, our group of seven friends unanimously decided that a good meal would undoubtedly help us make the big jump to our new military life.

Among us was Théodore, a somewhat simple-minded hostler ironically with an equine profile; Émile, a tenor who led our local choir; Jean, an erudite joker who worked in a hardware store and could play billiards with one eye fixed on the ball while the other kept track of the score; Pierre, a shoemaker who was undoubtedly the worst shod; Alphonse, a farmer who had left behind two young children and a pregnant wife; Léon, a teacher who was extremely pessimistic because he knew too well the recurrent and tumultuous History of France; and finally Fanch, an ogre with a well-rounded belly, who was already grousing with impatience, "I'm starving. I should have packed a snack for the road. I would have given a lot on the train for a slice of country bread spread with Hénaff pâté. He had a good nose, Jean Hénaff, when he began to mass produce his pâté with pork tenderloins and ham more than twenty years ago!"

Licking his lips and sighing heavily, Fanch continued, "Now I really can't take it anymore, just thinking about it made me even hungrier. Let's quickly find a little restaurant to quench our cravings and our thirst."

"You only think about your stomach," Théo retorted, even though he was in a bad position to lecture him as his weight was approaching a hundred kilos too, "but I agree with you Fanch. Let's find a good place to dine."

Across the station, the bar restaurant Aux Bons Amis seemed to have been established there just for us and we decided without wasting any more time to head there.

"*Bonsoir*. Would you have a table for seven?" I asked the restaurant owner, a little plump man with a reddish face, showing off a mustache worthy of the one worn by the Maréchal Pétain – Henri-Philippe Benoni Omer-Joseph to his close friends – who although victorious in Verdun during The Great War was going to shame France in the months to come and end his days compunctious, in exile on the Île d'Yeu.

"You can sit down over there. I'll put these three tables end to end," the *Lion de Verdun* lookalike told us with a deference proportional to his menu prices.

The dinner was delicious. The *charcuterie*, followed by a *pot-au-feu*, and a caramel flan for dessert filled our bellies; the many bottles of inexpensive red wine aided with digestion.

Sated with this gourmet meal, after paying and thanking our host with the impressive hairiness under his nose, we headed for the barracks located near the station. After viewing our enlistment orders and our identity cards, the sentry let us pass through a large austere *porte cochère* flanked by two small symmetrical buildings. A duty officer then accompanied us to our quarters for the night, large drab dormitories where a concert of snores from comrades who had arrived earlier could already be heard. We went to the unique bathroom, where some had gathered to smoke their Gauloises Troupes, packets of twenty troops cigarettes which they had been given upon their arrival; these extolled the prestige of the uniform, representing the soldiers of the three Armed Forces smiling in profile, wearing a cap, a sailor hat, and a helmet. After refreshing ourselves summarily, we quickly went to bed with saggy and squeaking spring mattresses that dated from before the previous war. Despite the improvised and dissonant concert of rhythmic snores, jerky coughs, and whispers accompanied by the lamentation of the tortured springs, I fell asleep as soon as I rested my head on what had been designed eons ago as a pillow.

I slept straight through until dawn.

Suddenly the sound of a bugle drew us from our cloudy dreams.

After getting ready and having swallowed a cup of black coffee in record time with a few slices of semi-stale bread with butter, I joined my comrades in the large interior courtyard in front of the tricolor French flag already hoisted on its pole and standing out against the nascent dawn. At the call of our names, we formed a single line to take possession of our equipment and then join our *6ᵉ Régiment du Génie* – the 6th Engineer Regiment – which was part of the 21st Division. Our company was specialized in mining and demining missions, opening and destroying routes, as well as providing support to the stationing of troops; our objective was to help the fastest possible deployment of our armed forces and to slow down the movement of enemy forces.

In a first room, where a huge sign reminded us of our motto – Sometimes destroy, often build, always serve – I received a uniform corresponding to my sergeant's military rank, with two chevrons attached to the cuffs of my khaki brown coat, trousers of the same color with beige suspenders, a khaki shirt and a brown tie, a cap, underwear, and undershirts with a few pairs of socks and the famous puttees. These consisted of a simple ribbon of cloth, wrapped around our calves from ankle to knee, having a restraining effect on our legs. They made us look like a *Poilu* of '39! While they were easier to put on than boots – and especially to put back on after a long walk – they unfortunately got soaked through on wet ground or in the rain.

On my frock coat, the recently designed badge of my regiment had been sewn. At the top of the badge, a helmet or *Pot en Tête* surmounted an anchor rope of the pontoniers; in the center, the silhouettes of the cathedral and the castle of Angers stood out. The three names inscribed on the tower of the castle – the Marne, Verdun, and the Aisne – recalled the famous battles of The Great War where our regiment particularly distinguished itself. Finally, the number six appeared in red, like a sun rising on the horizon behind the spire of the cathedral, and the badge rested at its bottom on a golden anchor.

We each were provided with a backpack and a haversack, a shoulder bag to store all these military articles. In the next room, we each were given new boots, a helmet, a gas mask in its case, a large leather belt with cartridge pockets and small pouches, a compass, a small pair of shears, a canteen, a mess tin with utensils, and a canvas tent. I was already wondering how we were going to transport all this when in the last room our equipment was completed by a rifle with its bayonet, as heavy as it was ancient. I immediately called this rifle, the famous Lebel of The Great War, "Babel," not because of the etymology of the name meaning the Gate of Gods in Akkadian – a name predestined for our enemies – but because it appeared as gigantic and imposing as the tower of the same name. Other soldiers nicknamed it "the Fishing Rod" but, loving and respecting fishing too much, I stuck to "Babel!"

Sometime later, we set out to walk to Trélazé, a village located a few kilometers away. We had put on our carapace of soldiers and said goodbye to our civilian lives. We were stationed at a place managed by a horticulturalist named Delaunay. We stayed there for a few days, trying to get used to our equipment and keeping ourselves in good physical and mental shape. During the day, we exercised and took several marches in quick time in the nearby forests and nurseries. I tried, most often in vain, to hit with Babel a few targets placed in a nearby field. We followed some training to refresh our memory on the handling of the different types of explosives for which we were responsible, from light petards to heavy loads of melinite with different types of exploders, fuses, or detonating cords.

On September 1, 1939, the general mobilization was decreed in France for five million men and, at twenty-nine, I found myself being one of the oldest.

I already terribly missed Gabrielle and my son. When my mind drifted towards them, I imagined them in our house or in our garden, but soon a wave of sadness washed over me.

Finally, the day came when we embarked for an unknown location in wagons marked with "8 horses in length, 40 men." Our destination was secret, but we were heading east, no doubt in the direction of Germany, towards an imminent war. We crossed Rouen then Nancy, where the train stopped at the end of the afternoon. We learned from the onlookers gathered on the train platform who had come to encourage us that the war unfortunately had just been declared.

In fact, on September 3, 1939, following the example of Great Britain's ultimatum to the German authorities, the French ambassador in Berlin also issued an ultimatum asking Germany to withdraw its troops from Poland which it had invaded a few days earlier. The sinister German Minister von Ribbentrop, who had shortly before signed the non-aggression pact with the USSR, replied, "France will be the aggressor," to which the French ambassador replied, "History will be the judge!"

We continued our journey and arrived in Alsace where most of the inhabitants did not even know how to speak French. The *garde champêtre*, a rural guard with his drum slung over his shoulder, informed them of our arrival and ordered them to gather their cattle. The village schoolteacher, Miss Dummy – a cantankerous old maid with an aquiline profile outlined by enormous iron-rimmed glasses, dressed in a gray smock with frayed cuffs – translated what the *garde champêtre* had just announced after his drum roll that rivaled the loudest roar of thunder.

That evening of early September, we went to sleep in a wood, each in an individual tent. It rained all night without interruption and in the early morning, numb with cold, we took the road to station in Fénétrange. On the way, we occasionally came across lines of ox-drawn wagons, where the civilians had hastily piled up pell-mell their most useful and precious goods.

Plans had been designed several months earlier by the French General Staff to protect our borders in the event of a conflict, by mobilizing and strategically deploying the French troops. In particular, the Saarland, which had been administered by the League of Nations from 1920 to 1935 following the Treaty of Versailles signed on June 28, 1919 – the anniversary of the Sarajevo attack on the same day in 1914 which had ignited the powder and started The Great War – had reversed back to Germany following a referendum in 1935. It had then become urgent for the French General Staff to protect the border with bunkers and artificial ponds, known as the aquatic Maginot line.

When I arrived in Fénétrange, I did not know that I was part of one of these plans, named the "Saar Offensive."

# Chapter 3

## *From First Offensive to First Relief*

At the beginning of the afternoon, the captain called me because there was a simple-minded soldier among us, a man named Mornay, whom I knew, having done our military service together. He was seeing Germans everywhere! As he demoralized everyone around him and constantly put us on alert, the captain ordered me to escort him, with the bayonet on, to the command post. There, I ran into François Godec, a guy from my village, and we drank a glass of red wine together. Later, I learned that Mornay had been sent back home.

Coming back from the command post, we were ordered to assemble immediately on the Fénétrange soccer field, not to attend or participate in a match – which would certainly have calmed the tempers – but for a harangue from the colonel. Standing on a barrel employed as a dais, he proclaimed in his baritone voice, "Soldiers of the 21$^{st}$ Division, war was declared with Germany on September 3. You are here on the front line to defend our border and force the enemy to engage their troops. Our strategic goal is to attract German forces to the border to help relieve our unjustly invaded Polish comrades who are defending themselves so gloriously."

Then he added emphatically, "History will remember you as the very first fighters who bravely drove the invader out. Tonight, we will advance towards the German border. Prepare yourself and may God help you! *Vive la France!*"

Indeed, in May of the same year, France and Poland had signed an agreement which forced France to launch a general offensive within a very short time after the mobilization. Therefore, our regiment got ready and, at nightfall, we began our long march in columns towards the border. The walk was difficult, interminable in the twilight. The hours passed slowly in this cold and damp journey. Some of us were lagging behind, the weight of our gear adding to fatigue and lack of sleep.

We arrived in the morning in a border town. There were no living souls here; this ghost town only increased our apprehension. The inhabitants had fled with loaded carts and wheelbarrows, or just suitcases, leaving their homes open to looting. The streets were littered with broken glass, flying papers, and other objects reminding that the heart of the village had still been hopeful and beating calmly yesterday. I bent down to pick up a photograph in a broken frame. A smiling couple, with a curly blonde haired little girl in her Sunday dress, was staring at me. Suddenly, I felt a flood of tears rise, ready to pour out. I swallowed my sadness while thinking of my son and my wife, far away in Brittany, who did not have the slightest idea of my fate.

After a brief lunch in the deserted village square, our walk resumed towards Sarreguemines. The city was located at the confluence of the Saar and Blies rivers, and our objective was to build bridges to help our division cross the rivers and enter Germany. The stone bridges which had spanned these rivers since the dawn of time had a great deal of charm and were decorated with beautiful planters adorned with multicolored flowers. However, they were far too narrow and unstable for our division's heavy vehicles to pass.

We therefore undertook to build the first bridge over the Blies river to access Germany. It consisted of shallow hard-hulled boats, linked together by ropes anchored from a point on the shore, to support the wooden spans through which soldiers and light vehicles would pass. According to the engineering regulations of 1939, most of the works built by our sappers were made of wood.

True to our motto, as soon as the bridge was completed, we stuffed it with explosive charges and incendiary substances to ensure its rapid destruction in the event of a German intrusion.

As we were finishing this first floating bridge, a roar suddenly arose above our heads. Raising my eyes to the heavens, I saw fighter planes chasing each other in an incessant dance, bursting the sky with their jerky gunfire. One of my comrades, a so-called expert in aviation – by virtue of his qualifications, not only as an auto mechanic-in-chief in civilian life but also as a Don Juan loving to send women to the seventh heaven – commented for me this aerial ballet, "Look Alex, the plane with the black cross on a white background on its fuselage is a German Messerschmitt. It's the fastest plane in the world and, unfortunately, it's also the flagship of the German Air Force. It is so fast and so maneuverable that the two French planes chasing it may not be sufficient."

"It's my first time seeing air combat," I replied. "I've never been on a plane, but it must be so intoxicating. With all those stunts, they probably feel like they are on the chair swing ride at the carnival. You know those flying seats suspended with chains from the top of a rotating carousel which run at breakneck speed over the ground?"

"Yes, Alex, I know that ride well. I call it 'the Women's Trap' because when I go to the fair, I always take my girlfriend of the day tossing around on that ride; as she gets down from her seat, she invariably falls into my arms, dizzy and scared to death. But watch the two French fighter planes with their proud tricolor cockade. These Morane-Saulnier are supposedly coined 'best combat aircraft in the world,' but it seems to me that the Messerschmitt is far more agile. They haven't even scratched it yet."

Suddenly, thick white smoke began to emerge from one of the two pursuit planes. "Alex, one of ours has been hit. No wonder when you think that the fire controls of his machine guns quickly freeze, even at low altitudes. Attention! The Morane has just entered a death spiral. The unfortunate pilot will not have time to eject!"

I watched in awe as the plane hit the ground in a final whirlwind. A deafening crash, followed by a fireball, and a thick black cloud rising towards the sky, accompanied the flight of the soul of this unfortunate pilot.

Stunned by this unexpected and thunderous explosion, I cried out, "Poor fellow! The war will have been very short for him. The other pilot did well to give up and return to base."

This is how the first aerial combat of this war unfolded sadly before our eyes. Was this German superiority in the air a bad omen for what awaited us here on earth?

That evening, in Sarreguemines, we had some free time. We decided to go to a brewery where we quickly contributed to a temporary shortage of aperitif bottles. Unsteady and tipsy when they came out of the brewery, Théo and Fanch, arm in arm, were singing at the top of their lungs, "La Madelon vient nous servir à boire." On the way back to camp, they continued by alternating, "Comme de Bien Entendu" with "Félicie aussi." I must admit that their talents of composer-performers made us cry with laughter when they started to improvise:

> "On the road to Sarreguemines, the fields were full of
> vermin, *Félicie aussi.*
> When we left for the border, it smelled like a foul
> odor, *Félicie aussi.*
> Arriving near a bridge, it was full of German midge.
> We blew up every fugly, Boom, it was really ugly,
> *Félicie aussi!*
> We all crossed with *savoir-faire,* we showed them our
> *derrière, Félicie aussi.*

They caught the Führer all wet, he smelled strongly
   of bad sweat, *Félicie aussi.*
We locked him in a big cage, so that all unleash their
   rage,
Adolf lashed in furor, releasing putrid vapor, *Félicie
aussi!*
We sent him to inferno, Lucifer told him hello,
   *Félicie aussi.*
We are the best Engineers, but our song is cavalier,
   *Félicie aussi!"*

There were many that evening who tried to forget for a moment their sadness and their fear of the next day.

In Sarreguemines, we received the order to stay in a border village very close to Frauenberg. From there, our mission was at nightfall, in small groups of three or four, to surreptitiously infiltrate German territory to identify the safest paths for our troops and vehicles, assess German defenses, and unearth the enemy mines. That first evening, with two comrades, we crossed a floating bridge that we had built over the Blies river, and we began our reconnaissance through the German fields and forests.

The night was dark, deep, and silent. A drizzle made this nocturnal scouting even more mysterious and frightening.

Suddenly, on the other side of an embankment, we heard whispering. A German patrol of the Wehrmacht, the army of the Third Reich, was patrolling down below on a muddy path, stopping from time to time. We watched them from our position, quietly, but it was too dark to make out what they were doing on that path. We let them pass in an easterly direction and when they were out of range, we set out to follow in their footsteps, looking for mines they might have freshly buried in the mud. We only had a rudimentary pointed iron rod that we attached at the end of a wooden stick, or sometimes we also affixed our bayonet to the end of our rifle to probe the ground while advancing step by step all three on the same line. We drove the metal point obliquely and carefully into the mud to avoid any pressure on a mine igniter that would have caused a deadly detonation.

At that time, we had no idea that it would take until the end of the war and the armistice for the delivery of the first French mine detection devices!

After a few minutes of dramatic intensity, Jean abruptly stopped and whispered, "I can feel something under my stick, and it feels metallic. Stand back while I clear the mud around with my hands."

"Be very careful Jean. Take it easy," I said, stepping back with our other comrade Léon, worried about Jean's dexterity because of his pronounced squint.

"Don't worry Alex. I'll take it very carefully. Can you shine your light on my hands?"

I immediately turned on a small flashlight, the pale beam diffusing in the mist and lighting up Jean's hands, which fortunately were not shaking. He began to push out the mud around where he had spotted the metallic object, gradually surrounding it, and getting closer to it. Time seemed suspended. Everything was silent, immobile. Jean seemed to be moving in slow motion, as in a scene from Marcel L'Herbier's movie "El Dorado." In a nearby chestnut tree, an owl hooted, another responding further away like an echo of sinister omen.

"I'm holding a metal part," Jean said in a low voice. Then extracting his booty, he gave a low chuckle. "All that angst for an old rusty horseshoe! I had to be careful, but all those precautions for a piece of junk! At least I hope it will bring us some luck."

We regrouped to continue exploring the muddy path side by side, unsure if and where the Germans might have buried murderous mines. These could possibly be anti-personnel mines, explosive charges placed in a way to be triggered unintentionally as our soldiers stepped on them, or anti-tank mines which would explode as our armored vehicles drove on them.

The Germans had developed the S mine, *Schrapnellmine*, a bouncing bomb, which projected the charge more than a meter above ground, ensuring an efficient and terrible dispersion of incandescent or shrapnel projectiles. Later Americans would nickname it "Bouncing Betty" and we would simply call it *"Piège à cons."* These haphazardly scattered mines would severely thwart the advances of our troops into German territory.

After taking a few steps, Jean stopped suddenly and whispered, "There is another metallic object under my stick. It's my lucky day! I hope this time I won't scare myself for nothing."

Kneeling, once again freeing the object from the mud with his bare hands, while Léon the teacher and I took our distances, Jean exclaimed, "I hit the jackpot, it's a *Tellermine*, an anti-tank mine. These anti-tank mines are much larger and heavier than jumping anti-personnel mines, but it takes a considerable weight to activate them. Here's one that won't detonate at the passage of one of our armored vehicles, even though it might have only damaged the wheels or the tracks."

The circular metal mine cleared from the ground, Jean observed its Machiavellian mechanism, with a central igniter which, if subjected to a strong pressure under the weight of a vehicle, would trigger a detonator which would explode the formidable charge.

"If we are extremely careful and avoid any pressure on the igniter, I think we can safely bring it back to camp. Our gunners will be amazed, and it might be very useful for them to practice defusing them and to improve our own mines."

It is true that our French engineers had waited until 1936 to develop an anti-vehicle mine of such weak power that it only had an impact on cars or trucks, but it could in no way stop the German tanks. After having indicated roughly on a map the path which seemed to have been mined by the German patrol, I took the precious deadly mine in my hands like a holy relic; sweating profusely, I carried it for a few kilometers to our camp, step by step, ceremoniously as at the penitential procession for Notre-Dame du Folgoët.

At daybreak, our find fueled conversations and a large crowd formed around us. We had heard of these types of German mines, but we had not seen any of them yet, due to the lack of practical training or even theory lessons on these new lethal weapons. Unfortunately, the "Infantry Officer Manual" was as silent as a grave on this subject.

Our captain went to fetch an artilleryman, a specialist in explosives. A gargantuan bald fellow, all in muscles, his sleeves rolled up, arrived shortly thereafter. He ordered us to move away, as far as possible, and leave him alone with our booty. Alone in the middle of our circle, like a druid with his offering at the heart of Stonehenge, we saw him kneel and make the sign of the cross. I wondered if God was really going to be able to guide his hands to neutralize the mechanism of the active mine.

To my surprise, I then saw him take a few tools and a piece of string from his bag. He began by securing the detonator with the string, then with infinitely slow movements, he removed the upper central part, the igniter, on which I had had to avoid any pressure. Suddenly, with a brisk gesture, he threw the lighter towards us. The circle burst into a terrible hubbub as we all took to our heels. The Hercules burst into a cavernous laugh, declaiming, "Come back! You are a bunch of cowards! There is no longer any danger. I've defused that damned mine and I'm going to take it back to my artillery regiment where we will dissect it religiously."

I later learned that the detailed examination of our find had enabled it to be copied quickly by our engineers, thus producing a more efficient French anti-tank mine and at the same time giving back to Adolf what belonged to Adolf!

As we dispersed, a motorized patrol appeared. It had been on reconnaissance during the night beyond the border and, unfortunately, one of the cars had exploded on one of the treacherous mines, killing four people and leaving one, who came from a village in Brittany that I knew well, with very serious injuries.

On that day, our regiment redoubled its efforts to enable our troops and tanks to reach Germany quickly and in force. We began the construction of a Model 35 bridge on the Blies river, consisting of crafts made of aluminum and copper alloy – an alloy ironically invented by a German metallurgist at the turn of the century. The bridge also utilized metal spans, as a bridge made of boats was too fragile and unstable to support vehicles which weighed several tons.

By the end of the day, the bridge was almost complete. Exhausted, we rested briefly for a few hours before setting out again, in small groups, to infiltrate Germany and continue identifying the safest passages through the woods. With Jean and Léon, we crossed another bridge that we had built on rafts anchored in the river and began our march for a few kilometers in the dark through an ominous forest. We were looking for unobstructed tracks, testing the ground at random for the possible presence of mines, then marking the clear path on our topographic map. We had walked safely for over an hour when, a little lower down a wooded slope where Léon had drifted away from us, he stepped on a mine and screamed his last word: "Mine!"

Immediately, Jean and I threw ourselves prone, face down on the ground. Before Léon had time to react to the terrifying click of the igniter, the charge exploded, throwing at random a multitude of metallic balls and various fragments. As Jean and I were higher up the slope from Léon and had dropped to the ground, luck was with us; the explosion spared us. Unfortunately, Léon had both legs torn off and died before we had time to get to him.

The History he so loved to teach would not remember his name, which would simply adorn one of the many war memorials in a public square at the end of the war.

At that moment, even though our efforts might have been essential to the advancement of our army into enemy territory, I realized with increasing dread the risks that we were taking, especially with no mine detectors available. Retracing our way through the woods, enveloped by the coolness of the night and our growing fear, we rushed back to the camp carrying our fellow teacher Léon's shredded and bloody body.

The next day, after paying a brief tribute to Léon, we completed the

Model 35 bridge which would allow a powerful penetration into Germany. Our 21$^{st}$ Infantry Division, supported by a battalion of battle tanks, then prepared to cross the Blies river to deploy the conflict into German territory. At dawn, as a thick fog blanketed the surrounding countryside, our division's infantrymen began to cross the bridge in organized columns, followed by Renault R35 tanks and various support vehicles. At the same moment, other divisions crossed the Saar and the Blies rivers, using nearly fifty passages built on boat bridges, wooden plank bridges and other footbridges but also many flotillas of Habert bag rafts, with the help of ropes stretched between the two banks. The Habert bag raft was another antique, as was our rifle. It consisted of simple envelopes of waterproof canvas, filled with straw or dry grass, connected by ropes. With these rudimentary passages, the crossing of the battalions took place until the beginning of the afternoon.

The French assault known as the "Saar Offensive" was launched.

It was not long until the alert for our offensive was given, and the German engineers responded by destroying several of our bridges. Other explosions echoed those blasts. Some of our armored vehicles, blinded by the thick morning fog, rolled over anti-tank mines, unfortunately failing to live up to their names of "Glorious" and "Victorious." The scale of the German mining was considerable, with thousands of anti-tank and anti-personnel mines, some with an igniter connected to a wire stretched between two trees or on barbed wire that our soldiers inadvertently unleashed in their path.

Despite these ominous beginnings, our troops and tanks made a breakthrough of several kilometers in width and depth into Germany on this first day of land combat, avoiding with great difficulty the mines and moderate German resistance. Part of our regiment stayed behind to defend the bridges we had built while we followed the advancing French troops from a distance.

Our order was to patrol the deserted villages and clear them of the many deadly traps that had been hidden there in addition to the German mines. In one of these villages, with some of my comrades we began to explore the abandoned houses. Entering the kitchen of one of these houses, from which an attractive aroma of rich and nutty coffee emanated, one of the sappers grabbed the coffee pot enthroned on an old stove. The tension on the wire attached to the underside of the kettle triggered the incendiary trap hidden in the stove and the entire room exploded in a vortex of fire, killing the coffee aficionado as well as two other soldiers. In another habitation, we discovered with stupor that some of the picture frames and paintings hanged on the wall of an upstairs bedroom were also linked to similar deadly explosives.

From now on, any object, even the most mundane one, was to be considered suspicious and potentially fatal.

In the following days, our troops continued their slow advance in the Saarland, approaching the Siegfried line, built a few years earlier along more than six hundred kilometers, from Holland to Switzerland. It was crammed with thousands of bunkers and tunnels rivaling our famous Maginot line which stretched from the English Channel to the Mediterranean Sea. The French defense line had been initiated ten years earlier, mainly on the eastern border, by the Minister of War, André Maginot, with his unambiguous motto – *On ne passe pas* – indicating that no one would cross it. The long static face-to-face of the two lines, Siegfried and Maginot, was beginning and would last many months.

At the beginning of October, the 21st Division, including our engineer regiment, was ordered to withdraw, and was replaced by the 45th Infantry Division. Our withdrawal was painful, both physically and morally. The fatigue of the past weeks was weighed down by the foggy and gloomy weather. We turned back painfully on foot, for lack of transport, only accompanied by equally exhausted horses. Walking on muddy roads, we thought of our families and all our comrades who would never see theirs again. Some of my Breton comrades felt depressed and sobbed over the fate of their late comrades who had disappeared too soon on German ground. Although our division had been relieved, we took this departure as a failure or even an abandonment.

Our morale was low, the withdrawal feeling like a hasty retreat, all the more difficult due to the recent and painful loss of our comrades.

The beginning of the conflict was followed by a period of several months that History would remember as the *Drôle de Guerre*. This name was later derived from a report on the French-British armies, with this period of the Second World War coined as "phony war" or "false war." French journalists would mistakenly understand "funny war," thus giving its name of *Drôle de Guerre*, due to a simple misunderstanding! The German troops would call it *Sitzkrieg*, or "sitting war," while Poles would call it *dziwna wojna*, or "amazing war."

This game of chess between the Siegfried line and the Maginot line would last for almost a year on the Western Front. French soldiers were on the lookout, ready to defend against any attack from German troops, while German forces sheltered by the Siegfried line patiently awaited the French assault. This analogous line would inspire the famous French song by Ray Ventura and his band "We Will Hang our Laundry on the Siegfried Line," that the Allied soldiers would later sing while marching to the front.

On the French side, our soldiers killed only time behind a fortified defensive line, giving a false impression of being impenetrable, despite being incomplete due to lack of budget further hampered by political battles. This line of continuous obstacles spread over different sections but also over several underground levels, with galleries up to nearly thirty meters deep extending over more than ten kilometers. It connected hundreds of forts or casemates for artillery and infantry, observation posts or turrets, and thousands of blockhouses. Unfortunately, the Maginot line had not been designed for agile and rapid warfare, but instead represented a passive, heavy and slow infrastructure.

The buildings were independent and self-sufficient, with their own electricity, radio communication, and food reserves. The underground network compared to a small modern town where soldiers, like in an anthill, worked from the stoves of a well-equipped kitchen to the power plant, passing through the ammunition stores, the dormitories, the infirmary, the operating room as well as the food and water reserves. In this maze of galleries, a small electric train connected the various combat stations, equipped with anti-tank guns, machine guns, other mortars and grenade launchers, or bombs.

In outposts, behind mined roads and various barriers, wide corridors of barbed wire were drawn up like the hair of the Gorgon, to slow down the German infantry and expose them to the deadly cross-fire of machine guns coming from the casemates. Vertical rail fields had also been erected, like a giant Mikado game, to slow down the enemy vehicles, making them more vulnerable to our anti-tank guns and artillery fire. The logistics support and command posts sat behind all these obstacles and buildings.

From time to time, the valve would release a little pressure, resulting in a few altercations between patrols. After the brutal "Saar Offensive", the prolonged wait on both sides resulted in the absence of any major fighting.

The slow and oppressing *Drôle de Guerre* also faced one of the harshest winters in over a hundred years, freezing and paralyzing troops in their positions. This chilling and agonizing wait would be relieved neither by the radios, parcels, and soccer balls sent to the soldiers for entertainment, nor by the visit in great pomp of the new king of England, George VI, to the most impressive fort in the Maginot line.

While this face-to-face of patience, worthy of the most intense game of chess, was starting between the two lines, we passed through Fénétrange once again; we then continued, under a pouring and continuous rain, an uninterrupted and exhausting march for over a week. Mid-October, we arrived near Lunéville where we were finally able to rest for several days. The conditions of withdrawal had been so difficult that nearly two hundred horses died of fatigue or illness on the return journey.

We felt that the "Saar Offensive", our first trial by fire, was a failure; we mourned our fallen comrades while the German forces had resisted fiercely with far fewer losses and had not loosened their grip on Poland at all.

Meanwhile, in our General Staff, the star-studded officers strutted and celebrated their glorious success dreaming of their next victory. They were once again seriously mistaken.

# Chapter 4

## *From Relief to Boeschepe*

At the end of October 1939, we were relieved to move up to the Somme. In columns of four, we walked to Nancy via Saint Nicolas de Port. The weather and morale were appalling. Billows of cigarette smoke rose in the morning drizzle above our marching column, barely advancing into the wind. By midday, we crossed the Meurthe River and finally stopped for a meal and a long-awaited rest near the flamboyant basilica of Saint Nicholas, a Gothic building with two towers stretched out towards the sky like two arms imploring God. While the mobile canteen was busy preparing our meal, we went with some comrades to visit the basilica. Inside, the famous blessing phalanx of Nicholas of Myra rose proudly in front of the multicolored stained-glass windows. In this peaceful and silent place, I implored Saint Nicholas to watch over my wife and my little boy, hoping to hear from them soon.

Two months of silence had elapsed with no news despite my letters.

With the declaration of war, time had also gone into conflict.

Coming out of the basilica, we went to take our mess tins from our backpacks, and we lined up in front of the *popote*, as if getting ready to receive communion; however, this field kitchen was only going to satiate our stomachs and not our faith. The cook served us the *rata* of the day, a potato ratatouille with a few thin and scattered pieces of meat, accompanied by a piece of bread; it was so stale that it would take a miracle for the juice of the stew to soften it and make it more edible. With my comrades we went to shelter under the forecourt of the basilica to eat this lukewarm but still welcome meal, and we shared a *piquette* that was supposedly red wine.

Warmed up by the *rata* and this indefinite-colored alcohol, the tongues loosened up progressively.

"Alex, do you think Saint Nicholas' finger will protect us in this bloody war? You saw what already happened to poor Léon! Do you believe in this poppycock of Christian magic?" Jean said to me inquisitively, while licking his fingers dripping with the brackish sauce of the stew that looked less and less like a roux.

"I don't know if it's nonsense Jean, but I know I want to get out of this war alive to see my wife again and watch my son grow up."

"Well, I wonder which finger they got from this Nicholas. Why not a full hand? Do you think he gave pieces of himself elsewhere? And who tells us if it's really his finger? Did they get it with a receipt or a certificate of authenticity?" Théo asked, puzzled, looking at the fingers of his hand which held his spoon immersed in the stew.

"You ask yourself too many questions Théo, logical and theological, but do you think you're going to finish your *rata*? Otherwise, I can help you," Fanch answered, as he had refused an apple for dessert, dreaming instead of chocolates, pastries, and other sweet treats.

"Nevertheless, Léon was a good guy. He attended mass with us before we left home, and he received the same blessing from Father Favé. So why him?" Jean retorted. "I don't know what this bloody war has in store for us, but I don't think that finger has any miraculous properties. If I wasn't so upset about our fate and afraid to get a rap on the knuckles, I would tell you without pointing the finger at Saint Nicholas that he obviously did not lift a finger for Léon!"

Despite our fatigue and depressing situation, I couldn't help but smile in response to this bad pun. Jean was known for both his wits and his eye features, suffering from a very pronounced strabismus. Jean joked for whomever wanted to hear it, "In '14, we had the *Poilus*, due to the lack of hairdressers in the trenches who could not find any 'short cuts' to get there," or even worse "Breaking news: Hitler was visiting an asylum, and each patient respectfully saluted him with a *Heil Hitler!* except for one, who obstinately refused to do so. Extremely annoyed, Hitler asked him why, and the man replied, 'I'm the doctor here, I'm the only one who isn't crazy!'"

After drinking a *jus*, a coffee so black that it gave us a cyanotic tongue, we gathered in front of the basilica to continue our walk to Nancy. At the end of the afternoon, we finally crammed ourselves and our gear into covered trucks that were waiting for us in the national forest of Haye to take us further north.

The rain lashed against the canvas of the truck which swayed us towards our destination. We passed through the valley of Omain at Bar-Le-Duc, where Pierre Michaux had many years earlier designed the pedal-operated velocipede, the famous *Michaudine*. The gusts of winds still swept over the canvas of the truck, accompanied by intense rain showers as we passed through Reims, the City of the Coronations. The bells rang the twelve strokes of midnight at the top of the cathedral which had seen the coronation of many Carolingian and Capetian kings.

Huge fields unfolded before our eyes, bordered by vineyards made famous by their champagne, the divine drink invented by the illustrious Dom Pérignon. Anecdotally, the Benedictine monk had used beeswax for the first time to tightly close wine bottles. Unexpectedly, the sugar in the wax had gradually dissolved in the bottle, generating a second fermentation, thus creating champagne according to the *méthode champenoise*.

These unknown landscapes reminded me that I had never before ventured beyond my native Brittany. With nostalgia I thought back to the moors of heather and gorse, mauve and gold, undulating on the hills of the Monts d'Arrée. I recalled the artichoke fields, the fine sand dunes, the rugged coastline where the sea spray caressed the granite rocks harboring rock and velvet crabs. The river where I used to go fishing for salmon trout, the wet bluish slates shining on the roofs of the houses in my village, the smell of wood and sawdust, my garden, my house – I missed all of them so much. But above all, the separation from Gabrielle and Jean-Pierre had become unbearable to me. I had never been so far from Gabrielle for so long. I imagined myself hopping off that truck, running back home and snuggling up in her arms, forgetting the rest of the world and crystallizing that moment for eternity.

The pain of alienation suddenly became physical, all my muscles aching, my breathing becoming more and more uneven and difficult, my eyesight turning to a blur and an eerie darkness insidiously invading my whole being. Fortunately, this panic attack vanished as quickly as it had happened and, remembering the moments of happiness with my wife and my son, I finally fell into the arms of Morpheus.

In the early hours of the morning, a kestrel woke me with a start, calling out with its shrill cry, flying into the wind and searching for a prey, ready to dive on it like the Messerschmitt on the Morane-Saulnier. The sky was beginning to clear over the wooded hills and Jean, who laboriously opened one eye after a spotty nap, cried out when he saw the sign announcing the town of Soissons, "Soissons! Why make such a big deal for a broken vase? Clovis could just have bought a new one instead of making such a fuss for a pot!"

The few comrades-in-arms who were not dozing undoubtedly wondered who this Clovis – the first king of the Franks – could possibly be, if he was one of Jean's relatives and if he had been able to replace his broken vase at last!

Later that day, we arrived in Amiens, with all its canals which earned it the name of Little Venice of the North. We passed the Notre Dame Cathedral as a shy sun rose between its two towers capping the largest religious building in France. It had suffered extensive damage from the shells that had hit its roof, its flying buttresses and its organ during The Great War and I did not know that it would this time be totally spared during the bombings to come.

Finally, on a cold and misty early morning we caught sight of a city: it was Abbeville, our final destination.

When we arrived in Abbeville, we stayed in the Saint-Frères factory. This wrapping fabric factory, located on an island bordered by the Somme River and linked to the city center by numerous bridges, did not have anything sacred despite its name. Inspired by the Manufacture Royale des Rames established in Abbeville in the seventeenth century to manufacture sheets and tapestries, a hundred years earlier three Saint brothers had the idea of producing jute cloths and bags for packing goods. Their family enterprise had flourished over the years, propelling their business to the forefront of burlap production in France. This inexpensive long solid fiber, extracted from the bark of jute plant in the British Indian Empire, was transported through the neighboring ports of Boulogne-sur-Mer and Dunkirk to the factory.

Of course, as soon as Jean learned the origin of the factory where we were stationed, he could not help declaring mischievously to whoever wanted to hear him, "It's indeed our luck. It must be Nicholas' finger that showed us the way to this destination. Now we will surely be well protected in this place supervised by the three Saints, the father, the son, and the 'holey' ghost!"

Our stay in Abbeville was short-lived. For a few weeks we built barracks near the marshaling yard for passing soldiers. We left our quarters at the factory early in the morning to walk to our construction site in generally cool and gloomy weather matching our mood. We passed by the bridge of the Jean Jaurès street to reach a place near the train station, one of the last wooden stations built in France, covered with red-orange bricks and a roof of the same shade, surmounted by a steeple which reminded us of the slowly passing hours, in chorus with the tolling of the bells at the Saint Vulfran collegiate church.

Sometimes at the end of the day, we had permission to go into town. We passed the monument dedicated to the Chevalier de La Barre, who shortly before the 1789 French Revolution had been tortured for not having greeted a religious procession by removing his headgear. This reckless young knight had been tortured in the public square, his bones broken, and his tongue torn, before being beheaded and burned. This monument reminded us of our own barbarism, driven by endless religious wars, and how fortunate we were to now live in a world where church and state were seemingly separate. We were unfortunately going to discover very soon that the war against certain religions, in particular Judaism, was already underway to decimate the Jewish people.

One day, after strolling through the picturesque streets of the town center where we encountered little girls playing hopscotch on the road while boys in shorts played marbles on the sidewalks, we met at the Café de la Colonne to try for a moment to forget our fate.

Jean, true to form, now a budding philosopher, uttered these words, "So, will the world ever change? Did we not learn anything in '14-'18? Here we are again in Somme. In sum, back to square one! We now have the Maginot line, and the Germans have the Siegfried line instead of smelly and unsanitary trenches. Is that what progress is, really?"

"Don't talk nonsense Jean," Émile replied in his harmonious voice. "Today we are free thinkers without risk of being killed for a lack of respect to a religion."

"Well, if La Barre had been like Fanch, the executioners would have had a hell of a job cutting him up into little pieces," Jean retorted.

"Hey, a little respect for me," Fanch cried, gulping down a tall glass of beer accompanied by two gigantic sausages topping a mountain of *frites*.

"Anyway, as long as we're stationed here, we only have to worry about the cold and the humidity," I replied. "The Germans are far away, and we are building barracks for our comrades who will then be sent east. We risk far less here than in the German forests riddled with mines, like those that took Léon's life, peace to his soul. I hope we will stay here as long as possible."

Unfortunately, mid-November, we had to leave Abbeville with the order to head for Norway the next day following an alert. Shortly after our departure, we received a counter-order asking us to move this time towards the Belgian border.

We arrived one Thursday morning in Bailleul, at the foot of the Flanders mountains, a few kilometers from Belgium.

It was market day.

In the main square, the Grand Place, opposite the town hall, a plethora of stalls were relatively well stocked. The city had been recently rebuilt following its complete annihilation by the Allies during The Great War to drive out the Germans who occupied it: only one house had survived this apocalyptic cataclysm!

The town hall was not very quaint, lacking for my taste in character with its motley mix of red and yellow bricks. The belfry of yellow bricks, placed anachronistically on a sandstone base extending the ground floor of the town hall, rivaled by its aesthetic mediocrity. I learned a little later, walking through the city, that the precious bricks, stones and historic sandstone blocks which could have gone into the restoration of the town hall and its belfry, had been collected after the destruction of these buildings and diverted for the recent construction of a monument dedicated to soldiers killed in previous wars, a massive amalgam stylized as a Gothic *trompe-l'oeil* ruin.

Under a thick blanket of grayish clouds hovering above the belfry, nestled snugly in a campanile, the belfry bells tinkled as if to welcome us with a local piece of music. Further down in the square, in a cacophony rivaling with the opening of Wagner's opera Tannhäuser, the merchants shouted out loud to tout the freshness of their eggs, the quality of their hens or rabbits, the incomparable savor of their fruits and vegetables, the efficiency of the knife sharpener grindstone, the sturdiness of the wicker baskets or the flexibility of the belts, suspenders and other clothing accessories.

I walked over to a jewelry store adjacent to the bustling plaza where I bought a bracelet for my wife, hoping I could offer it to her in person for Christmas, if only I had the chance to get a leave.

In the afternoon, we marched about ten kilometers to the north with a small detachment to reach a small, picturesque village, named Boeschepe, perched on a hill on the edge of the Belgian border. Jean and Fanch, as well as a few other comrades, accompanied me while the rest of the regiment settled down in the vicinity of Bailleul.

We found temporary refuge in the small communal hall, near the church, while we would build a barrack to house us for the months to come. The first evening, exhausted from our journey of the previous days, we went to bed as soon as night fell.

# Chapter 5

## *From Mill to Letters*

The next day, awakened at dawn by the Franco-Flemish crowing of a most irritated rooster, we decided to set off on a scouting mission while the morning mist gradually vanished. The village of Boeschepe offered a good view of the surroundings, bordered by fields, sheltering some draft horses *Trait du Nord* for plowing and milking cows for milk and cheese.

Curiously, as far as the eye could see, some spaces were covered with wooden poles several meters high to which was attached a tangle of threads, like a web woven by a giant spider emerging from the depths of the center of the earth, as in a novel by Jules Verne. I was wondering what these fields could produce when Jean, now promoted to budding botanist, told whoever wanted to listen, "I hope the villagers have had a good harvest and that we can taste the fruit of their hard labor later today. Look, these are fields of hops, the vine of the north."

Then, he added proud as a peacock, "This plant is from the same family as cannabis and in the spring the underground stumps will cause immense bines to emerge from the earth which will twine on these scaffoldings. I have read a lot of articles on this plant because I was thinking that maybe one day I would embark on its cultivation to produce my own Breton beer."

I had heard of hops of course and I certainly enjoyed a good beer from time to time, sometimes cut with lemon soda, especially on hot days in the summer.

Jean continued, encouraged by our astonished looks, "Here growers will harvest hop flowers, little yellow-green flowers resembling cedar cones, around the same time that grapes are harvested. They contain substances that will give beer its taste while stabilizing its smooth foam, but they also have sedative properties. No wonder why I feel so tired when I'm done drinking a one-liter beer bottle!"

Then he concluded, "All these explanations made me thirsty. Let's go back to the village."

At every street corner and crossroads, we discovered with astonishment a multitude of tiny chapels. We stopped in front of one of them, a red brick building the size of a bus stop. Jean, true to form, joked, "The villagers must all be dwarves to fit together in such a tight chapel."

"You think so," Fanch replied incredulously, wondering if he could pull off the feat of stepping through the door that seemed to be so narrow.

"Look, this is the Chapel of Marie-Consolation-de-la-Peur," I exclaimed. "We will come back later to light up a candle with our comrades to provide us courage and free us from our fears!"

On the way, we passed a few villagers who, by their normal size and build, reassured Fanch of his fears of having arrived in a village of gnomes. They greeted us with *bonjour*, but more often with *welkom* in their Flemish dialect, *Vlaemsch*.

In an alley, we passed a brick building covered with a corrugated iron roof displaying under the attic a protruding brick monogram of the founder of the establishment, PDL, Pierre Decanter Leynaert. In this place, he had installed a hop dryer a century ago that was still in full operation. Hops from neighboring fields were dried there overnight in a tower in the presence of sulfur vapors. Later, the desiccated hops were compressed in a power press into large hessian bales, then transported to breweries where they would be used to flavor the beer with the resin, lupulin. The practice of purification by smelly sulfur vapors dated back to ancient times. Ulysses had asked to purify in this way a room where he had massacred all the suitors of his faithful wife Penelope. In the Middle Age, premises, objects, and individuals were thus purified during the plague epidemics.

On our way back to the parish hall, we were passing in front of the church when, coming out of the small adjacent cemetery in a black cassock, bundled up in a long black cloak and muffler, wearing a beret of matching color, a priest approached us and welcomed us, "*Bonjour*, gentlemen. I am Father Émile Galloo. I am happy to meet you. Welcome to Boeschepe, even if the circumstances are not the best."

He asked us our names and where we were originally from, then added, "Let's hope that the war will spare us, and that God will protect you as well as France. You are in front of the church of Saint-Martin, the patron saint of France and of the soldiers, therefore I expect to see you all on Sunday at Mass."

As Jean would say after the clergyman's departure jokingly, "For a priest from French Flanders in northern France, he does not lose his 'north' bearing!"

Father Galloo then introduced us to his church, expressing his pride to watch over his flock, "The church of Saint-Martin was thus named in recognition of the kindness of this Roman legionary who, in the days of the Gauls, had shared in Amiens the lining of his chlamys, a military cape, with a poor homeless man who was facing the harshness of winter. Just like you all, Martin the Legionnaire had also fought against the Alamans during a campaign on the Rhine. After Christ appeared to him wrapped in his chlamys, Martin gave up his military life and took Holy orders. He was later acclaimed as the Bishop of Tours."

He then told us that we had narrowly missed the annual Saint-Martin celebration on November 10, "If you had been here last week, you would have enjoyed all of our kids walking the streets with head-shaped lanterns, called *grigne-dents*, carved out of candle-lit sugar beets, singing as they paraded:

> 'Saint Martin,
> Drink wine
> In the street of Capuchin friars.
> He drank hard liquor,
> He didn't pay.
> We kicked him out with a
> Swift sweep.'"

The priest of Boeschepe continued, "After the parade of the children in the streets, we gathered in the village hall where you are now staying and, as is customary, before judging the most beautiful lantern, we gave each kid an orange and a *folard*, also called *craquandoule*, a traditional milk roll containing raisins or sometimes chocolate chips instead."

As we were approaching lunch time, starting to be frozen to the marrow by the icy wind which had risen, the ecclesiastic offered generously to accompany us to the village bakery where he bought a famous *folard* for each of us. He explained its origin, "While Saint Martin was passing through Flanders with his donkey to spread the Word, the animal fled while the holy man was asleep. The next day, the poor man's horse unfortunately could not be found. At nightfall, the children had set out in search of the donkey, equipped with lanterns like *grigne-dents*, and had finally found it on the dunes where he was quietly enjoying thistles. So happy to have been reunited with his mount, Saint Martin had thanked the children by transforming the droppings of the donkey – *Voolaeren* in Flemish that we pronounce *folard* – into those succulent raisin-containing brioche buns of suggestive shape."

After savoring our *folards*, we left Father Galloo, promising to visit his church another day, but to surely attend his Sunday Mass.

Satiated by the *craquandoules*, we took a quick and light meal in the communal room, then decided to go up to the heights above the village. With some comrades, we followed a path through the fields and the woods to finally arrive at the top of Boeschepe's hill. The panorama unfolding before our eyes was remarkable on this grayish afternoon at the end of November 1939.

From our vantage point, we observed the gentle slopes of French Flanders, with the hop fields bristling with wooden poles, greenish pastures dotted with small woods of chestnut, beech, and poplar trees, where we would soon go to pick up mushrooms like ceps, amethyst deceivers, chanterelles, even the false ones, and with a little luck a few wood hedgehogs.

We also had a bird's eye view of the village, with the brick church, topped by an octagonal spire, where we had previously met Father Galloo, the many pygmy chapels, a dovecote with its pigeons nestled in the nesting holes, and the traditional houses of the region with bluish smoke rising from the red brick chimneys. We also discovered with surprise an imposing windmill next to the village, its wings turning rhythmically in the breeze. We absorbed in silence this tranquility, this normality of a peaceful and carefree village. We realized at that moment that we had already reached an unknown land, so distant and so different from our Breton countryside. After having rested for a short while, as clouds of a similar shade as the bluish black slates of Brittany seemed to descend towards us, we decided to go down in the direction of the mill.

West of the village center, we crossed an alley lined with cypress trees which brought us to a gigantic wooden mill, on a pivot, which was in full operation to grind grain. The mill was impressive in size, overlooking a charming two-story crisscross brick house with a sloping gambrel roof. This mill, made of wooden planks, with its pivot allowing the orientation of the wings to face the wind, appeared to be at least twice as high as the house.

Having seen us from his mill, the miller came out to meet us and introduced himself, "Hello, my dear friends, I am André the Miller! Your arrival is already like a thriller."

Jean whispered in my ear, "This miller also seems to be a poet at heart, and he honors you, Alex, in alexandrine!"

André the Miller added, "Here is our notorious Mill of Ingratitude. It is on a pivot to change its attitude. Its name comes from a problem with the carpenter, but to grind the grain it remains a true master. Two years ago, the storm destroyed one of its wings, but now that it has been repaired it turns and wrings!"

Jean, unable to keep from laughing, said to the miller, "I'm Jean, simple sapper from 6th Engineering. Glad to meet you in this beautiful gathering!"

The miller was wondering why Jean was laughing so hard when the latter added, "We observed earlier the humongous fields of hops; where can we get a beer from those wonderful crops?"

"You have come to the right place, see this great tavern," André replied, pointing to the house nestled timidly under the wings of the mill. "It's the *estaminet De Vierpot*, my cavern!"

We then headed towards the long-established brick building, in the shade of the mill. The *estaminet De Vierpot*, André explained, was a traditional Flemish tavern where we could consume local beer, but also have a good meal while stocking up on tobacco. In fact, as soon as we had passed the doorstep, we discovered that *vierpot* was the Flemish word for firepot, a receptacle into which the embers of the coal stove, which warmed the room and its customers, were regularly transferred. The copper *vierpot* was placed on a corner of the bar, facing the entrance to the room, and regulars used it to light their pipes or cigarettes.

The room was warm, decorated like a family dining room, with small tables arranged neatly along the walls. On the walls of this low-ceilinged room, lit by a few windows at the front of the house, monochrome family photographs retraced the fate of a few intertwined lives: from the newborn in his embroidered rompers to the kid in a suit for his first communion holding in his hands a bible that he would probably never read; from the little girl in her Sunday best holding a rag doll near a well to the stoic bride in a white gown holding a bouquet of lilies in front of a fake painted background; from scowling families to several lonely ancestors, one of whom proudly displayed his stripes of chief warrant officer before going to The Great War where he would get disemboweled in a sordid trench. Various trinkets accentuated this family and friendly atmosphere from floor to ceiling.

Joseph, the owner of the tavern and his wife Marie-Louise were busy behind the bar serving customers who had joined the establishment after a day's work.

*"Goeienavond heren, en welkom in uw favoriete oord van verdef,"* Joseph said cheerfully. André translated for our benefit that Jo was welcoming us to his favorite place of perdition!

We followed André to a wooden table next to a window, near the stove which warmed the room. This heat was most welcome after enduring the damp cold that had gradually permeated our bodies during our getaway to the top of the hill.

Marie-Louise, a three-apples-high *bon vivant*, with scarlet cheeks and short, curly, reddish hair, showing off curves as plump as buxom – which testified to the richness of her cuisine – came towards us, *"Welkom! Wilt u een biertje gaan drinken?"*

This unknown guttural language reminded us once again painfully of the distance from our families as it did not have the slightest resemblance to the Breton of our region, but sometimes seemed to resonate more like the language of our Germanic enemy.

André asked us if we all wanted to taste the local beer or if we preferred a glass of wine, an aperitif or for the less brave ones a farm apple juice or a purple lemonade. We all readily accepted, without the slightest reluctance, his generous offer of a round of beers. Shortly after, all seated around our giant beer mugs filled with a lager covered with a thick and smooth foam, we toasted to a swift victory and to an upcoming peace.

"Let's raise our glasses to the nigh end of this war," André said.

"To your return, safe and sound, to your family! May God help you! Welcome to our gorgeous country!"

"Thank you very much, André, for this warm welcome! May this beer give us all happiness and wisdom!" Jean replied, still in alexandrine, giving me a complicit wink.

"*Yec'hed mat*, to your health, and *Vive la France*," I replied.

A few beers later, Marie-Louise was back and asked us, "*Wil er iemand iets eten?*" André translated, "For dinner, would you like a tasty Flemish plank? Bacon, cheese, potatoes, gourmet food to be frank?"

We were starving and a real meal would be a nice change from our field rations and military meals. André ordered a memorable dinner for us which Marie-Louise brought us on wooden planks.

"Hear ye, hear ye, hear ye, my friends observe this feast! You will all be force-fed until morning at least!" Jean joked, while his gaze devoured bacon, cheese, pâté, pickles, and potatoes covered in melting garlic butter.

"Save room for delicious desserts in a moment. Waffle or pie, from chef Jo will be complement!" André bloviated, as he now seemed to be feeling the euphoric but also sedative effects of the hops.

This delicious meal was to leave for a long time the perception of an indelible savor on our taste buds as well as in our memories.

At nightfall, we thanked these new friends from Boeschepe and joined our comrades back in the communal hall.

The next morning, as we emerged from a deep night's sleep, undoubtedly helped somewhat by the sheer number of beers that we had consumed the day before, a truck from our regiment burst into the courtyard adjacent to the parish hall.

"Hi, Alex," Théo called out to me. He had accompanied the driver and obtained the order to join our detachment.

"Hello, Théo. What brings you so early this morning to visit us?"

"I had the permission to join and bring you all the material stored in the back of the truck. I will now stay with you to help you build a barrack," Théo replied, while lifting the tarp at the back of the vehicle to show me stacks of wooden planks, canvas, nails, rivets, and various tools, essential for the construction.

"But first of all, I have a major surprise for all of you!"

Théo grabbed a canvas bag from the truck and placed it at my feet, uttering, "I feel like Santa Claus a bit early, even though I don't have a beard and the right costume, but the content is actually extremely late."

I hurriedly opened the bag, now surrounded by all my comrades. Its content was what I had dreamed of night and day. They were finally here, right in front of me, waiting only to be taken and disseminated, after having traveled through time and space. I had waited impatiently for this moment, imagining it with so many scenarios, fulfilling my sweetest dreams, hoping.

Trembling with excitement, I began distributing the packets of letters that we had finally received!

The letters were handed out as everyone waited, champing at the bit. Once the packages of letters distributed, we isolated ourselves in the four corners of the building to read the long-awaited news, while Théo and the driver began to unload the truck. It had taken nearly three months for these letters to find our trail, like Sherlock Holmes in pursuit of the Baskervilles hound in the English moors, but now I was going to delight in this moment of happiness.

I sorted the letters chronologically and began to read them:

*"Sunday, August 27, 1939*

*Mon Alexandre,*

*Here you are in this train that takes you far away from me, towards Angers and then the unknown. Jean-Pierre fell asleep after his feed in our home, now empty and very quiet, and I am therefore taking this moment of respite to write* to you.

I miss you so much already!

Only a few hours ago, I was hugging you so tenderly. I still breathe you whole and my mouth still remembers your lips. I have stopped crying as I want to be strong and wait for you with Jean-Pierre. I do hope that you will be back very soon. Here they say that a war with the Germans may be imminent, but I pray that peace will be maintained.

It's so unfair that you, a father with a newborn baby, had to be drafted. Take care of yourself and come back to us soon! Be careful wherever you go, think of me, think of our family, promise me to stay alive.

I am writing to you sitting in front of our wedding portrait, in our bedroom. Two years already ... Two years of pure bliss! We are so proud, innocent, and happy in this photo, so delicately colored by Mr. Gardarin, the photographer. Your ocean-blue eyes are so sweet, your lips so full, your face so beautiful and tender, your curly hair so attractive; you look admirable in your black suit, white shirt with its wing collar, and black satin bow tie. A real dandy!

I was only twenty-one, but I knew you were the one I wanted to spend the rest of my life with. I still remember that day like it was yesterday, pulling on my white dress and tying my veil over my kiss curls. Do you remember how much the white flowers of my bouquet, lilies, carnations, and roses, arranged with emerald-green ferns, perfumed the room where we posed for this portrait?

We did not yet know that from our love a little boy would be born, who now sleeps so peacefully in the wooden cradle that you built for him. When I look at him, I see you

*too. You are everywhere in front of my eyes, at each
moment, like an apparition haunting the household.*

*Jean–Pierre seems to be waking up and I'm going to
have to leave you for tonight. I will post this first letter
tomorrow so that you receive it very quickly and I promise
to write to you more extensively the next times. I hope I will
receive reassuring news from you as soon as possible. I don't
even know where you will be when you receive this letter ...*

*I miss you terribly. I am going to sleep, hugging your
pillow very tightly and breathing in your still remnant
scent. Come back to us quickly Alexandre.*

*I long to kiss you passionately and very tenderly when
you return.*

*Your Gaby,
who loves you for life and waits impatiently for you."*

I reread these sweet words, my heart racing, oblivious to my
surroundings, secluded in a parallel world. Then, with a dry throat
and wet eyes, I opened the other letters, one by one, filling the empty
void of the past few months. Gabrielle told me about the progress that
Jean-Pierre was making from day to day, aroused to a tumultuous
world with such an uncertain tomorrow. He now slept without interruption for most of the night and only took a few short naps. His
teeth were starting to pierce through as evidenced by his flushed
cheeks and his nibbling of whatever came to hand. Shortly after I left,
he had smiled at Gabrielle for the first time, "with the same smile as
mine, tender and loving," she wrote.

She described to me the passage into autumn, with nature
turning into varied colors intermingled with wine-red, ocher, emerald, amethyst, and bronze. The beautiful days had also given way to
the Breton drizzle, the days becoming shorter and shorter, cold,

windy, and humid. François and his wife Herveline also wished me well and Father Favé lavished prayers to protect me until my homecoming. The rabbits were putting on weight every day and would soon contribute a stew as only Gaby knew how to cook. The garden continued to supply the meals and Jean-Pierre was beginning to feast on delicious homemade purées. Neighbors took turns with François to keep the vegetable garden in good condition and harvest the potatoes and carrots.

Back home people claimed that the war was gradually spreading. All feared that the *Drôle de Guerre* would be broken suddenly by a German invasion of France as it previously happened in Poland. The *coup de grâce* inflicted by the USSR, following Stalin's order to the Red Army to finish off defenseless Poland after the German aggression, foreshadowed a global and ruthless escalation. However, it seemed that Hitler had offered peace talks to France and England, but he wanted to impose his own drastic conditions. The situation seemed extremely confused and unstable. I also learned about the dissolution of the French Communist Party and the flight to Moscow of its General Secretary, Maurice Torez, a sapper like me, but now a deserter from the 3rd Engineering regiment.

In one of the letters, Gabrielle had inserted a black and white photograph, where she was carrying my little son in her arms in one of the garden paths. They both stared at me with frozen, helpless faces, wondering where I could possibly be. François was probably behind the lens, and I placed this image of happiness delicately in my wallet.

I read and reread all the letters, while most of my comrades, for a moment also in another world, did the same. At last, rousing them from their reveries, I asked them with a hoarse voice to come and help unload the truck and store the construction equipment in the yard.

That evening, the emotions were divided between the joy of having finally heard from our families and the pain of feeling so far away from them. The evening was silent, accompanied only by the rustle of sheets of letters being turned over repeatedly, as well as some sniffles that were not due solely to a change in the weather.

# Chapter 6

## *From First Snow to Divine Child*

The next day, Sunday, we got ready to attend the nine-thirty mass on an empty stomach. With our entire detachment, we left the communal hall under a blue sky covered with high transparent clouds; it looked like the veil of a bride floating up there. An icy wind lashed our faces and numbed our hands. We passed in front of some imposing mansions dating from the last century, built with bricks of various colors and roofed with slates. The bakery with its various breads and *folards* was still open, as well as the butcher's shop with its tempting dishes, but the blacksmith near the church had already abandoned his forge with its anvils and horseshoes. The inhabitants hurried in part not to be late, for fear of a public remonstrance from the priest during his sermon, but mainly to flee the bitter cold which foreshadowed some impending snowfall.

We arrived at the church of Saint-Martin with its unmissable octagonal bell tower where two bells were pealing vigorously, calling the flocks to assemble as quickly as possible in one of the three naves. It seemed that the whole village had answered the call. We sat down in the heart of the church, among the villagers, prompting a few muffled murmurs as we passed. Mademoiselle Person, the schoolteacher, old-maid-in-chief of the village, stood behind the organ case, echoing long, squeaky notes resembling lamentations. The church was relatively sober despite some paintings depicting religious scenes, in particular Saint Martin preaching the word of God, without his donkey. Beautiful multicolored stained-glass windows projected onto the flagstones of the church a watercolor of luminous rainbows and polychrome spots resembling the northern lights.

Punctual, Father Galloo made a masterful entrance, accompanied by two altar boys in white lace cassocks, while the assembly and the organ suddenly fell silent. I wondered if the altar boys had been chosen for their vocation or rather as a punishment for clowning during religious teachings after school. One of them, a mischievous reincarnation of Poil de Carotte in Julien Duvivier's film, seemed to be engaged in a frantic race with his sidekick.

He looked as though butter wouldn't melt in his mouth!

The cassock of this Lepic lookalike was far too long for him; he almost tripped as he climbed the steps leading to the altar, stepping on a piece of lace. Both whirled around the altar, swinging out of control heavy censers, like a Foucault pendulum, from which escaped the fragrant smoke of incense.

Mass dragged on until almost eleven o'clock and before Communion, Father Galloo took the pulpit and gave a very long sermon which was undoubtedly partly directed at us. He preached unconditional love to each other, with reactions neither natural nor protective in times of war, such as offering the other cheek after being struck on the opposite one.

Sitting next to me, true to form, Jean whispered in my ear during the sermon, "Easy to say when you are wearing a soutane, far away from the battlefield. If someone shoots at me, I will surely not turn the other cheek but rather take aim and retaliate as quickly as possible with my rifle to save my skin."

Then he carried on sarcastically, "It's easy for him to pontificate from the ambo while declaiming his mumbo jumbo, but I wouldn't give much of his chances against the Germans and he would probably end up in a limbo!"

If these wisecracks from Jean were not always timely and tasteful, at least they helped endure this interminable mass that was starting to drag on like the *Drôle de Guerre.*

At Communion, the two acolytes continued to distinguish themselves. One suddenly poured a flood of water from a cruet onto the priest's hands at Offertory, splashing profusely on the cassock of the priest who turned red with anger; the other vigorously and maddeningly shook a handbell without interruption as Father Galloo raised the Sacred Host during the Eucharist.

Finally, the mass ended. The two bells started a dement peal while the organist, no doubt also tired of this interminable celebration, intoned a tune that seemed surprisingly quite familiar; at times, I thought I recognized flights similar to those of the popular song "La Java Bleue"! Despite her spinster airs and her official status as a cantankerous old maid, Miss Person also had a touch of humor. Fortunately, Father Galloo could not hear it from the sacristy where he had already retired with his two henchmen to whom, at this precise moment, he was giving a really hard time.

Villagers lingered in small groups in front of the church despite the cold that had intensified while Father Galloo had attempted to warm up the souls attending the worship service. Some greeted us by taking off their caps or hats while others looked at us sideways while conversing in undertones. Unfortunately, in their eyes, we represented the reminder of the war declared more than two months earlier. Their worried faces spoke volumes, no doubt wondering if we had been stationed near the Belgian border in preparation for an imminent invasion by German troops. We tried to reassure them, although our information was in truth very scarce, and we had in fact no idea what our real objective was.

André saw us and came to meet us with some of his friends, "*Bonjour!* You survived this interminable mass! Well done for this feat and for turning up *en masse.*"

I could not help but surreptitiously give a knowing wink to Jean that said a lot about my appreciation of the miller's alexandrines.

"After the Sunday Mass of the chatty pontiff, tradition is to go for an aperitif! *En route, mauvaise troupe*, towards the tavern, our shrine. The Rue de la Soif is fortunately not mined!" declaimed our poet miller who, unlike Monsieur Jourdain in The Bourgeois Gentleman, spoke in alexandrines quite intentionally.

We headed for the *estaminet De Vierpot*, where it seemed that all the men from the village had arranged to meet for an intense post-mass debate. The atmosphere was much more cordial and cheerful than during the liturgy. The various aperitifs – Dubonnet, a generous Byrrh wine of quinine, Pastis from Provence or Marseilles, a simple glass of plonk or hooch, or even absinthe, the green fairy, being poured on a sugar placed on a pierced spoon on the sly behind the bar – undoubtedly contributed to this better mood. We had to stay standing because the room now seemed very cramped with this sudden influx of dry throats. In this smoky room, conversations drifted from the war to the government, and from the price of bread to the future hop harvest. To help with the service, Jo and Marie-Louise had enlisted a stuttering and hunchbacked young girl who would have preferred to be a hundred leagues away, as well as the illustrious Mademoiselle Person who, between services, seemed to take an infinite pleasure in swallowing to the last drop the remnants of liquid in each of the glasses.

After having fueled many conversations while enjoying a few slices of bread with homemade pâté and small cornichons as well as cheese slices, we were about to go back to our quarters when, leaving the tavern, we saw a small crowd standing behind the mill. Necks outstretched to the sky, all were looking upwards, fascinated, silent and motionless. We decided to go see what was going on.

Onlookers had in fact surrounded a pole about thirty meters high where targets, some sporting multicolored feathers, had been positioned. These fake "birds" were used as targets by archers standing below them, attempting to hit them with their bow and arrows. One of the spectators explained to us that the artificial birds were worth different points, depending on their height and accessibility, when the flat tip of the arrow reached its goal. He also taught us that this ancestral activity of vertical pole archery had its origin in the Middle Ages. In peacetime, archers thus trained to reach the enemy at the curtain walls or at the crenels with more precision, and for the most skillful ones, at the bartizan and even loopholes of the fortified castles. These *francs-tireurs* also challenged each other to this game, called the *papegai*.

Hearing about *papegai*, which Jean literally interpreted as gay pope, he could not help saying to me mischievously, "You see Alex, I have always told you that I found it suspicious that the Pope dresses in a white robe. Even in the Middle Ages, they had already noticed it!"

Finding his interjection somewhat inappropriate and offensive, I ignored it, but Théo, who unfortunately was far from having a good head on his shoulders, asked Jean, "You know a thing or two about popes! That's absolutely true, I hadn't even thought about it. Why are the Pope and all the other clergymen wearing cassocks?"

"Prattling about the papacy, did you know that when the cardinal camerlengo was elected as our new Pope Pius XII, a few months ago, the smoke which came out of the Sistine Chapel was white at first to announce the great news, but in the end, oddly enough, it turned black? The person responsible for the smoke in the Vatican is probably of Normand origin; as they say there, maybe yes, maybe no!" Jean added.

"But do you really believe what you say about ecclesiastics? You will end up in Hell, Jean, for always blaspheming."

"Easy Théo. We can laugh a bit in times of war, right?"

"You can't laugh at everything Jean; the holy sacrament is sacred!"

"You're right, I shouldn't be joking about religion, but all these beers are starting to kick in on me. I now have to make an urgent run behind the mill to piss in the Pope's pocket!" Jean replied, bursting into obsequious laughter.

Under the reproachful looks of the villagers, we adopted a profound silence so as not to disturb the archers who tried to focus, their eyes sharp on the targets. This game did not seem so easy because the "birds" continued to sit unharmed at the top of the mast, as proud as a peacock. Suddenly, one of the archers, a muscular middle-aged man, dislodged at last the "bird" perched at the top of the pole.

Some archers offered us their bows to try to reach the targets but, despite our perseverance, we left empty-handed from this synthetic hunt.

André and his friends then invited us to return to the village for a game of boules. We thought it was a bit cold for a *pétanque* tournament when we discovered with bewilderment that the boules alley, the *bourloire*, was indoor. We were not at the end of our surprises. In the *bourloire* room, we discovered not a flat bowling alley, but a curved concave court, about twenty meters long and three meters wide.

André explained to us that the Flemish boules game was very different from *pétanque*, which obviously we had already noticed! But when he showed us the boules, which he called *bourles*, we then figured out that we were going to have major difficulties to play this unknown and surprising game.

Indeed, André gave us each a set of *bourles*, large flat and cylindrical wooden discs covered with rubber. Not only were these Flemish *bourles* not spherical, but they were also weighted!

We started a game, already regretting having accepted this challenge of boules game. The first games were disastrous and, if our *bourle* managed to roll, pitch and land sometimes by luck, and not by skill, near the *étaque*, a copper puck that we called the jack, most of our boules ended up either at a considerable distance from the target or in the pit at the end of the alley. After several unsuccessful games, we began to understand the handling of the *bourle* a little better and at the end of the afternoon we finally emerged victorious from an ultimate game. At that point, we decided that it was better to stick with this sole victory and return to our Flemish fold.

The next day, we began to transport our equipment to an available land near the church to begin the construction of our wooden barrack. As the days went by, our progress was as slow as the days were short and glacial.

Soon after we got down to work, the snow began to fall. One morning in December, we found the village in an immense white silence, the snowflakes falling down profusely, thus isolating and camouflaging everything under a thick bluish shimmering blanket. For most of us, this snowstorm was a first experience!

Despite the cold and the lack of visibility, we immediately found ourselves in the courtyard for an epic snowball fight. I had never before walked in powdered snow that crunched under our feet. It muffled the slightest noise and rounded all shapes into a mysterious landscape. This snowy village lost in the middle of a white immensity, the flames of the fireplaces dancing on the frosted windows, their plumes of smoke adorning the milky sky, everything reminded me that Christmas was near. It was unlikely though that a leave would now be granted in time for the holidays.

The snowy roads had cut us off from the outside world for a while and the construction of our barrack was on hold. I took advantage of these respite days to write long letters to Gabrielle, sharing with her this fabulous and unforgettable spectacle as well as our rare hikes to the summits.

Secluded in this cocoon of snow, time seemed suspended ...

The arrival of Christmas took us by surprise. In the early morning of December 24, 1939, the village was still frozen as in one of those glass globes that one turns upside down to see the snow twirl and settle in a thick white coat. Father Galloo, braving the bone-freezing wind and the snow falling down in a thick muslin, came to pay us a surprise visit.

"Hello gentlemen. How are you on this day before Christmas?"

Father Galloo said, taking off his black frock coat covered with a white melting powder, his woolen scarf of the same color and his beret.

"*Bonjour*, Monsieur le Curé," I replied. "What brings you so early in the morning? It must be very important for you to brave the elements."

"I wanted to remind you that today you will have the chance to listen to not one but two of my sermons, the first at the half past nine mass and the other at the midnight mass! If you don't mind, I will then come and celebrate Christmas Eve with you and a few villagers who have offered to prepare a festive dinner for you."

"Of course, we will be happy to host you all in this communal hall," retorted Fanch, our ogre on duty.

As he was licking his chops at the thought of the kings' feast the villagers were going to prepare for us, I added, "It is very kind of you and your flock to think of us during the Christmas holiday when we are unfortunately so far away from our own. It is with great pleasure that we will spend Christmas Eve with all of you here."

"Very well, you will feel a little less alone during this traditional family celebration. I must now return to the church to prepare for mass. I'll see you soon there as well as tonight."

"Hold on," Émile called out, as the priest bundled up, ready to go on his way. "I would like to ask you a favor. Would it be possible for me to sing 'O, Holy Night' at Christmas Mass? If possible, might Miss Person be able to accompany me with the organ?"

"Of course, Émile, it will be with great pleasure that we will listen to your singing this evening in the church, and I will speak to Violette, umm, I mean Mademoiselle Person," the clergyman replied as his blushing cheeks betrayed either a change in temperature or his hidden feelings for the organist!

After morning mass, we spent the rest of the day tidying up, cleaning, and airing the communal room, then setting up a few tables in a square for the evening. Some villagers came to join us in the evening to set up a festive table and decorate the room for Christmas

Eve dinner. They also brought large homemade loaves of bread, some appetizers and enticing bottles of wine.

A little before midnight, we walked out by the light of the full moon on the snow which sparkled under our feet, while some inhabitants were already arriving at the church guided by their lanterns. This procession in the lanes of the village cast phantasmagorical shadows on the snow-covered facades.

The church was crowded and lit with multiple candles that burned in the four corners of the naves. Near the altar, a manger commemorated the birth of Jesus in Bethlehem. Miss Person, helped by other women from the village, had arranged an exquisite miniature stable, where Mary and Joseph already stood around the empty manger, filled with fresh straw. Around the Nativity, other terracotta subjects were displayed on a shimmering green moss, scattered with twigs and fallen leaves. A donkey and an ox were impatiently awaiting the arrival of the newborn, as I had awaited the birth of Jean-Pierre several months earlier. The shepherds and their flock of sheep were heading towards the stable and other local figures had been arranged here and there: a baker, a farrier, a couple of old peasants carrying bundles of wood on their bent backs, a few children and farmers with dairy cows also seemed to await the advent.

Suddenly the twelve strokes of midnight rang. Mademoiselle Person intoned with great pomp, "He is Born, the Divine Child," while all resumed in chorus in full voice:

> "He is born, the divine Child,
> Play, oboes, resound, musettes!
> He is born, the divine Child,
> Let all sing His Nativity!"

I gave a disapproving look at Jean who had just stood out once more by asking me and my neighbor if these musettes – in fact a French bagpipe played during the 17th and 18th centuries – were the same as the musette bags we wore over our shoulder.

At the first notes of the song, Father Galloo made his entrance with great pomp through the door of the sacristy, preceded by the same two altar boys, one holding a long candle which he placed in front of the Nativity scene, and the other carrying with veneration Baby Jesus in the palm of his hands, like an Inca treasure discovered deep into the Amazon jungle. He laid the holy child in the manger, while awkwardly toppling a few sheep and characters who were inadvertently in his path.

Mass then followed without major problems and just before the end of the celebration, Émile got up and went to stand next to Mademoiselle Person. The priest solemnly announced, "We are fortunate to have with us tonight, on this Christmas Eve, soldiers of the 6th Engineer Regiment. They have been with us for the past few weeks and one of them, Émile, will sing '*Minuit Chrétien*' – 'O Holy Night' – for us. Go in peace! Merry Christmas to everyone!"

Émile sang in his melodious voice and many were moved to tears by these very apt words on this solemn night, "The Redeemer has broken all shackles ... The Earth is free, and Heaven is open ... Love unites those that iron had chained ... People, stand up! Sing your deliverance." These words of hope echoed in the house of God as the locals made their way to the exit greeting us with "Merry Christmas" or "God bless you."

After this moving celebration of the Nativity, we returned to the parish hall where some villagers were already waiting for us to celebrate Christmas Eve. Father Galloo and his two acolytes arrived just as we were sitting down at the table for an aperitif.

The Vermeulens, a peasant couple chatting in patois with profusion, had brought in bottles of their home-made aperitif, an exquisite walnut wine that they had concocted in their barn by macerating green walnuts with wine and alcohol. The widow Devos, who ran the small village grocery store, had cooked a *flamiche*, a delicious traditional hot leek pie. She had also brought a *tarte au Maroilles*, a bread dough covered with slices of the famous cow milk cheese with its orange rind on, topped with heavy cream mixed with egg yolks. The pies had been kept warm on the edge of our stove during mass. Fanch, attracted by the tempting odor, had been hopping up and down with impatience as he circled the stove endlessly since our return from midnight mass, excitedly waiting for us to sit down and eat.

Father Galloo raised his glass of the home-made walnut wine to toast, "I don't want to bore you with a third sermon but simply wish to tell all of you, my friends, that it is an honor to have you in our village. I know you would love to be with your families, wives, and children, on this Christmas Eve and I pray that you join them as soon as possible, safe and sound."

We all raised our glasses, moved by this warm hospitality and I replied, "Monsieur le Curé, on behalf of all my comrades and myself, we thank you from the bottom of our hearts for having organized this surprise celebratory dinner. We also thank the villagers who joined us this evening and assembled this divine meal. It is true that the separation from our families is more burdensome day by day, especially since we have not yet had the chance to be granted a leave. Let us try for one evening to forget the war, to savor this marvelous feast which you have so kindly prepared for us, and let's celebrate with joy this 1939 Christmas Eve."

The meal was sumptuous and after the aperitif we discovered the *Potjevleesch*, a traditional dish that the Dubois couple had simmered since the day before. This small pot of meat containing rabbit, chicken, pork, and veal meat, simmered in stout with various spices and herbs, served with potatoes, would remain in our olfactory and gustatory memory for many years to come.

Father Galloo and his altar boys had brought a few bottles of wine, which probably came from his reserve of wine bottles for the dominical Communion. We had already opened a few bottles of red wine and conversations were going well when Émile offered to sing. He began by singing *a cappella* "He is born the Divine Child," but quickly Francis Vermeulen grabbed his diatonic accordion; we all drifted in chorus to the song by Ray Ventura and his Collegians,

"Everything's Fine, Madame la Marquise," where Émile replied solo to our "there is just one thing I mention, if you please." The songs followed one another, and I was afraid that at any time Théo and Fanch would once again venture as a duet another improvisation of "Félicie aussi"!

For dessert, Mademoiselle Lefebvre, the village postwoman, had prepared a traditional Christmas log for us, a little too creamy and pasty for my taste; the priest uncovered some bottles of sparkling white wine. Coffee was then accompanied by a home-made rotgut from the Vermeulens who seemed to have an impressive reserve of handcrafted alcoholic beverages. The songs followed on from one another, gradually slipping into ribald ones. In response to the song "What Are We Waiting for to Be Happy? What Are We Waiting for to Party?" some of my comrades answered with the song by Ouvrard, "I am Not in Good Health," declaiming faster and faster, "I have got my spleen that's swelling, my liver that's not straight, my belly that's pulling in, my pylorus that's coloring, my gullet that's anemic, my stomach that's far too low," and a litany of other ailments associated with certain organs that Father Galloo, tired of his day and by the various alcohols, would have preferred not to hear. However, he was the first to sing the chorus with renewed vigor, "Ah! Good God! How annoying it is to be always unwell, Ah! Good God! How annoying it is, I am not in good health."

The evening, or rather the now well-advanced morning, continued with less respectable songs, such as that of Jeanne Aubert, "Sur la Commode," where we took a malicious pleasure in singing the virtues of sitting on a commode to refresh one's full behind, while laughing out loud and censoring or replacing some of the words, especially the *derrière* with a shrill whistle.

The abundance of camaraderie, the overflow of kindness from the villagers, the plethora of sumptuous food and drinks, had unfortunately not totally erased our loneliness and nostalgia. Once the guests had gone and the day began to dawn on the horizon, we found ourselves exhausted and sad not to know how our families were celebrating Christmas. Would we ever see them again? Would we soon be granted leave? Would this war end in the weeks or months to come? Would the Germans be crazy enough to try to invade France like Poland a few months earlier? If the conflict dragged on, who among us might be injured, or worse, killed? All these questions were circling back and forth in my head and those of my comrades too.

After a few hours of rest, the snow still being present, we decided to get some fresh air and build snowmen in the courtyard of the communal hall. As amazed as children by the magic of snow, we, the sappers of the 6th Engineer Regiment, started a contest for the most original snowman. This activity, as well as the coolness of this Christmas afternoon, invigorated us, making us forget for an instant our precarious situation.

The competition became fiery, even fierce, everyone endeavoring to bring an original touch to the traditional debonair fellow.

A little later, we watched the result of this improvised game, splitting our sides with laughter! One of the snowmen looked like the spitting image of Father Galloo, wearing a black beret and scarf, as well as a gray blanket serving as the cassock. Further on, another more traditional subject, with a straw hat, coal pieces for the eyes, a carrot for the nose and pebbles for the buttons of his white coat, might have been the perfect archetype if it weren't for a superfluous carrot that had been added as an appendage below the waistband.

The last character, although sinister, made everyone burst out laughing; a piece of soiled Christmas Eve tablecloth as a skirt twisted under disproportionate snow breasts first made us think of a "snow-woman" phantasm; it is true that we were so deprived of a feminine presence. But the lock of brown wool, well pressed on the left of the forehead, the small rectangular mustache under the potato nose, the tattoos of swastikas in twigs left no doubt: Adolfine looked at us pitifully.

She was taking the world by storm!

The hilarity was at its height; we were writhing with laughter with great reinforcements of slaps on the thighs or on the back of the neighbor. The insults and obscenities fused. Suddenly it turned into hysteria as if the sadness and the frustrations contained until that Christmas day sprang from our exasperated bodies; everything that was within reach was thrown violently on this puppet of snow. A true shelling!

Someone shouted, "Board, board! Attack!"

It was the quarry, a merciless hand-to-hand combat with the grotesque effigy. It was who would tear out the eyes and the hated mustache, who would give the most frenzied kicks to abort this belly impregnated with future misfortune.

Soon Adolfine was no more than a shapeless and filthy mound that we ended up crushing under our feet.

Stunned by our own violence, we returned in silence.

The next day, a car from our company came to visit us as we had resumed construction of our barrack. *Le Juteux*, the adjutant Pirioux, brought us a few letters but above all a wonderful, even though slightly delayed, Christmas present. Indeed, some of us were finally granted, with wonder, official leaves for the beginning of January. I was the happiest man on Earth to be in this first wave of leaves. I couldn't believe that I would be seeing my son and my wife again in about two weeks. From that day forward, I impatiently counted down the hours that were bringing me closer to my loves, dreaming up everything I would do while on leave. I imagined my arrival at the train station, Gabrielle and Jean-Pierre waiting for me on the platform. I saw myself running towards them, hugging, and kissing them tenderly. The journey by train would be long but who cared! I wrote a letter to Gabrielle to announce the wonderful news of my upcoming arrival. A few days before my departure, I would also send her a telegram to confirm the time of my arrival.

The New Year arrived after a simple but cheerful New Year's Eve amongst soldiers. We wished each other a safe and happy year 1940, with a prompt resolution of the conflict and a return to normal civilian life.

We did not know then what the future held in store for us.

We were all so happy to see the leaves finally granted; we wanted to forget that we were at war. We all hoped that this situation would soon improve, and that the history of The Great War would at least serve as a lesson so that this war would not get bogged down.

The last few months had toughened us up, even though the fighting had been sporadic. We had already rubbed shoulders with Death and lost comrades under atrocious circumstances. Isolated in this peaceful village, we had gradually started to turn a blind eye to the pains of war. The separation from our loved ones, the uncertainty of tomorrow, the harshness of military life, the permanent fatigue and cold had begun insidiously to fracture our morale. It was high time to go on leave to restore our energy and optimism.

# Chapter 7

## From First Leave to Blockhouse

On January 13, 1940, I finally left for my first leave.

For four long months, I had waited for this moment. I could hardly believe that in a few hours I was going to see my wife and my son again.

I later learned that I had been extremely lucky because the day after my departure, the leaves had been suspended for a few days following the forced landing of a German plane in Belgium due to mechanical problems. The Belgian authorities had seen a dark auspice in this event, suspecting an imminent German invasion of their country. Consequently, all leaves of the French troops stationed near Belgium, of which we were a part, had been suspended. During that time, I spent countless hours in many trains stopping in an infinite number of stations, accompanied by a multitude of soldiers on leave, all impatient to be with their relatives again.

I remembered how Gaby had looked at me with a disarming smile a few years back when I had finally approached her, timidly, to ask her for a walk with me in the woods on an autumn day. I had learned about her sometimes-strained relationship with her stepmother. Indeed, after her mother succumbed to the Spanish flu in

1918 when she was only a child, her father Pierre had remarried his sister-in-law, Maria, a young widow from The Great War, who had found herself with four stepchildren overnight. In addition, in 1931 she had had the immense sorrow of losing her only daughter, Jeannette, who was just turning eight. Overwhelmed with grief and no longer able to face the tough responsibility of raising all the children, Maria had then convinced her husband to board Gabrielle in the Ursulines convent in Saint-Pol-de-Léon.

This secular order of nuns was dedicated to Saint Ursula, a Breton princess kidnapped and pierced with arrows by the Huns in Germany. Her companions – eleven martyr virgins, who, through an erroneous translation of their funeral inscription, found themselves to have grown to eleven thousand when arriving in the legend – had suffered the same fate. In reality, the founder of the Order of Saint Ursula was Saint Angela Merici, but out of humility she referred to the courage and wisdom of Saint Ursula.

Little Gaby had thus found herself a boarder at the Rue des Minimes convent for many years, and at the threshold of adolescence she had felt like an orphan, abandoned by her family. She had retained an acute aversion to community life. In addition to traditional teachings, she had to recite her rosary every day and attend vespers every afternoon at the neighboring chapel. She had painful memories of the Reverend Mother Prioress who made it a point of honor to provide a strict education, even very severe, to the young girls. The Reverend Mother, Marie de Saint Jean, the Mistress of Novices, had even urged her to become a novice, but as a teenager Gabrielle had been more intrigued by the boarders of the Kreisker. The boys of this nearby college run by priest-teachers regularly passed in lines in front of the windows of the convent during their weekly walk. Even if a vicar of the parish had composed a song in Breton, Kastel-Paol, which proclaimed, "*E skeud da douriou, ô Kastel, Eo brao beva ha mervel*" (in the shade of your bell towers, O Saint Pol, it feels good to live and die), she had not had the slightest intention after so many wasted years to continue living in the convent and eventually die in there in isolation.

Therefore, on the very day of her majority, she had given up the veil and quickly left her life as a recluse. Soon after, I had met her and enabled her to wear a completely different veil!

At last, in the early morning, I gradually recognized the country-side, the villages, the houses of my region. Everything seemed calm, so far from this terrible war and the atrocities of the first combats.

Under a January drizzle and a very low sky, my train entered the station of Landivisiau.

The train slowed down. On the platform, I saw Gabrielle carrying Jean-Pierre, a baby I barely recognized. I stepped out of the train, my bag on my back. Despite the fatigue of the journey and the long months of separation, I dropped my bag on the practically deserted platform and ran towards my two loves. Gabrielle smiled, her blue eyes tearful with tenderness, but my little boy seemed to wonder what he was doing here. He was standing upright in Gaby's arms, bundled up warmly, watching me with surprise, curious to observe the reactions of this stranger who had come running with a smile in his direction. Somewhere deep inside, he had probably felt an indelible bond and perhaps recognized my looks, for he gave me a grin from ear to ear that would have melted all the snow fallen on Boeschepe these past few weeks.

Wordlessly, cherishing this moment of pure happiness, I hugged them both together, and time suddenly stopped. There was no more rain, no more station, no more train leaving in a shrill fracas, no more living soul around us. I was only feeling their hearts beating in harmony against mine, their warmth invading me little by little, their scents intoxicating me to ecstasy.

I was back!

The war had increased my love so much for these two beings huddled silently and tenderly in the hollow of my arms.

I was so happy!

The giddiness of that moment enveloped me in a whirlwind of pleasure and tenderness.

After this long moment of bewilderment and immense joy, our azure eyes met, and I kissed Gabrielle in a long and passionate kiss. Staring at us with intense curiosity, like Christopher Columbus discovering the natives of the New World, Jean-Pierre stammered, surprised by this overflow of emotions, and initiated a succession of babbles, trying to attract his mother's attention.

We went through the small, empty train station and walked across the road to the Hôtel de la Gare. This imposing freestone building of several floors was in fact run by Pierre Bizien, Gabrielle's father, and her stepmother Maria. Her brother Alain cut a fine figure and worked there with his wife Anna. The hotel had a large bar at the entrance, always buzzing, leading in the back to the restaurant which had built its reputation with the horse dealers and brokers from the surroundings.

"We are going to wait for your brother François who will come to pick us up and drive us home," Gabrielle told me.

"That's fine," I replied. "As long as I'm with you I could be anywhere and be the happiest man in the world."

She couldn't wait to meet Alain and Anna at the Hôtel de la Gare because she had an unconditional affection for both of them. She was so happy to see them again in my company and with our baby who continued to observe me fixedly, like a new specimen discovered for the first time in the depths of the jungle.

It felt good to be back here, in a familiar environment, surrounded by family and friends. We sat in a back room and Anna brought us coffee with freshly baked croissants. Alain joined us there and, after long hugs, I told them about my first months of war, sparing them painful details, such as the horrible death of Léon and other comrades.

It was difficult for me to express the anguish and isolation I had felt over the past few months. Moreover, I didn't want to worry Gabrielle. I took out of my bag the bracelet that I had bought for her in Bailleul, that market day a few months earlier, and I gave her this late Christmas present. Then, I described the warmest moments, in particular Boeschepe with its unusual *bourles* game, the vertical archery, the fields of hops, the gigantic mill, the tavern with its familial atmosphere, the Christmas Eve dinner with its traditional dishes, and most importantly the crushing of the "snowwoman" Adolfine which made them laugh to tears too.

A short while later, François arrived in his black Traction Avant. I had also missed my brother, as well as working at the carpentry shop. He was so happy to see me again in good health! He told me about the care he had taken to keep our garden in good order, and I thanked him profusely.

He drove us back to our house. Nothing had changed since my departure, except for this little fellow who was now crisscrossing the house on all fours. François proudly showed me the improvements he had made in the garden and took the opportunity to talk to me in a *tête-à-tête*, "You know Alexandre, Herveline and I often came to see Gaby and your little boy. She is very courageous and her rough upbringing with the nuns has prepared her well for such tough times. She was waiting so impatiently to hear from you. To reassure her, I kept telling her that the mail was unreliable in wartime. She watched for Ernest the postman every day, hoping he would hand her one of your letters. The day she finally heard from you, she was so radiant."

"I shared a similarly difficult and straining experience. I had to wait until the beginning of December to receive her first letters, all at once. I knew that, with our moves and the ongoing war, mail would be disrupted, but I was starting to imagine so many horrible scenarios in my head. When I figured out that I wouldn't be back for the holidays, I was so distraught, but finally the time for leave arrived. What a joy to see you all again! Jean-Pierre now travels on his own. He's growing so fast!"

"You know Gaby loves you more than anything. She will always be waiting for you and despite her worry of tomorrow, she remains positive. You are so lucky to have her in your life and you need to take care of yourself. Do not take unnecessary risks and may God protect you!"

"Thank you, François, I appreciate everything you do for us. One of these evenings, you must visit us with Herveline, and perhaps Alain and his wife too. We will celebrate my return and we will play card games."

"It will be my pleasure Alexandre, but first get some good rest. You look so tired! Have a good time with your little family and we'll talk about it again."

I then confided to my brother the difficult times we had experienced in the Saarland, the treacherous and murderous mines, the soldiers killed head-on during our mission, the shameful retreat of our regiment and the disillusion. It seemed that by telling all that I had kept to myself, deep inside me, I was exorcising my nightmares, driving out all my demons of war. Here, in this peaceful garden, it felt like my story was about someone else, like a forgotten film that we involuntarily watch time and time again.

My first night back home was all sweetness and tenderness, intertwined with pure love. How happy I was to finally fall asleep in Gabrielle's arms!

The following days, life resumed its course after this interlude of a few months. I did not return to work in the carpentry shop, but sometimes in the morning I went to give François a hand. When I went into town to get bread or the newspaper, I became inextricably engaged answering questions from the inhabitants who kept asking for news from the front and my opinion on the future of the *Drôle de Guerre*. I was careful not to alarm them and appeared optimistic about a rapid resolution of the conflict.

The weather was cloudy or rainy most of the time and temperatures, although better than in the east, remained relatively cold. One afternoon, while Gabrielle was resting, I walked Jean-Pierre in a stroller, and we went to meditate at the graves of our ancestors. My boy had totally adopted me, and that afternoon filled me with happiness when, taking him from his pram after our walk, he looked at me with a big smile as he reached up to embrace me. I was so proud that I went to wake up Gaby, who was taking a short nap, to tell her about this wonderful step!

Another day with better weather, we drove to the coast. We went to Carantec via Saint-Pol-de-Léon where Gabrielle did not want to stop because of her dark memories as a boarder and then as a novice at the Ursulines convent. In Carantec, we walked on a coastal trail, in front of the Château du Taureau, the only maritime fortress in Brittany which had seen its image restored by the famous Vauban, the poliorcetic expert of Louis XIV.

The sea was beautiful, with emerald and azure reflections, the same color as Gabrielle's eyes. I felt good facing the ocean, free, deeply breathing in the mixed scent of wet seaweed and salty iodine. Jean-Pierre also seemed to enjoy the wind which blushed his cheeks; he vocalized a series of waxing and waning murmurs, which filled us both with happiness. Then, the tide being low, we were able to walk towards the Île Callot, opposite Carantec. The passage was cleared for only a few hours, the island transforming as if by magic into a peninsula. We seized the opportunity to take a walk there.

The air was fresh, but this walk was most invigorating. Gabrielle and I walked the trails side by side. I was carrying Jean-Pierre who snuggled up on my shoulder. The landscape was fabulous, beautiful secluded sandy beaches succeeding one another, nestled between small rocky coves. To the west, beyond the cottony sea spray on a metallic blue sea, we discovered the port of Roscoff, from where the "Johnnies" crossed the Channel on their barge to Plymouth to sell their onions in England. In the center of the island, on a promontory, a small chapel stood out. We headed towards it, attracted like hummingbirds by nectar flowers of vibrant colors.

From this chapel of Our Lady of Kallod, we had a panoramic view of the bay and before entering the holy place, we savored the tranquility and serenity of the moment.

The small chapel, also named for Our Mighty Lady, was deserted, and breathed piety. The decoration was extremely sober, encouraging meditation. Above the altar, a polychrome statue of the Blessed Virgin carrying in her left arm the crowned child Jesus made me think of Gabrielle who, holding Jean-Pierre in her arms, was heading towards the remnants of a few candles which were gradually burning away.

I saw her kneel before the Blessed Virgin and say prayers, her eyes half closed. Then she got up, went to light a candle, and dropped a few coins in the trunk of offerings, near a series of ex-votos. I joined her and she whispered to me, looking at me with her ocean blue gaze, "I have recited a few Hail Marys to the Holy Virgin who carries her son in her arms too. She will easily understand the wishes I expressed to her. I only want us to be all three together, happy, far from wars, and to continue to grow our family. I know she will listen to me, but promise me anyway, Alexandre, to be very careful when you return to war."

At that precise moment, Jean-Pierre, looking at me with affection, started a serenade of prattles that would have broken the heart of the most hardened. "I promise you Gaby, I have already been extremely cautious, and I hope that the conflict will not drag on and that we will all live in peace very soon," I replied, moved by this moment of intense feelings at the heart of this humble but sublime chapel.

Gabrielle placed a tender kiss on my cheek and whispered, "I love you, Alexandre."

"Me too, Gaby. It's now time to turn back if we do not want to see our retreat cut off by the rising tide."

The following Sunday, we had invited Anna and Alain for lunch at home. After Mass, Father Favé, a jovial *bon vivant* with progressive ideas, curly brown hair, a sparkling gaze, and a permanent mocking smile at the corner of his lips, joined us as we had just sat down at the kitchen table.

"Hello everybody. I can see that the earthly food could not wait any longer because the spiritual food lavished during my Mass has already been well digested," the priest said with a mischievous wink.

"Come join us at the table, Louis," Gabrielle replied, allowing herself to call him by his first name, being on familiar terms with him. "Come tell us the latest news and Alexandre will tell you what he saw on the front line."

While drinking a home-made aperitif *quarante-quatre*, Gaby's specialty based on an orange with forty-four holes filled with forty-four coffee beans, macerated with forty-four sugar lumps for forty-four days in alcohol, the priest told us about some recent events, "It looks like the Germans won't stop at the invasion of Poland. This Adolf has Napoleonic plans and delusions of grandeur. The Russians are also worrying since they, in turn, also invaded Poland following the example of Germany. They then attacked Finland a few weeks ago. They try little by little to nibble their passage towards the west, but they have met a fierce resistance in the far north. The Finns stand up to them in the snowy forests and were even victorious in a counterattack on Christmas Eve! Now Denmark, Sweden and Norway have proclaimed their neutrality!"

"I'm glad to hear that the Germans and the Russians don't have it easy – serves them right! This resistance in the north gives me hope that they won't make it to France," Alain replied. "But what is the Good Lord doing in all of this? How can he let these invasions, these killings, this obscene obsession towards certain peoples be? It is said that Nazi Germany performs atrocities on its disabled in the name of a pure race. This is insane!"

Red with anger, Alain added, "This is beyond belief! What is the Church doing to protest such extermination practices, Father?"

"What you report is terrible Alain, if it turns out to be true. I find it hard to believe in so much cruelty. Certainly, the German clerics would revolt against such sinister and criminal practices."

His face turned crimson, flushed with rage. Unable to take it any longer, Alain exploded, "You see Father, that's the problem with religion. You are good at condemning sometimes, but concretely what are your actions against this damned war? The new pope says nothing, sitting comfortably numb in Vatican City. He even commended Franco's victory in the Spanish Civil War, supported by Germany and Italy. He did not deign to denounce the invasion of Poland publicly and he certainly did not join in the Franco-British condemnation. It is also said that the Gypsies are being deported from Germany and the Jews are supposed to wear the Star of David, some with the inscription 'Jude'."

"Calm down Alain," Gabrielle said, well acquainted with her brother's fiery and hotheaded temper. "Louis has nothing to do with it and he tries to help his parishioners in these difficult times. Enough about war and atrocities. Let's start eating."

Conversations continued in a lighter tone for the appetizer, deviled eggs accompanied by rolls of ham stuffed with a mixed vegetables macédoine. Next, Gaby brought her famous rabbit stew, with a delicious sauce whose secret ingredient was a generous dose of port, accompanied by boiled potatoes. Our garden and our rabbit hutches had once again furnished our *table d'hôte* well.

The conversations became more mundane, switching from the historic harshness of this winter to the victories of Marcel Cerdan and the triumph of the Môme Piaf, whom Gaby loved to listen to on the radio, singing, "Les Mômes de la Cloche," "It's Him that My Heart Chose," or "My Legionnaire."

To end the meal, Gaby had prepared my favorite dessert, a Far Breton with raisins – and not with prunes that I hated more than anything – accompanied by a glass of Grand Marnier.

"Gaby, your Far Breton is a delight! You are a real *cordon bleu*," the clergyman said while sipping his glass of digestif. "I will gladly come back every Sunday if you invite me, but now I have to take leave of you to visit Madame Bellec, who seems to have reached the end of the road. I hope that my prayers will help her move on to a more serene hereafter as she has suffered terribly in recent months. Disease has no truce either."

"Thank you for your visit," I replied. "I hope to see you again before I leave."

"I will pray for you, and I will visit Gaby and your son from time to time. May God protect you and take care, Alexandre. Good luck and keep faith!"

As Father Favé was leaving us, we had the good surprise to see François and Herveline arrive. On this gray and rainy Sunday, they had decided to pay us an impromptu visit.

"I hope we haven't scared the priest away!" François said mockingly. "We came over for coffee and now that we are six of us, we could perhaps play a game of rummy if that sounds like fun to you. But first, I have a little surprise for Jean-Pierre."

Hearing his name, Jean-Pierre crawled pronto on all fours to his uncle François, wondering what he was hiding in the large paper bag. The latter unwrapped a series of wooden cubes that he had fashioned himself in the carpentry shop, with letters of the alphabet engraved on some faces and numbers on others. Jean-Pierre was ecstatic in front of these unexpected toys; he would later learn to read and count thanks to this ingenious gift.

"Looks like I made one happy little boy with these modest pieces of scrap wood," exulted François. "Now let's get down to business, a *centime* a point, okay? Gaby, can you pull out two decks of fifty-four cards?"

Sitting around the kitchen table lined with its floral oilcloth, a steaming coffee in our cups, the rain drumming on the windowpanes while the coal stove warmed us from its radiant heat, the afternoon was shaping up well with the family.

After having dealt fourteen cards per person, Alain arranged his cards and got rid of the three of clubs for the discard pile next to the draw pile. Herveline, sitting to his left, drew a card and got rid of the queen of hearts. Gaby, with a big smile, swiftly took hold of the queen of hearts and spread out in front of her two runs of hearts – eight, nine, ten, and queen, king, ace – then triumphantly laid a pair of twos and a tierce including a joker, then discarded the eight of diamonds.

"Dry rummy," she exclaimed! "I feel like luck has given me

rendezvous and you are all going to start with a lot of points. Tough handicap! It seems to me that I am going to get richer today!"

"Either you have been cheating or the cards weren't shuffled well enough," sighed Anna, who was a renowned sore loser.

The afternoon flew by quickly, only briefly interrupted by Jean-Pierre's greedy feed. The card games followed one another, fierce, and Gaby had warded off bad luck because, when tired of losing we decided that it was soon supper time, Gaby had won hands down. We paid her a few francs, like defeated Gaul chiefs laying stacks of staters at the feet of a victorious Roman general.

Alain and Anna left for the Hôtel de la Gare where they had to join the evening service. We had dinner with François and Herveline following Jean-Pierre's bath; he had spent a wonderful afternoon going from lap to lap and trying to understand our excitement for these colored pieces of paper that we threw in turn on the table. The wooden cubes were also a great success, and François promised to carve him some wooden skittles for the next time.

The next day, I went to the carpentry shop. I found again those incomparable scents, the rhythmic symphony of saws and hammers, and the beauty of the furniture that François continued to produce. In my absence, he had hired an apprentice, Yves, a young, beard-less, stocky spring chicken with an impressive build and callused hands. He was helping François assemble an oak armoire with two large side doors and a small door in the middle surmounted by two large shelves. Just before noon, I invited François and Yves to go have a drink in a small café near the fairground, run by Joséphine, our dear "Tante Fine". Alone behind the bar, in a grey smock, a greying bun enthroned on her emaciated face, she greeted us warmly in Breton with *"Yen eo an amzer!"* reminding us that the weather was very cold. Then recognizing me, she added *"Mont a ra mat ganit Alexandre? Yac'h an dud du-se?"* worrying about my health and that of the family. Tante Fine served us a small glass of red wine, but Yves was only entitled to a grenadine lemonade. In the afternoon, I went to the hairdresser Crogennec, near the church; he provided me his one and only *coupe courte*, the short haircut I wanted before my departure which was approaching with great strides in an agonizing way.

The days passed quickly, far too quickly.

A Friday morning, after almost two weeks, I unfortunately had to go back to war, leaving my wife and my son once again, sad, and alone, on the platform wetted by a fine mist.

"I will be back soon, Gaby. The leaves now seem to be more regular and numerous. I will write to you from Boeschepe as often as possible. I'll be careful, I promise. I'll be thinking about you all the time. I love you both, forever," I said to Gabrielle, kissing her tenderly on the deserted platform and hugging them both. Then, I boarded that cursed train where I found myself alone, distraught, and powerless in the face of this monstrous and uncontrollable war machine.

At the end of January 1940, I returned to Boeschepe and joined my comrades. Winter was still here, oppressing and freezing, but the snow had stopped falling. During my short absence, the construction of our barrack had made good progress and we moved in the following weeks, returning the village hall to the parishioners.

"*Bonjour*, Alexandre. How did your leave go?" the priest asked me one morning during one of his visits to our barrack where we had just moved in.

"I was so happy to see my wife Gabrielle and my little boy Jean-Pierre again," I replied, proudly showing him a recent photograph. "He is now crawling on all fours. He recognized me despite the long months of absence and smiled at me time and time again. I miss them both so much, and coming back here feels like landing on another planet."

"I understand your dismay and I am here for you and your comrades if you need to confide. It has been quiet here, apart from several cases of bad flu which unfortunately took away suddenly Mademoiselle Lefebvre, our valiant postwoman."

"I am saddened to hear this awful news. She was so kind and had spoiled us so much for the Christmas Eve dinner with her Christmas log. Hopefully this flu season will not be as bad as the one that broke out after The Great War in 1918!"

Indeed, the extremely contagious and virulent so-called Spanish influenza pandemic – curiously imported from the United States of America – had landed in Europe with American soldiers during The Great War. It had caused the deaths of tens of millions of people around the world.

"I pray that this time the epidemic remains contained because we already have enough worries with this bloody war. Now that your barrack is done and you have settled in, what are your plans?"

"We have been ordered to build a blockhouse on the hill. It is a strategic place that will allow us to watch the surroundings."

"Good luck to you all and may God protect you!"

The priest continued on his way, and we began to search for the ideal location for our new construction.

The following days, while the snow had stopped but the cold and black ice dragged on over scintillating landscapes of frost, we set to clear the ground armed with shovels and pickaxes. With the blueprint of the bunker in hands, we had to build a passive fortified casemate to observe the enemy in the event of an invasion, safe from deadly fire. We had found a relatively flat spot near the top of Mount Boeschepe. The work was hard as the ground was deep frozen. The digging for the blockhouse took us many days and, despite our gloves, our fingers were numb with cold in the early morning before the sun sometimes timidly came to warm us up.

Once the groundwork was completed, we prepared a formwork to pour the raft, a reinforced concrete base platform with a foundation armoring. The day the raft was to be poured, men from a company stationed in the vicinity arrived to lend us a hand.

The following weeks, we prepared the scaffolding to erect the formwork of the block with our detachment of sappers.

Finally ready for the pouring of the block, two dozen men from the neighboring company returned to the site. The weather, which had become much milder, had meanwhile transformed the site into a filthy quagmire. We were wading through a thick and sticky mud, rendering the terrain extremely dangerous and difficult to access. Our concrete mixer had to be moved because it was gradually sinking into the mud. At last, we wedged it on a few wooden planks. On this ground as slippery as an ice rink, Théo stumbled and inadvertently sank a long nail in his left palm. The medical officer was called to urgently cleanse and bandage his open wound. He decided to give him an injection of anti-tetanus serum since Théo had not been vaccinated.

"Here you are in a pickle. Do you know my brave Théo that tetanus was described and named so by Hippocrates?" Jean explained with a gloomy air.

Our budding nurse, always ready to boost the morale of his comrades, continued, "Hippocrate is the one who also examined Democrite because of his unusual laugh, sad and critical," Jean said, using the French names of the "Father of Medicine" and of the Greek philosopher.

While we wondered where he was going with this, he produced a bad punchline. "It is important that one does not confuse Hippocrate who examines Democrite with the hypocrite who examines the democrat!"

As proud as a peacock of this more than doubtful pun, he concluded with a taunting look, "When you think about it, it beats everything that you, a horse broker, received a serum from a horse! You will surely now be as fit as a racehorse to help us, and I hope you won't kick over the traces," Jean continued, mockingly.

After administering the tetanus antitoxin in his left arm, the medical officer gave him the tetanus vaccine in the other arm. Théo was seriously starting to wonder how many more injections he was going to receive and if this doctor was obsessed with syringes! Confirming our growing fears, the medical officer told us that he would return the following days for our anti-typhoid vaccination. We then all turned in unison towards Théo and gave him the evil eye, as if he had drawn the curse of the devilish syringe upon us!

Every day, trucks brought us the materials needed to pour the concrete. The trucks of sand, cement, gravel, and dross – the scoria used in the manufacture of cement – followed one another in a hellish dance, and we worked long, exhausting hours unloading them, then preparing the concrete for its pouring. Little by little, like a mushroom emerging from the earth after a salutary rain, the blockhouse was taking shape, but the coordination of the plans left something to be desired, these being constantly reassessed.

One day we had a visit from artillery officers, curious to see what weapons could be installed in the bunker. Given the strategic position of the blockhouse and its dimensions, they debated on the most suitable type of artillery, either machine guns, grenade launchers, or small caliber anti-tank guns. It was a real turn-up for the books for us that they could not agree on the types of weapons, their positioning, or even the direction of fire!

We were beginning to seriously wonder how many more times we would have to adjust our plans and if this edifice would ever be completed!

At the end of the day, we returned exhausted to our barrack and our reinforcements slept in the now vacant communal hall. One evening, the parish priest arrived at our barrack in a panic and asked us to accompany him immediately. He directed us towards the parish hall, from which we could hear clamors and great fracas. When we arrived, we noticed that the soldiers were all, without exception, dead drunk and that for some unknown reason they had started a general free-for-all, breaking everything in their path. Some were lying outside, barely moving, others were staggering, moaning, and holding their ribs or their heads. The strongest continued to fight, dealing imprecise blows at an invisible foe. We managed to control and calm them with great difficulty.

We learned the next morning, when they arrived at the site – this one with a black eye, that one with a toothless smile or even a broken nose – that some of these soldiers had surreptitiously crossed the border to enter Belgium clandestinely the night before. The announcement of the closure of the border between Belgium and Germany on March 1 had probably made them very worried and they had therefore been eager to get a quarter cask of wine in a border village. Unfortunately, these men had not known how to drink in moderation, as the empty wooden barrel testified. Alcohol helping, the spirits had heated up, verbal aggressions had followed simple disagreements, and they had finally come to blows very quickly.

That morning, this troop of *Pieds Nickelés* was of no help and delayed the pouring of concrete. At nearly a thousand francs the cost of a cubic meter of concrete, this delay caused by our allied masons would further increase the total cost of our construction which was already estimated at more than three hundred thousand francs! We hoped that with these expenses our work would at least be ready and useful if Germany decided to invade France via Belgium.

Another day, we learned that one of the comrades from our detachment, who had gone on leave after me, had not returned on the scheduled day. After three days of delay, he arrived claiming that his train had encountered mechanical problems, making him miss his connections; he was immediately put in prison for a period equivalent to his late arrival. He did not complain because, during that time, he didn't have to work hard and tirelessly like us on the construction site.

# Chapter 8

## *From Vaccination to Last Leave*

While the day was slowly rising one sleepy and silent morning, the growing hum of a car passing through the village woke us abruptly. The vehicle stopped near our home and two doors slammed. We saw the medical officer enter our barrack, accompanied by a nurse carrying a large box.

"Hello gentlemen. After my last visit to treat your comrade's hand and prevent a case of tetanus, I remembered that your detachment had inadvertently escaped the anti-typhoid vaccination campaign that I had carried out in your regiment just before Christmas. So, I came back here today with nurse Armandine to remedy this oversight."

Our eyes, initially fixed on Armandine – a pretty young blonde and busty woman in a very tight and revealing white dress-uniform – then reluctantly turned all at once toward Théo, who had despite himself drawn this curse on our detachment.

"Rest assured, the side effects of the vaccine should be minor compared to typhoid fever. In addition, I'll be back for two more injections, a month apart, for the boosters," the medical officer called out to us, sketching a wicked smile.

"You probably know that an injection is better than a high fever transmitted by contaminated water. If it weren't for this TAB vaccine, we would probably have lost the war in '14-'18!"

During the first year of The Great War, more than one hundred thousand cases of typhoid had emerged on the front lines, causing death by septicemia of nearly a quarter of the soldiers contaminated by this harmful bacillus.

"I'm sure you'll agree with me that it's better to be vaccinated than dead, right?"

We were still wondering what other microscopic plague the medical officer might have in store for us, when the nurse opened the box and unveiled a syringe and vials of the vaccine that was going to be injected under our skin.

We passed in a single file in front of Armandine who, captivating our gazes, made some of us forget for a moment their belonephobia. Unfortunately, many of us developed unwanted and incapacitating side effects for a few days, making us fear the next two injections even more.

Fortunately, as we were struggling to recover from our vaccination, we received letters and packages that cheered us up. Gabrielle had sent me some provisions to brighten up my days: cans of Hénaff pâté, dry garlic sausages, Extra Poulain dark chocolate bars, Banania powdered chocolate, caramel candies, licorice Lajaunie cachous, Nescafé soluble coffee, packets of Petit Beurre Lu and Choco Cas' Croûte biscuits. I was also very happy to learn that I had been granted a second leave for March 10, and I started the countdown to my departure.

That evening, after tasting some of the treats from our packages, I joined Théo, Jean, and Fanch to play belote. The cards seemed to give us a few hours of normalcy and insouciance. For a week, the days had become more and more tense with the endless pouring of concrete and many planes, especially German ones, flying frequently over us. It had stopped snowing, and the weather was starting to warm up. Thus, with flyovers on the rise, we unfortunately expected the worst very soon. I hoped, however, that my leave would not be canceled at the last moment.

Fortune having smiled at me, on Sunday March 10, 1940, I finally left on leave. I had a joyous heart to see my family again, but I was also worried about the evolution of the war.

Jean-Pierre had grown even more during these last months and had not forgotten me. He was more and more active, crawling all over the place and now standing on his own against each piece of furniture, which necessitated a doubling of our surveillance. He grabbed everything that came within easy reach and consequently posted an impressive record of breakage!

The village had also changed a lot since my last visit. French soldiers were now stationed in town in the parish hall. One morning, I made up my mind to visit them to learn the latest news. I introduced myself to a lieutenant who was on duty, "*Bonjour*, Lieutenant. I'm Sergeant Alexandre Rolland, 6th Engineer Regiment, 21st Division. I am on leave to visit my wife and my ten-month-old son. I took part in the battle of Saarland, and I am currently stationed near Bailleul next to the Belgian border."

"*Bonjour*, Sergeant Rolland, I'm Lieutenant Lemoine, 19th Battalion of Light Infantry from the 24th Brigade. We arrived in Landerneau last weekend, and we walked here, the town having made this place available to us."

"Do you know how long you will be staying here? Do you have an idea of your next mission? In the east, we are still building many bunkers and the overflight of enemy planes has recently intensified at the border."

"Our mission order is still uncertain, but we are ready to join the port of Brest one of these days to embark to a Nordic country. In the meantime, morale has been greatly affected by the recent gunshot suicide of one of our captains and other soldiers have also tried to hang themselves."

"I am really sorry to hear that sad news and I hope that you are holding on. If you wish, come join us this evening for dinner. My wife is a fine *cordon bleu*, and we will make you taste our specialties."

"It's very kind of you, Sergeant Rolland, and if you don't mind, I will gladly accept your invitation. I will be happy to escape the daily routine and meet your wife and your little boy."

"See you tonight then Lieutenant but call me Alex!"

After providing him directions to join us for dinner, I went home to tell Gabrielle of his coming for dinner. Punctual, the lieutenant arrived at seven o'clock sharp, a bouquet of carnations in his hand which he graciously offered to Gabrielle.

After the aperitif and tasty dishes accompanied with red wine, Lieutenant Lemoine told us a little more about his future mission.

"We are looking forward to our deployment, probably in Norway. Finland fiercely resisted repeated enemy assaults, but it has just accepted devastating peace terms imposed by Russia. With the neutrality of the other Nordic countries, we must control the North Sea and the Baltic Sea at all costs," confided the lieutenant, who was telling us much more than he was probably allowed.

"But why is this control in the north so critical? How can these countries declare their neutrality when the Nazi threat looms all over Europe?" I asked naively.

"With our British allies, we must absolutely block the transport of Swedish iron to Germany to reduce their military production. These neutral countries must be shaking in their shoes after Finland's defeat; they will be glad to have our support."

I nodded and asked him with a worried look, "With the onset of spring, I also fear that the German troops will soon come out of hibernation. Do you have any other news?"

"I shouldn't tell too much, but it appears that German forces are indeed concentrating near the borders of other neutral countries, in particular Holland, Belgium and Switzerland."

"Belgium?" Gabrielle cried out with a terrifying apprehension, thinking of my cantonment near the Belgian border.

"Yes, unfortunately the latest information confirms these regroupings at the borders. An invasion could take place soon."

Seeing Gaby turn as white as a sheet, I tried to reassure her by saying, "Don't worry Gaby. We are ready to engage them and to defend ourselves. These long months of waiting were put to good use to build a plethora of bunkers and other fortifications. The Germans will not be able to break through our defenses."

"I sincerely hope so, but we cannot underestimate their strength and determination. The Germans have already started to occupy many Norwegian ports and they will probably move towards Denmark as well."

"I'm afraid you're right, Lieutenant. The German time bomb is ready to explode, and I fear the conflict will escalate soon."

After the lieutenant's departure, I tried to reassure Gabrielle about this uncertain future. But words were no longer sufficient. Her worry, anchored deep inside her, had reached its climax and she was now trembling all over while sobbing.

"I don't want you to go back. I do not want to lose you. Jean-Pierre needs a father. I have a bad feeling. I can no longer get rid of this permanent fear that is slowly eating away at me."

"This war is terrible, Gaby, but sooner or later it will end, one way or another. I promised you to be careful and to come back alive from this bloody war. Trust me. I will come back safe and sound."

Drying her tears and pretending to believe me, she took me in her arms and said, "I trust you, Alexandre, but I'm afraid for you. War is such a terrible and unpredictable scourge. I can't imagine a life without you. You must live and come back to me as soon as possible. Don't leave us alone. I will wait for your return, and I hope you will never leave again. Before your upcoming departure, to ward off fate, we will go to the chapel of Saint Michel de Brasparts to ask for divine protection."

The following Sunday, we thus rode in our Simca 8 to the Monts d'Arrée.

The Arrée Mounts, located in Argoat which literally means

"near the woods" in Breton, did not correspond to that description in the slightest. Indeed, the mountains stretched as far as the eye could see, in the very heart of Brittany, but on treeless land, made up mainly of legendary moors, covered with heather and rocks.

The desolate, surreal, otherworldly landscape, punctuated with rocky escarpments, perfectly represented the Breton character, harsh, resilient, and sometimes stubborn like this thousand-year-old rugged moor, but also proud and sharp like the hard rocky peaks rising from this arid land.

The rounded summits or *Menez* succeeded one another, giving a magical and majestic aspect to this place lost at the end of the earth. As the author Anatole le Braz had described so well in his book, "Legend of Death among the Armorican Bretons," we were standing here at the Balcony of the West. This moor, the land of the Korrigans, mischievous goblins, was dressed in a multicolored coat: green mosses and verdigris lichens, purple heather, golden gorse, bluish gentians, and whitish sedges. This sea of pastels undulated under a north wind, giving life to this grandiose landscape.

At last, the pot-bellied silhouette of the Saint Michel de Brasparts mount loomed on the horizon.

After parking the car, we walked up a winding path leading to the top of the rock. All of a sudden, coming out of the moor, an ermine crossed our path. Its white winter coat with a black tail end was beginning to take on spring colors. This incongruous encounter with the symbol of Brittany was most surprising. I saw in it a good omen for the future. Indeed, wasn't the ermine the symbol of courage, purity, and honesty since the dawn of time?

At the top, the small Saint Michel chapel – humble but robust – was perched on a flat ridge, open to the elements. Alone on this rocky summit, we absorbed a magnificent and changing landscape at each of the cardinal points. Towards the north, a succession of rocks loomed beyond Roc'h Trevezel, like the backbone of a gigantic skeleton of dinosaur that once haunted these places. Turning our gaze to the right, we could see with awe the bogs of Yeun Elez. This

Marsh of Hell, dark and unfathomable, was according to legend the Gates of Hell which welcomed the ungodly souls of the condemned. A shiver ran through my back at the thought of the Ankou, a spectral figure clothed in a black shroud and armed with his inverted scythe to sever the souls piled up in his cart before delivering them to the swamp forever.

Another legend told how the ghosts of men who had led a dreadful life came back to haunt their house and had to be exorcised by transferring their spirit into the body of a black dog. Then, at nightfall, a priest entered the black and icy water of the marshes to throw the beast into the abyss of Hell, also called *Youdig*.

Recently, part of the bog had been used to create a huge artificial lake in which the ominous dark clouds, wandering over the horizon, were now reflected. Continuing our panoramic observation, we discovered in the distance more fertile valleys opening onto the Black Mountains tearing the sky with their sharp ridges.

His cheeks reddened by the wind whipping his face, Jean-Pierre seemed happy to spend these moments in the great outdoors with his family. We held his hand, each on his side, and he awkwardly ventured to take a few strides towards the chapel.

The seventeenth century Chapel of the Shepherds, consecrated on the day of Saint Michel, stood before us, majestic in its austerity: a simple chapel made of local granite stones, surmounted by a timid spire, and sheltered by shale slates quarried from neighboring areas. We descended the few stone steps worn by the footsteps of pilgrims from olden times, in particular those who, invoking the Archangel Saint Michel, prayed for the return of the soldiers from The Great War, safe and sound, and for peace. Stooping down, we passed a small, low side door. The chapel was deserted. A row of raw oak benches faced a bare altar, flanked by two stained-glass windows painfully lighting up the interior on this gloomy day.

Gabrielle knelt on a bench, facing the stained-glass windows illuminating her serene face. I fixed in my memory her angelic face, her gaze of such pure blue, the line of her lips, her graceful figure and in that instant, I fully appreciated the blessing of our reciprocal and ever-growing love. After having dropped a few coins into a trunk which sounded mostly empty, I walked with Jean-Pierre to a dark corner of the chapel to light a candle. In front of this dawning glow, I begged Saint Michel to protect me and to quickly end this cursed war. Gabrielle, collected, eyes lowered, intoned a prayer in Breton in a low voice, *"Euz ho trôn saret huet, var lein Menez Are,"* imploring the Archangel, "From your throne raised on top of the Monts d'Arrée" to watch over our family. Jean-Pierre seemed to understand the gravity of the moment and suddenly began to cry with scalding tears. My kisses and gentle words could not calm his long and tormented sobs amplified by the empty chapel. Gabrielle stood up, made the sign of the cross, and took the inconsolable toddler in her arms. We left the chapel in a hurry, at the very moment when the heavens started to tear apart. A typical Breton deluge poured down on us as if to signify that the Archangel had decided to absolve our sins and seal our pact of protection.

A few days later, I found myself alone with Gabrielle on the train station platform. Jean-Pierre had caught a cold during our trip to the Monts d'Arrée and had stayed warm indoor with his *tonton* François. The drizzle mingled with our tears as we kissed tenderly on the platform while waiting for the train which was already whistling its arrival in the distance. Gabrielle clung to me as if to hold me back desperately and prevent me from boarding the train where only loneliness, sadness, and disquietude awaited me.

I was far from suspecting the interminable separation that now awaited us.

I had sworn once again to Gabrielle not to take any unnecessary risks and to get back to her as soon as possible.

But the future unfortunately would decide otherwise.

On the train, to take my mind off my worries, I read the latest news. The headlines of the Dépêche de Brest announced that Paul Reynaud had become Prime Minister after a cabinet reshuffle in which the government of Édouard Daladier had been overthrown.

Despite his cowardly inaction following the attack on Finland by the Soviet Union the past few months, Daladier nevertheless found another post, and not the least, as Minister of War and National Defense in the new Reynaud cabinet. His apparent incompetence, rewarded by such a critical government position, did not foreshadow a favorable outcome of the war, as the months to come would reveal. Then, to kill time, I immersed myself in a new novel by my favorite author, Agatha Christie. "And Then There Were None" would become one of my favorite novels, which I would reread several times, with "The Murder of Roger Ackroyd," another masterful *tour de force* of this genius writer and English queen of suspense.

On March 22, 1940, I was back in Boeschepe. My heart was heavy to have left my wife and my son, but seeing my comrades in arms again gave me comfort and renewed energy. I learned that the construction of the blockhouse was soon to be completed, but Jean gave me the sad news of the death of career Captain Lejeune, just before his fiftieth birthday. Following extremely violent words vociferated by his commanding officer against him, he had committed suicide. Commandant Billot, a gruff runt, full of himself, with a huge, repressed inferiority complex, had no tact and was unfortunately notorious for verbally assaulting his officers in public, barking insults and baseless accusations. The unfortunate captain had no longer been able to stand this recurring bullying from the commander and had shot himself in the head the day before his birthday. This news upset me greatly; I had met the captain on several occasions, and he had inspired my respect and confidence. In a secluded farm of a remote hamlet in his native Ardèche, he left behind a grieving widow and three teenagers with now a more than uncertain future.

The day of my return happened to be Good Friday. I therefore expected a meal of fish or white beans, which I particularly liked seasoned with a good dose of vinegar. To my great surprise, the beans were replaced by potatoes and the fish by red meat. Gabrielle would have undoubtedly considered it sacrilege! But the intendance had to quickly dispose of the excess meat, and we gladly accepted this sin –

probably not mortal – swearing to confess to the good Father Galloo one of these upcoming days.

The next day, to boost the morale of the troops, we decided to engage in a soccer game against our reinforcements, now sober, stationed in the communal hall. We found ourselves at the soccer field where some locals had joined to support us. I was a goalkeeper, the least compromising position for our team, as this sport was not my cup of tea, except as a spectator. A swimming competition would have been more appropriate for my physical skills but, short of the ocean, I had ample opportunity to repeatedly dive into the puddles and mud lining the goal. Despite a few saves, as remarkable as lucky, and the efforts of my teammates, we were flatly crushed, like Napoleon at Waterloo; our defeat was qualified by Jean, our center-forward with a single shot on goal during the whole game, as the "hammering of the century." Despite our stinging defeat – it is indeed difficult to qualify a result of nine goals to zero in any other way – we all met again at the tavern for the post-game where, this time with more intoxicating highballs, we quickly settled the score!

On April 9, in the only estaminet of the village, we celebrated the completion of the blockhouse construction, having backfilled all around it with the soil removed from the excavation many months earlier. We learned from the TSF Radio that Jo and Marie-Louise had turned on that the Germans had invaded Denmark, without any consideration for the neutrality of the country; they were now occupying Copenhagen. As a consequence, all leaves were suspended until further notice, and I wondered if I would be lucky enough to see Gabrielle once again in May.

I also thought about Lieutenant Lemoine who had undoubtedly gone to Brest to embark and defend Norway, where many German troops had taken up positions. With the return of sunny days, it seemed that Germany was preparing for a massive invasion of the Nordic countries followed by Holland and Belgium on the way to France. We also learned that Norway and Sweden had decreed a general draft.

Without the shadow of a doubt, Germany had already lit the fuse that would ignite destructive fires across Europe, and I feared that a point of no return had been crossed.

My fears were confirmed in the following days. Ominous news announced German troops concentrating in front of our Maginot line and at the Belgian, Dutch and Luxembourg borders. For several days, German planes had been flying overhead, dumping leaflets, trying to sow discord between the Allied troops. We thus discovered satirical drawings, against the English, reminding us of the contemptible judgment of Joan of Arc by Bishop Cauchon and her brutal death at the stake in Rouen, fueled by the Englishmen.

Jean, who was looking at these propaganda drawings with us, could not restrain himself and declaimed with a fake solemn air, "What a *cochon* this Bishop Cauchon! It is he who should have been roasted for his collaboration with the *Rosbifs* of the country of the Beefeaters, and for having handled the Pucelle of Orleans."

"Jean, your tongue will be your downfall if you continue to insult our Allies! It is true that we have had more than one conflict with our neighbors across the Channel, but they are now fighting at our side. Our unity is strength," I replied, frustrated by Jean's too easy jokes.

Jean examined another caricature representing Napoleon Bonaparte in exile on the island of Saint Helena, lost in the middle of the Atlantic, under severe watch by an English guard. He added in a slightly more restrained tone, "Of course, Alex, you're right. But the Brits weren't kind to our Little Corporal either. Bonaparte was a good guy; he gave us a Civil Code for the first time in our history, guaranteeing equality between all French citizens. In addition, he also left us his famous Cognac!"

"These cartoons are just a bad, defamatory propaganda trying to demoralize us, but if the Germans need such Machiavellian manipulation, they aren't so sure of themselves," I said looking at another cartoon illustrating a French soldier emerging from a trench to go on the attack while a phlegmatic mustached Englishman, leaning on a parapet, sipping a whiskey, a cigar in his hand, cried mockingly, "Charge, comrades!"

The following weeks were most agonizing. The increasingly frequent overflights of enemy or allied planes and the alarming news on the radio made our anxiety palpable. We were bundles of nerves as we started a new project to build barracks in a neighboring village for troops passing through. Every day we expected to see tanks looming on the horizon, flanked by German troops, supported by the Luftwaffe air force.

So, when Wednesday evenings arrived, with the showing of a film for our regiment in Bailleul, we walked light-footedly towards town. After the presentation of some news, often obsolete, we tried to escape our anxiety by watching the movies selected by the General Staff.

"Tonight, we are going to know the sequel to 'Marius' that we saw last week," Fanch said, walking briskly down the road to Bailleul.

"It was all the same a pillock this Marius, dropping Fanny to keep mum and go to sea instead," Théo replied.

"You are talking nonsense. Marius did not keep Fanny's mum, Honorine, the fishmonger with her constant fisheye!" Jean replied with a smirk at the corner of his lips.

"But, no, not keeping her mum. Just keeping mum! I don't have sea legs and I get seasick, so I would definitely have chosen the girl over the ocean."

"Of course, I too would have loved to go to a 'fish market' while trying to avoid catching an assortment of 'crabs'," Jean said, giving me a mischievous wink.

To cut short Jean's fallacious allusions, I declared, "Still, marrying the widower Panisse for his money! Fanny disappointed me," I replied. "Perhaps she had some unknown reasons and 'César' will undoubtedly enlighten us more this evening. I have to admit that I haven't read the saga written by Marcel Pagnol so I can't wait to watch the sequel. In any case, it is fortunate that we don't cheat at belote like César when he declaimed, 'You break my heart' at the attention of Escartefigue."

"That remains to be seen! The last time we played belote I was left with another Fanny – Sweet Fanny Adams – and I wonder if you and Jean didn't use some secret signs," Théo replied.

After the screening of the picturesque and sunny film "César," which had been released in cinemas recently, conversations resumed excitedly more than ever.

"What a shame to sacrifice a whole life out of spite! Césariot lacked nothing and succeeded in life but at what cost. Fanny sacrificed her best years for her son, but luckily in the end all's well that ends well," Théo said with a tear in his eye.

"I really liked this melodrama, and the accent from Marseilles always makes me laugh, even if it is quite soapy."

Seeing that no one reacted to his comment, Jean added, laughing out loud, "Soapy! For the Marseilles soap. Do you get it?"

"Well, I wash my hands of your Marseilles soap and your cheap jokes. At the movies, we were completely packed and now I'm whacked, so stop your quack, wack!" Théo replied surprisingly, suddenly inspired by the air of the Mediterranean.

But on May 10, 1940, returning from the village where we had continued to build wooden barracks for our soldiers in transit, we learned that German troops had finally invaded Belgium, Luxembourg, and the Netherlands. Before the sun rose on the horizon, a swarm of paratroopers had been dropped from silent gliders inland in these countries, followed by massive attacks by tanks and the German army.

The "Battle of France" was well and truly underway!

# "Prisoner"

*A man who deprives another man of his freedom is a prisoner of hatred, prejudice and narrow-mindedness.*
Nelson Mandela (1918-2013)

*It is a mistake to believe that average men can only make average sacrifices.*
Georges Bernanos (1888-1948)

*A courageous prisoner sets himself free in his prison.*
Fenelon (1651-1715)

# Chapter 9

## *From Liberty to Submission*

The sun had not yet appeared on the horizon as the convertible Peugeot 402 sped along the deserted country roads. Lieutenant Faurie slowed down as he entered the village, still asleep, while seven knells echoed from the octagonal bell tower. The car stopped near the wooden barrack and the lieutenant burst into the room where we were barely awakening.

"Rise and shine, fainéants, the Germans are at our gates. We have been ordered to leave for Belgium, which they attacked at the same time as Holland. Get your things ready and meet this afternoon on the Grand Place in Bailleul where you will receive your mission order."

"Yes, Sir. At your orders, Lieutenant. We will get ready and join the regiment as quickly as possible. We were already on alert since yesterday when we heard the latest news," I replied, worried about this hasty departure to an unknown destination that would undoubtedly bring us face to face with the enemy.

Indeed, this Friday, May 10, 1940, the German forces had not contented themselves with invading Belgium, Holland, and Luxembourg in a massive and carefully coordinated attack, but they had also started their insidious penetration into France through the Ardennes. The French High Command had decided to ignore the lessons of The Great War and the alarming, but well-founded information provided by the King of Belgium, Leopold III, and his staff, indicating the Germans' intention to enter France once again through the Ardennes. The Maginot line had even been previously interrupted along the Belgian border at this exact location, the topography of the Ardennes with its very dense forests being considered a sufficient deterrent.

The narrow-minded and traditional French General Staff had preferred to continue to believe in a more likely breakthrough via Belgium or Luxembourg for which it had defined a defense strategy a few years back and had decided to stick to it.

We were far from imagining that this Lightning War, *Blitzkrieg*, would end less than three weeks later with a landslide German victory.

The enemy success of this 18-day campaign would in no way reflect the courage and frenzied resistance of the Allied forces, their numbers and armaments, but it would in part be the result of the tactical daring and cunning of the German troops, infiltrating France through the Ardennes, considered impassable.

We set about preparing our bags and equipment, and we said our goodbyes to Father Galloo and some of the villagers who, with lumps in their throats, lavished blessings and encouragements on us. Then, in deep silence, we started walking to Bailleul where we arrived in the afternoon.

The bustling square we had arrived at on a market day several months earlier was now crowded with soldiers and all sorts of military vehicles that seemed to move in a Brownian motion accompanied by a surreal cacophony. After joining our regiment to learn our mission, we headed for the train station to be transported to Belgium to lend a hand.

Through the train windows, we could see the panic that this sudden attack had already engendered. Long lines of bicycles loaded with hastily prepared suitcases succeeded crowded cars, their roofs overloaded with trunks and other luggage, as well as carts drawn by horses panicked by this forced and frenzied migration towards the west. In the distance, muffled explosions illuminated the landscape while thick baneful plumes of smoke made our imagination drift towards the most morbid thoughts.

A few long hours later, we arrived at Saint-Pierre station in Ghent, Belgium. A staggering number of trains were parked on parallel tracks, and the station and its surroundings were teeming with soldiers and military equipment. We learned that after crossing the Ardennes, the German troops had taken control of the bridges over the Meuse River, allowing a dazzling breakthrough at Sedan, on a front only a few kilometers wide, just as in the two previous wars.

The French General Staff was once again ridiculously mistaken.

One more time, History repeated itself, despite the warnings and common sense.

From the heights of his Eagle's Nest, Adolf was already celebrating, with his generals and his Eva, the overwhelming success of his daring trap. He had bet on the element of surprise and the well-known stubbornness of the French, determined to protect the center of Belgium as a priority. He knew full well that the Reich could not have endured a war of position and attrition.

He had had to act quickly, cross the Ardennes and then the Meuse in three or four days, not one more. His daring strategy was not to allow the Allied forces time to redirect and concentrate against his troops. Unfortunately, we had already been directed to Ghent while the enemy entered France via Sedan under limited resistance.

It is true that the German forces had done everything to put the odds on their side. An armada of tanks and planes had spilled over Sedan while the German soldiers had been bestowed a feeling of invulnerability thanks to their doping with the Göring's pill. Indeed, twenty thousand Pervitin methamphetamine pills had been distributed to the troops for this attack, eliminating their angst and their need for sleep, while boosting their morale and giving them the perception of being invincible! In addition, at the controls of the swarm of German planes which supported the ground invasion, the pilots were also ecstatic, heads in the clouds. After having glutted methamphetamine chocolate, *Fliegerschokolade* or aviator's chocolate, they too felt superhuman!

For hours the French troops had been paralyzed under a deluge of bombs dropped by hundreds of Junkers dive bombers and Heinkel horizontal bombers, accompanied by the staccato fire from the machine guns of the Messerschmitt fighters. Meanwhile, the *Panzer-kampfwagen* assault tanks – formidable and impenetrable armored combat vehicles – had spread with the German infantrymen like wildfire across French territory. They were stunned to discover that most of the French blockhouses were not even finished, the armored access doors not having yet been installed.

We were trying to grasp the power of such a swift breakthrough. The earth and the dwellings had shuddered, reminding us of the terrible earthquake that had ravaged Turkey the previous year, killing tens of thousands of people.

Suddenly, a high-pitched alert sounded in the train station where we had temporarily settled.

Having taken shelter in the hall of the train station, we waited helplessly for the outcome of this lightning attack. The anti-aircraft machine guns huddled behind piles of sandbags tried to reach these birds of doom in flight. In a flash, under the shock wave of the first explosions, the windowpanes of the train station shattered into a thousand sharp and deadly pieces. The ceiling and walls cracked as a thick cloud of dust enveloped and blinded us.

The explosions were deafening.

We curled up on the tiled station floor in a survival reflex. Luckily, the bombs narrowly missed three ammunition trains parked on the railroad tracks near the station. We could hear Allied fighters chasing the enemy planes. At last, with the support of machine guns on the ground, they managed to deter the bombers from returning to their original target.

Still reeling from this brief but devastating attack, we gathered in front of the train station, covered in dust and rubble. We had narrowly escaped a certain death, had the ammunition trains been hit by the bombers. Nevertheless, our regiment lost a lieutenant, the doctor who had insisted so much to vaccinate us, a chief warrant officer from Tours, a young aspirant from Rennes and a master sergeant from Brest, a man named Ligniez. Around us, the dead and the wounded were everywhere; bloody, burnt, limbs torn off, guts winding from their open bellies like a nest of snakes, some stretched their hands towards the heavens in an ultimate plea.

The confusion was at its paroxysm. It was not until several hours after the tracks were cleared and repaired that we learned that we had to leave immediately by train to Holland. Our objective was to blow up a bridge at a strategic junction to delay the German invasion. On our way, we learned that the Dutch troops had stood up to the German forces, deprived of the support of the Luftwaffe air force which was concentrated on Sedan. A German regiment had been ready to surrender; the encircled SS officers of the *Waffen Schutzstaffel* had already prepared a white flag. Unfortunately, for lack of sufficient communication, the Dutch troops decided to stop the fighting abruptly. The German forces seized that opportunity to regroup and return to the offensive. When we arrived beyond the Dutch border, we learned that the Germans had since advanced rapidly and already crossed the bridge we were supposed to mine.

As soon as we arrived in Holland, we were therefore ordered to retreat.

We marched for days on end to fall back towards France, while by mid-May Holland had surrendered. After passing through Sedan, the German soldiers and Panzer tanks also moved rapidly, overtaking the Allied forces, and gradually tightening their grip towards the English Channel. They took Amiens, posing for posterity in front of its cathedral and approaching dangerously close to the capital. A few days later, Boulogne and Calais also fell into enemy hands.

The Battle of Dunkirk began brutally on May 26, 1940.

Meanwhile, as we walked cautiously without too much trouble towards France through Belgium, one afternoon we were ordered to take up our position in a field, on a hillock, armed with our obsolete rifles from The Great War. Intelligence indicated that German troops were advancing rapidly in our direction. Lying down, taking aim with my Babel, I watched the horizon nervously, knowing that soon we would have to face the enemy. Gradually, a cloud of dust rose in the distance and a low rumble resounded over the plain. A pack of German tanks grew and sprawled out before our frightened gazes, like an uncontrollable giant metastasis, while an inordinate infantry strode at a fast pace. Pinned to the ground, holding our breaths, we felt what the Lilliputians had probably felt as Gulliver approached: an immense and treacherous terror. Meanwhile, the German air force was circling over us in incessant revolutions. We were undoubtedly going to be run over and crushed when our lieutenant shouted, "*Sauve qui peut!*"

Without having fired a single bullet, which would have been futile considering the magnitude of the forces threatening us, we took to our heels. Seeing our flight, the Germans began to take aim. We ran for our lives without looking back, as fast as we could, amid the explosions and bullets whistling all around us. Panting and exhausted, we soon found ourselves together in the shelter of a wood, except for one man. After a few moments to catch our breath and collect ourselves, the lieutenant encouraged us to continue our journey at a run to reach France as quickly as possible, leaving behind our missing comrade and the German hordes on our heels.

As we continued our marathon towards the border, Operation Dynamo had been activated in Dunkirk. Caught in a pincer maneuver, the Allied troops could no longer advance. Their last resort was to cross the Channel to reach England. These last days of May saw tens of thousands of British and French soldiers embark every day on military vessels supported by an armada of fishing and pleasure boats that endured relentless raids by German airplanes. Explosive and incendiary bombs rained down by the thousands on Dunkirk, cloaked in a thick veil of black smoke. Water and fire mingled in a macabre dance over the English Channel.

The enemy's objective was very simple and radical: to erase Dunkirk from the map of France forever, pulverizing any house or other building, destroying any vehicle, and ruthlessly eliminating not only the Allied soldiers but also all inhabitants – men, women, and children.

The formations of German bombers followed one another at a metronomic rhythm in the darkened sky, creating a deafening din. In Dunkirk, ambulances tried in vain to sneak through the rutted streets littered with shattered bodies, shredded vehicles, as well as piles of bricks and fallen stones from destroyed homes. The stretcher bearers ran bravely, oblivious to the surrounding explosions, carrying the wounded to the nearest emergency stations. One of these stretcher bearers, Louis Aragon, would later express all the horror of these cowardly bombings of the civilian population in one of his poems:

> "... I will scream, I will wail louder than the bomb-
> shells, those who are injured, and those who have
> been drinking ...
> ... I remember the eyes of those who embarked ...
> ... In the sea where the dead mingle with the seaweed
> The overturned boats make bishops' hats ..."

Indeed, of the thousands of boats that left the port of Dunkirk during these terrible days, many were those that found eternal rest at the bottom of the dark and menacing abyss.

Dunkirk and its port were being decimated. The perilous evacuation of Allied troops continued towards England, taking advantage of a slowdown in the bombardments due to bad weather and smoke from the fires which eliminated all visibility. Meanwhile, we finally crossed the Franco-Belgian border.

The Germans were on our heels; our squadron moved with difficulty on the roads congested with refugees who had left their homes to take refuge further west. Lines of families on foot, carrying children, suitcases, and bundles, succeeded the peloton of overloaded bicycles. Carts, drawn by hand or by sluggish horses, on which had been piled pell-mell most of their goods, added to this throng; more seldom cars or trucks accompanied this crush.

When, with machine guns in action, enemy Stukas dove on crowded roads like birds of prey thirsty for violence, we dispersed hastily into the surrounding fields or woods. These attacks were returning more and more frequently. We were now passing through ghost villages that had been deserted and sometimes looted by German soldiers. As we approached one of those villages, we noticed an isolated farm on the edge of an undergrowth.

We could hear frightened lamentations coming from a wooden hut near the farm. Suddenly, we saw two German soldiers unpin hand grenades and throw them inside. The cries of terror morphed into moans of agony and then gradually into a heavy silence. As the smoke cleared, the soldiers entered the barn, pointing their rifles. They came out with a handful of men in a state of shock, haggard eyes, dribbling with blood. The Germans had captured British soldiers and locked them up in this hut. With a smirk on their lips, they had without warning thrown their murderous grenades at these despondent unarmed men; some of the officers made a final sacrifice, throwing themselves face down on the explosive charges to protect their comrades. The survivors were now being escorted in our direction. The threatening and sadistic looks on the Germans' faces foreshadowed the worst.

We began to walk briskly, hunched over and crawling in their direction. Other sentries joined them as the British soldiers were being forced to kneel down under the threat of strikes with rifle butts. At that precise moment, we rushed towards them, firing our rifles in endless bursts at these torturers. The lives of these British soldiers were spared for a second time in the space of a few minutes. Running towards the farm with my comrades, seized with a sullen and uncontrollable rage, we continued to shoot endlessly at any enemy silhouette. One of them was crouched behind a bush. He was relieving himself of a pressing urge, now trying to put his pants back in a hurry. I freed him of any other envy for eternity, with a clean shot to the head.

Sustained gunfire began to rain from a small wood on the other side of the farm. We quickly took cover and responded blindly, without any damage. When the gunshots started to lessen, we were ordered to fall back towards the suburbs of Dunkirk.

At nightfall, we arrived at Coudekerque-Branche. At the bend of a canal, we met a teacher who directed us to a school where, he informed us, many women were already gathered with their children in a cellar. Our arrival did not ease up on them; the look of the women spoke volumes about the days of anguish they had already spent underground in terrible conditions, without water or electricity, helplessly going through repeated bombardments. Some children shed tears, from hunger and fear, inconsolable. We gave them the meager rations we had left and decided to spend the night in this cold and humid place before sneaking into Dunkirk the next day.

The school was near a canal spanned by an ordinary looking bridge. However, this bridge was at a strategic crossroads, and we learned that it had already been mined as a last resort to slow down the German breakthrough. I was ordered to go with two of my men to check in the middle of the night whether the explosive charges were still intact under the bridge.

We sneaked out, armed with our legendary rifles. The night was dark. The stars had deserted the heavens, and the moon was veiled by the thick smoke of fires from Dunkirk. We hugged the walls of the school to the canal and then crawled through tall grass. Arrived near the bridge, hidden under a large stone on the bank, I found the electric wires which had previously been connected to the explosives installed out of sight on the piles of the bridge. While my comrades stood guard, I took off my helmet, my shoes, and my jacket which I put in a bag. I entered the brackish and cool water.

I swam hushfully from pillar to pillar, each time checking that the connection of the conducting wires to the detonators, the latter connected to the explosive charges, had remained intact. Then I swam back to my two comrades waiting on the bank. As I was getting dressed, despite my careful attention to making no noise, a German sentry on the other side of the canal noticed me. An unrelenting strafing ripped through the night. In all haste, I pulled an exploder out of my bag and connected it to the lead wires.

Bullets whistled above our heads and exploded all around us. My comrades fell to the ground; I threw myself face down on the handle of the exploder which sank, generating an electrical impulse which fired the detonators. These, in a chain reaction, activated the detonating cords which instantly set fire to the powerful explosive charges. With a deafening detonation, the pillars exploded, and the bridge collapsed into the canal, throwing stone debris in all directions.

This destructive fireworks display took the Krauts by surprise, stopping in their tracks the blind hail of bullets. This instant of calm allowed us to crawl away quickly. We did not shoot so as not to indicate our position.

I do not know which saint was on duty that evening to watch over us, but he made sure that we returned to the school safe and sound, after allowing us to detonate all the explosive charges from a distance, thus cutting us off temporarily from the enemy.

Back in the school cellar, while drying myself off and trying to regain some warmth, I narrated to Jean and others who were still not asleep our nightly adventure and how luck had smiled upon us, "Our lucky star guided us this evening. We narrowly escaped the bullets of those damned Boches, but at least we didn't come back empty-handed; they won't go through this bridge either tonight or tomorrow!"

"Alex, you are the king of the mines, even though your appearance does not look royal at the moment. You were lucky with these Heinies swarming across the canal, invisible but stubborn. True parasites!"

I thought to myself that I had indeed been lucky in my mission, and with a shudder I remembered the promise made to Gabrielle to be most careful.

"You know Jean, tomorrow we may be on the beaches of Dunkirk; I hope we can embark for England to regroup and come back *en masse* to crush the enemy."

"I pray to God that we will find a place on these ships which, rumor has it, have already evacuated hundreds of thousands of soldiers. However, it will be neither a cakewalk to get to the sea, nor a pleasure cruise afterwards with all the floating mines."

"The captain told me that hundreds of ships have been sunk, and the Germans have given no quarters on the dunes or in the city. But we must try reaching England."

The previous days, the German pilots had indeed concentrated their fire on the Allied soldiers who tried to embark, sometimes by stepping on the roofs of vehicles aligned side by side on the beach to serve as jetty. Thousands of soldiers jostled each other, sometimes violently, carried by this human tide onto the various embarkation piers, some trying to pass their turn under some dubious pretexts.

"It'll be funny, Alex, to drive on the left side of the road and eat roast beef with peas and mint. I bet we'll sing, 'God Save the King' for King George VI. When I think about it, it's not the same thing over there; it's not in France that Puritans would dethrone the President as they forced Edward VIII to abdicate in favor of George! Kicking up a row just because he wanted to marry a twice divorced American woman, a certain Wallis Simpson. A little birdie told me that the British government did everything in their power to remove this princely couple because they had too much sympathy for Nazi Germany."

"Jean, you spend far too much time in the dentist's waiting room reading gossip in magazines. You are probably making this up once again. Anyhow, I will be happy when we approach the white shores of Albion."

Jean, now focused on the English monarchy, hastened to add,

"When you think that it was the father of George VI who changed the name of their foreign-sounding, double-barreled Saxe dynasty to Windsor during The Great War to make it less Germanic! Taking the name of an English castle to bury the lede. It's really good to be the king!"

Proud to play Mr. Know-it-all by showing off his knowledge acquired during his too frequent visits to the tooth puller, Jean added, "Did you know that Adolf knows this area quite well? During The Great War he painted watercolors of neighboring villages. It is a pity that he did not confine himself to this art instead of playing dictator."

"I hope there will be justice in this world! Let's try to rest a little because the road to the port, even though only a few kilometers long, will not be a cinch tomorrow. *Bonne nuit*, Jean."

After a few hours of rest, on Monday June 3, 1940, when the day had not yet risen, we set out for Dunkirk.

We crossed apocalyptic landscapes, civil and military machines of all kinds littering the canals as well as the deserted streets. We were advancing step by step, guns aimed, on the lookout. The Allies had formed a formidable resistance around the Dunkirk pocket to allow British troops and French soldiers to evacuate this death trap which was inexorably closing in on them. Allied trucks, automobiles, machine guns, tanks, motorcycles, and cannons had been abandoned here and there, thus providing an extraordinary barrier against the invader. Progressing with difficulty through this mechanical ossuary, we observed with surprise rows of hundreds of motorcycles and side-cars, arranged like the megalithic alignments of Carnac, anachronistically in perfect working order but abandoned in a field by their dispatch riders.

We walked in amazement through the cobbled streets, rendered impassable by the devastating impact of bombs and shells. They were littered with canine and feline remains but also charred and torn human bodies. The smell was unbearable. A haze of smoke and dust hung over this phantasmagorical landscape. Our incredulous gazes anchored forever in our memories the specter of the devastated habitations, strewn with rubble, heaps of stones and intertwined scrap metal, enveloped in a mourning veil of smoke.

We had landed on a lunar landscape, surreal, defying all logic.

The air combats that continued were now at their apotheosis. The English Spitfire fighter planes had finally been deployed with their machine guns twice as numerous as those of the Messerschmitt. These fighters were also much faster than the German fighters, inflicting many losses on the enemy.

We walked very slowly and carefully, step by step, from house to house, under a veritable deluge of fire. From time to time, while the heroic defense of Dunkirk continued unabated, we encountered enemy detachments; the fighting was extremely violent. During one of these fierce skirmishes, while we were lying in a defensive position behind the remains of a Panhard armored car, my company suffered two injuries, one of them life-threatening to the belly. We had to be constantly on the alert because snipers could surprise us at any moment, posted at the window of one of these gaunt buildings. We did not know who we might meet around these collapsed miners' houses. Passing on the cobblestones of the Rue de la Marine, between the piles of rubble and the ruins, we realized the magnitude of the calculated annihilation which had been going on for endless days. In the middle of these chimerical remains, only the remnants of the door frame of a café entrance, whose irony of fate had afflicted the name of "Impeccable," reminded us that these ruins had recently had a soul, a life, now destroyed forever.

At the end of that day, the Germans were still contained at the gates of the city. They had not been able to enter Dunkirk.

Under the cover of darkness, as a thick fog settled over the sea, we approached the dunes where a continuous stream of Allied soldiers poured in from all the passages converging to the beach. Thousands of men, some seriously injured, limping or barely able to stand, desperately clinging to their comrades for support, attempted to approach the pier to board one of the fifty ships anchored in the port. All kinds of vehicles were lined up for miles out to the sea, serving as temporary and precarious jetties on which soldiers struggled to walk to the boats.

With the other men of our company, we tried in vain to get closer to the embarkation points. We were tossed about by this human tide which by its ebb threw us back endlessly on the sand, in the middle of the carcasses of boats and other military equipment. The dunes and the beaches morphed into a human and mechanical necropolis. They were littered with the tragic corpses of soldiers so close to their saving escape, with overturned and broken boats, wrecks of downed planes and vehicles or weapons of all kinds, abandoned forever. We could no longer move forward; the tens of thousands of soldiers who had already preceded us were trying to escape certain death and board the boats. They were stepping over the dead and elbowing their way, thus blocking all access.

When the day dawned on the horizon, we were still on that cursed beach, exhausted, behind a swarm of angry men. Indeed, thirty thousand soldiers had had the chance to embark in these ultimate moments, but when the last vessel, a British torpedo boat, the Shikari, left port, nearly forty thousand soldiers were forsaken without any possible way out. In addition, we learned that the last two ships had been scuttled to block the port of Dunkirk. We had tried to flee to England, but we had to face the evidence: there would be no more boats!

All hope had now vanished.

We were collapsing from exhaustion, unable to take one more step. We let ourselves fall down on the wet sand, in this apocalyptic landscape. All my comrades had the same blank stare, reflecting despair, abandonment, or death. Some were gazing at the ocean, their eyes clouded with tears and sea spray. In nine days, nearly three hundred and fifty thousand Allied soldiers had been evacuated, at the cost of enormous sacrifices and heroic resistance to save the Dunkirk pocket. Many were those who had found eternal rest in the abyss of these frigid and austere waters after more than two hundred boats had sunk to the bottom.

Jean tried to cheer us up, proclaiming that we had escaped a slow, painful but certain death, had we had to taste the English culinary curiosities and convert to teatime. But our heart was not in it and his bitter puns remained without response. Little by little an uneasiness began to eat away at me.

A deep silence ...

Disturbing and unexpected.

Something abnormal was happening.

Heaven and earth had become mute. The explosions, the jerky detonations from the machine guns, the gunshots, all had suddenly gone silent. This sudden silence was becoming more and more frightening, foretelling baleful auspices.

In the early hours of that morning, the Germans had finally succeeded in setting foot in Dunkirk, a decomposed city, reduced to ashes, annihilated. The shadow of Death lurked in the city as the soldiers of the Reich advanced from house to house, wiping out yet more lives and slaughtering all resistance.

On the morning of June 4, a white flag was hoisted on a building.

We were forced to lay down our weapons in a town square, to our great regret and dismay. Shortly thereafter, the German soldiers arrived, taunting us, and pointing their weapons at us. The men of my company piled up their rifles, bayonets, handguns, grenades, or other ammunitions. With sorrow, I put down my old Babel, ending its career in this chaotic place. My feelings were clouded, amplified by extreme fatigue from lack of sleep and food; shame, helplessness, abandonment, confusion, pride, and sadness intertwined.

From peaceful civilians, we had become helpless soldiers, and now desperate prisoners of war.

A multitude of soldiers gathered in the town square, arms in the air, aimless and haggard. We were taking in these events as a scathing defeat, forgetting that the British army and thousands of French soldiers had achieved the impossible: in just a few days they had reached England, safe and sound, and many were already back on French soil to defend the homeland.

We stood in small groups, the German soldiers barking orders that few of us could understand. However, their threatening demeanor and the scorching tone of their words left no doubt about their state of mind.

Nervous, on the verge of hysteria, Théo looked at us with a distressed countenance and said, "I wonder what will become of us. Do you think that they will keep us in prison somewhere in France? Or will they send us back to our civilian life? Perhaps they will execute us summarily; no one will ever know. All those dead for nothing!"

"Théo, calm down. The die is unfortunately cast. We must stay as calm as possible so as not to stand out. Let's not increase their evil pleasure of winners," I replied, trying to keep a cool head, while deep inside I trembled with fear, thinking of Gabrielle and Jean-Pierre. Would I ever see them again? What was going to happen to us? We were still in France but now at the whim of the enemy.

"You know Théo, if they intended to make us all disappear, they wouldn't be filming us and taking pictures for posterity," Fanch added, nodding in the direction of an SS officer.

Feet planted in shiny leather boots, a long black leather coat flapping in the wind over an immaculate uniform, he exuded a haughty look, his sinister cap with its ominous skull badge worn with pride.

It was the winner filming the losers, boxing them up for posterity.

As he passed near us, his steely blue gaze fixed Théo insistently. Why was he staring at him like that? What had he done to draw that inquisitive stare full of hatred? His heart was pounding and, feeling panic overcome him, he began to gasp. He had to get away from the group at all costs, become invisible.

To our surprise, he began to stride away from us.

"*Komm her!*" the officer yelled.

Théo did not understand what the German wanted. The officer's peremptory tone, the accumulated fatigue, the tragedy of the situation, and fear mingled in outmost confusion in his mind.

"*Komm her!*"

Théo began to run, panic-stricken, completely losing track of the danger. The officer drew a Luger Parabellum from his holster and in a final warning shouted, *"Hör auf zu rennen,"* ordering him to stop running.

Théo, his spirit already fled elsewhere, was running with his friends in the fields of his childhood, laughing, his arms open to life and to the sun; carefree, he did not slow down.

A gunshot rang out.

The conversations abruptly ended.

At some distance, the soldiers had formed an empty space where Théo laid motionless, his face against the cobblestones of the town square, a dribble of blood trickling from his head. An amaranth stain gradually widened, a vibrant and anachronistic burst of color amongst this desolate and monochrome environment.

Théo had finally stopped running.

He was smiling, peaceful now, as if he were sleeping in green pastures amidst daisies and poppies, lulled by a tender spring breeze. On this shimmering carpet of a thousand colors, he was now at peace, forever ...

At least that's how I imagined the end of my comrade, to forget the unjust death of this young man, almost still a child, so far from his family, from his village that he had never left before and would never see again.

# Chapter 10

## *From France to Poland*

"*Schneller, faule Franzosen!*"

"Faster, lazy Frenchmen!" shouted fiercely at us the German soldiers, while we dragged our feet from fatigue, hunger, and despair on the roads to nowhere. We could not move faster and the hours of forced marching, under the incessant and hateful screams accompanied by the blows of the rifle butts, had brought us down.

We were gathered on a marketplace in Dunkirk, which was nothing but ruins. A German officer asked our captain if the population of the town had been evacuated.

"No, *Oberstleutnant*, my lieutenant-colonel. They almost all died under the bombardments. Thousands! They could not flee the endless bombardments. Maybe there are a few survivors in the cellars. I don't know."

"Really?" The officer seemed surprised and disconcerted by the answer, as if he, the German, did not understand how a town and its inhabitants could be annihilated in this way.

He collected himself and ordered us to form two groups: the officers on the left and the privates on the right.

That afternoon, in rows of eights, they made us leave the ghost town. Our human tide rippled slowly towards the outskirts of the city. We had been on empty stomachs for almost two days already. We began hastily rummaging through the garbage cans for a meager pittance, like stray dogs, under the smirk of the German soldiers and their repeated blows.

In the evening, after a grueling twenty-kilometer march, we arrived at Rexpoëde in an archaic camp located in the middle of the fields. Morale was extremely low, and we had no idea about our potential fate. Where were we going? What tasks would we be subjected to? Or worse, would we be summarily slaughtered and forgotten in a mass grave? Discussions were flying around, each speculating on our fate and the future of France.

Jean, who had stayed with me since our surrender, lamented his fate.

"Everything is lost Alex. We could not contain this lightning war, despite all our sacrifices and the bloodshed. Poor Théo! Soon the Krauts will be in Paris, strutting around the Champs-Élysées and drinking our champagne. And we, meanwhile, where will we be? Slaves of these Fritz in Germany or God knows where!"

"Jean, I know it's difficult to accept our fate, but we are still alive. And we are not alone. We are thousands of prisoners; they will not be able to make us all disappear so easily. I think they're going to exploit us by giving us irksome, difficult tasks, but at least we still have hope for a reversal of the situation."

Jean looked at me with a sad, distraught air.

"Alex, who will fight if we lose the war? How can you still believe in change?"

"As long as people keep hope and aspire to freedom, anything could happen. Through our fierce combats over the past few days, we have enabled most of the British troops to regroup, free in England. Hundreds of thousands of French soldiers were also able to escape, and they will be able to resume combat. Believe me, Dunkirk, despite its annihilation and all its deaths, will remain in history as a victory for the Allies. All is not finished, Jean, keep hope and keep your chin up. We will be fine, trust me."

As I said these words of comfort to Jean, I thought of Gabrielle who, in the depths of Brittany, knew nothing of our fate. I had to be strong for her and Jean-Pierre and keep my promise that I would come back alive.

One day ...

For the moment we had to rest, to hold out under the yoke of these tyrannical Teutons. Under the cover of the night, a few desperate soldiers tried to flee from the camp, but they were all shot dead during their attempted escape or brought back to the camp.

With dismay, we saw Fanch in the middle of a group of French soldiers, hands in the air, eyes panicked, escorted by German soldiers who were pushing him forward with terrible rifle butts. Fanch, exhausted and starving, had joined this small group to attempt a desperate escape towards a nearby forest.

The soldiers ordered them to kneel, side by side, in the middle of the camp. After a moment of silence that seemed to last for eternity, an officer armed with a Walther P38 pistol passed behind the kneeling men. Some trembled, others prayed or bravely sang the Marseillaise. One after the other, he shot them in the back of the neck in front of our aghast eyes.

Fanch was one of the first to collapse, face down.

We had just lost another of our comrades in a horrifying way. From now on, fear would never leave us.

Frightened and emaciated, we walked day after day towards Belgium, accompanied by motorized German troops, sometimes on horseback or even on bicycle. Our ranks were gradually getting thinner. The wounded agonized, some coldly gunned down if they could no longer walk or because of a look or a misinterpreted word. Others were falling dead from exhaustion and malnutrition.

In the evening, hungry and dehydrated, we threw ourselves on our bowl filled with an undefined mixture. Nevertheless, that meager meal eliminated, at least temporarily, our stomach cramps and allowed us to fall asleep, lying under the stars. As I observed the night sky, I often thought of Gabrielle who at the same instant was perhaps also looking at the same half-moon or the same planets. United with her through the Milky Way, I usually fell asleep very quickly, exhausted.

Each morning, after a bad night, we took the road again towards an unknown destination. Weary, hirsute, hungry, we dragged ourselves, a lamentable herd on uncertain roads, our feet hurt by our boots already worn out.

We were approaching Bruges.

The column, too tired to chat, moved on in silence, disturbed only by the scraping of shoes on the road. A dull humming, faint at first then increasing in crescendo, made me raise my head: an airplane! Were we going to be bombarded? End up riddled with bullets on this road of misfortune?

It didn't look like a Messerschmitt. It wasn't a French plane either. I recognized the Fascist symbol under its wings: an Italian biplane! They had just entered the war alongside the Germans. It was flying low, in wide circles above our heads. What was he doing here?

The sound of a distant engine on the road made me turn my head; behind us came a convoy of German trucks. Soon they began to pass the column of prisoners. The German soldiers could be heard vociferating while standing in the back of the trucks; they seemed to throw something that caused an incomprehensible chaos in the last rows of prisoners. As the trucks moved forward, a wave of commotion spread forward.

I discovered that the Germans were throwing bread balls from the platform of the vehicles; starving prisoners rushed at this pitiful manna as if they were nuggets of gold. The men jostled and even fought to recover this meager pittance. I threw myself into the fray, the black bread rolling in the dust between the feet of the men who were tearing it away.

The Germans were laughing at the spectacle and pointing a

finger at the Italian plane. We learned later that this plane was filming the distribution of bread; this film would serve the enemy propaganda and further humiliate the French.

Torn with beastly hunger, like my comrades, I tore off a piece of bread with my teeth to calm my cravings. It was so hard that I had difficulty chewing it; then I put it away in my haversack in anticipation of future privations.

We resumed our walk.

We walked with our heads and shoulders down, shuffling our feet past Bruges, while the German soldiers entered Paris, parading chins high, goose-stepping down the Champs-Élysées.

The Battle of France was well and truly lost.

Paris had fallen!

A flag with a swastika now waved at the top of the Eiffel Tower.

Having overheard German sentries listening to a radio, an Alsatian corporal, Gustave Nolte, whom we called Gus, and who understood German perfectly, translated some of the latest news for us, "Hitler came to Paris on a whirlwind visit for his winner's lap. At the same time, on June 18, General de Gaulle broadcasted a call on London radio inciting the French people to resist and liberate France."

The Appeal from a French general, who had led the 4th armored Division since the beginning of the German offensive and then moved to London, restored our faith; our fate might change quickly, and we might finally get back to our homeland.

We continued our bumpy march towards the Netherlands with renewed optimism despite the redoubled brutality of our guards. Meanwhile, as we were crossing the border a few days later, we were stunned to learn that the Maréchal Pétain had replaced Paul Reynaud as the prime minister and had immediately accepted an armistice with the Third Reich. This armistice hit us head-on, like a sudden burst of shots from a firing squad.

To heighten revenge and humiliation, Hitler had insisted that the wagon, in which the armistice of 1918 had been concluded, be driven from the museum where it was stationed to the same exact location where the German defeat had been signed in the forest of Compiègne, in Rethondes.

He finally had his revenge, cynical and cold. Indeed, he had been particularly humiliated and disappointed by the signing of the armistice of 1918, feeling the acceptance of the German defeat as a deep betrayal.

The following days, he strutted in front of the cameras and for the newsreels facing famous Parisian monuments – the Eiffel Tower, the Trocadéro esplanade, the Notre-Dame cathedral, the Louvre Museum, the Sacré Coeur basilica in Montmartre – and he went to the Invalides to meditate in front of Napoleon's tomb. Accompanied by his entourage, he went up to a balcony overlooking the tomb of the Little Corporal, dressed in a white gabardine. He took his cap off; his deranged gaze wandered in his Napoleonic dreams, savoring this paramount moment of his life. He, the "two-bit little corporal" as Marshal von Rundstedt described him, stood above the Little Corporal; alive and feeling so much superior, even invincible.

A few days' walk from the border, we finally arrived in a charming little harbor in southern Holland to board one of the docked vessels. A few months later, this same port would become much more sinister; the bodies of many French soldiers would run aground, after having drifted during all this time with the currents following the bombardment of their boats which had attempted the perilous crossing from Dunkirk to Dover.

Among the various boats that anchored in this picturesque harbor, we were ordered to board a very long barge that carried coal. We had to sit directly on the open piles of chestnut coal. The crossing on the high seas was billowy and interminable. We were tossed by the waves on the unstable mounds of coal, with no space to move. Some, afflicted with seasickness, looked all the whiter as it contrasted with their hands and clothes blackened in contact with the anthracite.

Jean who had followed me with Gus at the front of the barge told us, "I did not realize, when they told us that we were going to get our hands dirty, that they literally meant it! Alex, we can only see your sparkling blue eyes piercing your 'ebony' face, the height for a carpenter!"

"Gus, if you didn't know it yet, Jean is a top prankster. He enjoys pulling our leg."

Gus, who also had his face as black as his hands, replied, "Don't worry Alex, it feels good to joke and it distracts us. During that time, we do not think about our miserable condition or the stench that emanates from those who unfortunately do not have sea legs; moreover, the billows of cigarette smoke intermixed with the oily smell of engines do not help!"

"You're right Gus. We have to try to stay positive and clear our minds. I don't know where this boat takes us, but it separates us even further away from our families. Fortunately, we are still together, and it is good for our morale."

A smile at the corner of his mouth, Gus then asked Jean, "Jean, you the joker in-chief, do you know the story of the SS officer who was wounded in Dunkirk while on patrol?"

"No, I don't think so. Go ahead, tell us!"

With his strong Alsatian accent which added spice to his story, Gus began:

"So, this is the story of Hans who is on patrol in the streets of Dunkirk, when his detachment gets shot at. They all die – good riddance – except for Hans who is seriously injured in the leg. He crawls painfully towards the first door that he finds to seek help. He bangs his fist on the door, 'Hallo, Hallo, *schnell*, du open ze door to help me.'

A small voice answers him timidly, 'Yeah, I'm 'p'tit Jean,' but I am not allowed to speak to the Boches.'

'*Ach so*, me understand,' the officer answers. 'Me talk to das daddy then?'

P'tit Jean replies, 'My father is not here. He left when my mom arrived.'

'Ach, du look for *Mutter*, *schnell*, me lose *mein blut!*'

'My mother left when my grandmother arrived.'

'*Suchen* grandma then, *schnell*,' Hans answers, feeling more and more unwell.

'My grandma left when my grandfather arrived.'

'*Ich habe schmerzen*,' Hans shouts in pain, 'tell Opa me be here, go, *schnell*.'

'My grandfather left when I arrived,' the exasperated kid replies.

'*Mein Gott, unglaublich!* Du never togezer, *nicht zusammen*, in the house?'

'Oh yes of course, in the house … This is the toilet!' p'tit Jean exclaims."

After a continuous duel of jokes between Gus and Jean that, worthy of a headliner at the Alhambra in Paris, embellished the long arduous hours of the crossing, we arrived in a German port, black as shoe polish.

After a laborious march, we arrived at a prison camp in Meppen. As soon as we entered the camp, our pulse accelerated uncontrollably. For the first time, we felt deeply that our freedom was definitely gone. All hope had left us.

We found ourselves in a dirt yard, in the middle of wooden barracks, surrounded by high fences topped with sharp barbed wire. From the top of the watchtowers, we were constantly under surveillance by soldiers, armed with MP38 submachine guns and MG34 machine guns. We were prisoners, cut off from the outside world, helpless at the mercy of our guards. We spent the night in this camp, with a majority of Belgian and French soldiers, replacing most of the early Polish prisoners. Only a few of these prisoners remained in the camp, continuing to build it up, or working in a nearby brick factory or at the construction of a canal.

The next day we boarded a freight train for an unknown destination. Sixty to seventy comrades per car! The German soldiers pushed us violently into the wagons with buttstrokes from their Mauser K98k rifles but also with their sticks, whips, and boots.

"*Voraus! Schneller! Steig in den Wagen!*"

Orders lashed at the same rate as the blows, ordering us to move quickly into these mobile prisons.

Meanwhile, they patrolled the station platforms with their dogs barking wildly, snarling with madness. Pressed against each other, we saw the sliding doors of the wagons slam with a loud snap, like the guillotine cleaver falling on the condemned man's neck. From the dazzling summer day, we suddenly found ourselves in an agonizing penumbra; the daylight barely filtered through two small openings high up obstructed by metallic bars.

The train started to move and gradually picked up speed. Suddenly, through the two openings, we saw English planes with their tricolor cockades flying over us. They dropped a shower of bombs which, miraculously, fell next to our train, without hitting us or damaging the rails.

The train journey lasted two long days, without any food, in a stifling furnace. On very rare occasions, doors opened onto stations teeming with enemy troops. In these fleeting moments of relief, we were given a little water to drink, and we could stretch our muscles. We also breathed more invigorating air than the stale one of these slums on wheels, engendered by our forced and unhealthy cohabitation. The stinking air of the wagons was finally diluted. We also took the opportunity to empty the buckets or cans that we had not been able to evacuate beforehand through the air vents after having relieved ourselves during the journey, against each other, without any privacy.

Our morale was at an all-time low.

After two days of this inhuman journey, feeling like an irrevocable descent to Hell, we arrived at the camp of Hammerstein, *Stammlager* or Stalag II-B. This camp for soldiers and non-commissioned officers, surrounded by moors and pines, was one of the first Nazi concentration camps that had been established about two kilometers west of the village in Pomerania. After passing through the large gate interlaced with barbed wire, we walked in a column in the central alley, flanked by numerous wooden buildings. We glimpsed furtively at the other prisoners already there who were staring at us, looking downcast, hoping to recognize a familiar face or exchange information.

*"Halt die Klappe! Sprich nicht. Beweg dein Arsch!"* spat in our face some big bullies in short sleeve shirts, forcing us to be silent while driving us with the whip to the back of the camp. Our parade in front of our comrades and the German soldiers was most humiliating but none of us tried to revolt. The machine guns installed in the numerous miradors, aiming in our direction, and following us with their threatening gun barrels, were indeed enough to dissuade us from doing so.

We raised a cloud of dust under our heavy and throbbing feet as we passed on this path of gray and sterile sand. At the end of the straight line, we crammed into large tents, directly on the ground. After spending two days in that camp without eating anything, in a suffocating heat, we embarked one last time for a new destination.

We arrived in a similar camp to the one we had just left: the Stargard camp, Stalag II-D, in Pomerania. As soon as we crossed its gate, we walked down the same glaucous central alley, lined with drab shacks of wood or brick. The other prisoners formed a guard of honor, asking us for news of the country and the war, looking in vain for comrades or forgotten faces.

In passing, some called us in French, Flemish or Dutch. I later learned that our jailers had already separated and isolated the Algerian, Tunisian or Senegalese soldiers. Kept apart in a separate area of the camp, SS torturers experimented with the poor souls.

Various races served as guinea pigs for these sinister and often fatal experiments, without the slightest consent, which some German doctors and other Germanic sadists imagined in their deranged brains. Under the pretext of treating certain infections or inflammation, they tested all kinds of molecules. In addition, they also evaluated different means of increasing blood coagulation by methods as barbaric as they were irresponsible, with the aim of supposedly better treating the wounded German soldiers. They also observed the survival of some of these prisoners in unbearable cold conditions. They threw these poor men naked in frozen baths or in the snow in winter to evaluate the kinetics of reduction of their body temperature before their inevitable death. Sometimes, those monsters would experiment with techniques as drastic as they were cruel to warm up these unfortunate people frozen to death, by dipping them directly into boiling water.

Flanked by Jean and Gus, I continued on this central path, harangued by all the prisoners eager for news. They also warned us of the upcoming searches. Some of these early prisoners encouraged us to surreptitiously pass them the rare objects that we may still have in our possession to hide them. They warned us that the searches would quickly strip us of these few relics that we had managed to protect until then.

I really had nothing of value except my wallet with my papers and a few pictures of Gabrielle and Jean-Pierre. However, I secretly passed my watch and a pocketknife to a fellow with a strong Breton accent, which immediately inspired my confidence. I felt even more reassured when he whispered to me that he was Father Pierre Gythiel, thinking that my meager possessions were safe with a man of God.

The sentries began to notice our ploy and the hits from the butt-stocks of their rifles began to rain haphazardly, accompanied by shouts and insults that had now become routine. They ordered us to be silent and move forward without contact with the early prisoners.

A German officer directed us to one of the wooden barracks, ordering us to put our belongings on one of the beds, and to assemble in the main courtyard.

The long, dark, dreary room was crowded with three-story bunk beds, the lowest almost at ground level and the highest over two meters high. One almost needed climbing skills to get up there! Nevertheless, in agreement with Jean and Gus, I climbed onto the upper bunk to find a sad excuse for a mattress containing a few handfuls of straw and a blanket. I would find out after the first night that

Jean and Gus found themselves sprinkled with hay dust and various mites, each time I turned around in this wooden crate that acted as a bed. In addition, the beds and the blankets turned out to be infested with vermin swarming erratically; we unfortunately had to fight lice, fleas, and other bedbugs on that memorable first night. In the dark, we were aroused without interruption by a parasitic Saint Vitus dance!

In the middle of the dormitory, with its small windows looking out onto the other barracks, stood an inert stove. Smelly latrines with few and far-between sinks sat at each end. We had no time to linger in our new lodgings; we had barely taken possession of the bedsteads before we were forced to assemble outside in haste.

"*In Reihen, schnell*," our guards ordered us, threatening us with their rifles.

We lined up as best we could in a dusty square, in full sun, surrounded by threatening guards and under the inquisitive gaze of the many watchtowers. An SS officer appeared in all his splendor – immaculate uniform, shiny boots and cap – his back to the setting sun, making him shine like a celestial apparition. But the *trompe-l'oeil* stopped right there! In charge of the camp, this demonic officer relished every moment of power and malice provided by his position, executing those he disliked for any reason, no matter how trivial. He also actively participated in human experimentation while listening on his gramophone to "The Valkyrie" or "The Rhinegold," composed by the anti-Judaic Richard Wagner.

In a stifling silence, the officer and his interpreter recited the main rules of the camp, which curiously always ended with threats of extreme isolation or summary execution if they were not followed to the letter.

Then we were directed to a group of brick houses where we were ordered to undress completely and make a pile of our clothes. We were told that these were collected and taken for disinfection. Fearing that we would be radically "disinfected" too *ad vitam aeternam*, we began to tremble in this empty, airtight, and aseptic room. Suddenly chairs were brought in. We were ordered to sit in the center of the room, three by three. With a gloomy purr, the clippers set to work; we watched with regret our hair, sometimes covered with swarming vermin, spread in a thick multi-colored layer on the white tiled floor. Like Samson having lost all his strength after Delilah betrayed him by cutting off his long hair, I now felt totally helpless, naked, and shaved.

A door opened and we were quickly directed into a windowless, dimly lit white room, tiled from floor to ceiling. Our guards closed the heavy doors. The tension grew. The minutes slowed down. Some began to whisper some prayers. They were answered when at last, falling from above our heads, jets of cold water began to spray us profusely. Our fear was gradually eliminated with our filth of the past weeks. This refreshing moment was short-lived but appreciated all the more so; we were still alive and now clean.

Back in an adjoining room, we waited there for a few hours to dry off. We were wondering what would become of us when another door opened. Soldiers threw in a jumble on the floor: underpants, pants, shirts, jackets, socks, and other garments which had been disinfected; they had also been lightened of any precious object inadvertently forgotten at the bottom of a pocket. We went on a treasure hunt, trying to find our clothes and shoes. Needless to say, the less fortunate found themselves in solely underwear or with only one shoe!

We were then transferred to another building where several tables were lined up, overflowing with piles of forms. Behind these makeshift desks, early French prisoners asked us questions while filling out a form on our identity.

"Last name, first name, age, and address?" asked a guy with a gaunt face, a resigned look, a cigarette on his lips.

"Rolland, Alexandre, 30 years old, 17 Place aux Poulains, Landivisiau, Finistère," I replied sadly, thinking back to our haven of peace in Brittany and to Gabrielle.

"Married or single? Children?"

"Married to Gabrielle Bizien. A 14-month-old baby boy. His name is Jean-Pierre."

"I'm sorry for you Alexandre, hold on tight. You will see them again but stay out of trouble because the camp commander is a mad sadist and you better avoid him," he whispered to me.

"Thanks for the advice. What's your name?"

"Francis Ambrière."

Years later, I would remember this name when he retroactively would receive the 1940 Goncourt Prize for his novel "Les Grandes Vacances," retracing our lives as prisoners in the stalags.

"Alexandre, you are now number 52593. Memorize your prisoner number. A word of advice, try to get yourself enrolled in an *Arbeitskommando*. Volunteer to join a work commando. It will be better than rotting in this seedy camp. Good luck!"

"Thank you for the advice, Francis, and may God protect you."

With the form completed, I found myself sitting on a bench with two other prisoners, holding a sign with my new identification number 52593, like a thug having his mugshot taken.

I had been stripped of everything, even of my name.

The harsh reality of being a prisoner of war hit me suddenly. I had the impression of no longer existing, of having lost everything – my freedom, identity, and love. Unable to find sleep, the first night passed extremely slowly in the dormitory; many were those who, like me, dreamed of escape, of returning to our country, to our faraway homes and loved ones.

In the morning, as daylight barely dawned, our guards burst in like an unexpected tornado. They whipped us while ordering to get ready and step out immediately. This was one of their many surprise searches that they loved so much, punctuating our day and continuing to strip us of any object that we may still have been able to hide.

In the meantime, we huddled together with our tin mugs around large basins containing a lukewarm yellowish liquid, acting as an ersatz coffee. This tasteless juice was nevertheless welcome. The sparse food in the camp was little varied; it was served as one meal in the middle of the day, indefinite mixtures with a piece of black bread.

On July 8, 1940, I celebrated my thirtieth birthday dreaming of a soft and fragrant omelet. I would have paid dearly for this simple dish! Eyes closed, I reveled in savoring it slowly, my imagination remembering those rustic but unforgettable flavors. My comrades tried to entertain me, but this birthday was the gloomiest by far. I knew Gabrielle would be thinking of me especially on this summer day, probably wondering if I was still alive and where fate had taken me.

This day of celebration turned into a deep grief, then into a nightmare when in the early evening hours two young Dutch soldiers, who had tried to escape by cutting off a piece of the first fence, were discovered by the light beam from a mirador. They were immediately hanged in the middle of the central courtyard. Their bodies remained there for all to see, under a blazing sun, for days on end: a reminder of our unconditional submission and a warning to the boldest or the most reckless of us.

The next day a German soldier randomly selected me along with three other prisoners and provided us with shovels and pickaxes. He ordered us to go and dig some graves at the other end of the camp. One of ours had succumbed during his transfer and would be buried there. The other graves would shelter for eternity the two hanged Dutch soldiers, and others for whom death would unfortunately be the only means of escape. Some also lost their minds, under the repeated bullying and mockery of the guards, and found themselves then the subject of barbaric experiments carried out under the cover of a "specialized" infirmary in the camp.

One morning, after drinking our *jus*, we were handed out in our room printed cards so that we could inform our families of our fate. These simple cards already drawn up left us no freedom to provide personal news. Indeed, these laconically mentioned, "I am in captivity at Stalag II-D, number -----. I am healthy." I wrote down my number, then added *"Ma Gabrielle"* and a furtive *"Je t'aime"* at the bottom of the card that I signed *"Ton Alexandre,"* hoping that the censors of the camp would accept those few extra benign notes. It wasn't much, but I consoled myself knowing that Gabrielle would recognize my handwriting and finally learn about my condition and where I was being held. She would be so reassured to know that I was alive; she would likely pray that I would stay that way until I got back home.

As a German non-commissioned officer was collecting the cards for our families, I said to Gus, "Gus, since you speak German, tell him that we want to volunteer for a work *kommando*. Sneak him a pack of cigarettes with our cards."

When the guard approached, Gus handed him our three cards with the cigarette pack and quickly asked him, in a low voice, to enroll us in a *kommando*, together if possible. He didn't answer but took our cards and pocketed the cigarettes.

In the afternoon, we talked with other French and Belgian prisoners around the barracks. Laundry was drying at the windows or hanging between stakes, exposed to all the winds and clouds of dust. Some had overheard guards murmuring about *Kanalkampf*, meaning that the German army had initiated plans to invade England. According to the snippets of conversation gathered, at this early stage of the Battle of Britain, the German air force was relentlessly attacking the British convoys in the Channel to cut off supplies to the United Kingdom. By this tactic, Germany hoped to isolate and weaken – if not completely annihilate – the British air force, known as the famous Royal Air Force or RAF.

Suddenly, cries resounded; our dorm room was being called to assemble urgently in front of our barrack.

The guards ordered us to form ten lines, facing the front of the barracks. Then, ten by ten we had to undress and place all our things on a blanket, laid on the ground in front of a guard who once again carried out a meticulous search. Some lost the little money they still had left, hidden at the bottom of their shoes or in their epaulets, or even for the most skillful in the lining of their jacket. I only had my wallet with my papers and family photos. When I appeared in front of the guard, he quickly realized that I had nothing more to contribute to the enrichment of their personal monetary fund.

To my astonishment, this guard, the same one who had come that morning to collect our cards, recognized me. He began to speak to me in German. Gus, who was just behind me, translated for me that he had made sure to assign us to a work *kommando* and that we would leave the camp the next day with several other comrades.

Surprised by this sudden help, supported by our tobacco contribution, I could only stammer a shy, *"Danke schön!"*

# Chapter 11

## *From Stalag to Schivelbein*

The next day, after drinking our *jus*, we hurriedly got our meager belongings together. Jean, Gus, and I arrived at the train station with ten or so additional French prisoners, forming our *kommando*, surrounded by guards who would escort us to our destination. Even though we were leaving for forced labor, we were relieved to leave this dangerous and depressing stalag. We did not have the slightest idea about what to expect. Would we be assigned to build roads or bridges, given our background in Engineering? Or would I end up as a carpenter helping in a sawmill deep in the woods? Some spoke of work in factories to help the German army, others of work in salt mines or in the fields. Our future was frightfully uncertain, but we were no longer under the yoke of this barbaric officer, absolute master of the camp and of our lives.

The train set off in the direction of Schivelbein in Pomerania, not far from the Baltic Sea.

The sky was low and the landscapes monotonous. The fields and forests passed by at the mechanical rhythm of the train, interrupted only by small, isolated villages. We arrived at Schivelbein station accompanied by six German soldiers. On that summer day, we marched in rows of three escorted by the Fritz. I was far from the escapades by the Iroise Sea that I shared with Gabrielle and our newborn baby, just a year earlier.

I knew now that the path of life could change in a flash.

We crossed a large square where a market was bustling. People looked askance at us, suspicious, likely because our coats had on their backs and on our hearts the inscription *KG, Kriegsgefangener*, in large letters. These humiliating letters reminded us of our condition as prisoners of war but would also serve as targets if we tried to escape.

The square cobblestones were covered with carts carrying calves and pigs. In another corner, onlookers were busy choosing goats from a herd. Some stalls sold cheeses, vegetables, fresh eggs, pâtés and pork products, or other products coming from the surrounding farms. At the sight of these feasts, our stomachs thought our throats had been cut. Unfortunately, we reluctantly only satiated ourselves with the local aromas. Further, the herders negotiated the sale of horses and cows in a language that was totally foreign to us. Even if this market resembled in some respects the one we had known in Bailleul, the architecture of the square and its houses, the brick church looming on the horizon and this unknown language, reminded us once again of the so painful separation from our families.

We left the square through an alley flanked by various shops leading to the only city gate, Brama Kamienna, the "Gothic-looking Stone Gate" which ironically was mostly built of bricks. We continued our walk, our footsteps echoing on the cobblestones of the alleys. In a distance, surrounded by large trees, we observed a castle; a circular tower of orange-colored brick dotted here and there with whitish and brownish hues was topped with a wooden roof with bell-shaped shingles.

We finally arrived in a small, abandoned factory, littered with rusty equipment and various tools. This shed, located near the Rega River flowing north into the Baltic Sea, had a single exit: a large sliding portal fitted with a padlock that our guards systematically closed when we were inside. This obsolete factory would become our home for the months to come. We immediately began to clear a corner to sleep, recovering some old rusty metal cabinets. We installed a few empty barrels that we would use to make fires to warm us up during the long cold nights ahead. Once cleaned, our space, although very basic, had officially become our residence – the "Ritz des Fritz," as Jean would call it – which indeed deserved many more stars than our quarters at Stalag II-D.

We would later learn that Schivelbein had gotten rid of its Jewish population before our arrival. The cleansing, as our guards described it, had begun in 1933, when the city was home to one of the region's largest Jewish communities and our artist at heart, the racist and anti-Semite Adolf, had seized power and had become the dictator-in-chief of the Third Reich. The motto of the Second Reich, *"Ein Volk, ein Reich, ein Gott,"* had suddenly morphed into *"Ein Volk, ein Reich, ein Führer,"* – "one nation, one empire, one leader," – raising the "two-bit little corporal" to the heavens in order to dethrone God! Having become the Führer and the Reichskanzler, the guide and the chancellor of the Reich, after a brutal and expeditious elimination of the opposition and any dissent during "The Night of the Long Knives," this new self-proclaimed "god" began his slow and cruel systematic elimination of the Jewish people. The Nazis, dazzled or blinded by the celestial aura of this perfidious fake idol, now controlled all of society, from the media to the indoctrination of children.

After being ordered by the National Socialist Party to boycott Jewish stores, shops went even further by displaying banners indicating that Jews would no longer be served in their stalls.

Hatred exuded by the Nazis spread like a lightning gangrene in the population, forcing many Jews to leave Schivelbein and many other cities of Pomerania and Germany. Some took refuge in Palestine or in South America; they thus escaped the pogrom, that fatal night of November 9, 1938, the "Crystal Night", when the Jews were arrested, summarily executed, or deported to Lublin and other concentration camps. That same night, the Schivelbein synagogue, like so many others, had been burnt down, the Jewish cemetery desecrated, and the Jewish shops looted. Schivelbein's last rabbi, Karl Richter, and many Jewish villagers had also been brutally murdered.

The Nazi madness seemed to have reached its apex.

But the following year, when many Jews had been freed from the camps in exchange for exorbitant ransoms that would fortify the Nazi coffers, the Jewish families were forced, under threat, to abandon their homes and possessions in haste; they found themselves crammed into ghettos, deprived of their liberty. Their humiliation continued by forcing them to add Israel or Sara to their first name. A new identity card specifying their Jewish origin was then imposed on them and the letter J was affixed to their passports. A little later, they would have to wear on their clothes the infamous yellow star, the Star of David with the inscription Jude, like cattle branded with an iron.

The *Shoah*, meaning calamity in Hebrew, or the Final Solution so named by the Nazis, was in full swing.

At Schivelbein, in the early days I was assigned to a small farm to help with the harvest work. Early in the morning, the guards accompanied us to our places of work and at the end of the day they directed us to our Ritz which they double locked for the night. The evenings were long, but we kept ourselves busy playing cards or writing to our families; others preferred to write in their diaries or draw sketches. We were allowed to write only two twenty-five-line letters and two seven-line postcards per month, only on printed forms provided by our jailers. Of course, those would be read and proofread by censors before being routed for weeks, or even months, to their destination.

In this first picturesque little farm, the boss, Wojtek, and his wife, Halina Goszczynski were already well into old age, at least their deep wrinkles and their deformed, callused hands suggested so. The recent loss of their two sons added to the weight of decades of hard work. One had followed his Jewish fiancée to Piaśnica after her arrest and, on a glacial morning in November 1939, they had both ended up at the bottom of a mass grave after being mown down, side by side, by a burst of machine guns, like thousands of other victims. The other son had decided to join the Polish army as a non-commissioned officer. He had bravely stood up to the invader in Warsaw, but he too had perished by the shrapnel of an enemy grenade. Their portraits sat proudly on the mantle of the fireplace in the kitchen but, from the very first day, I detected a fatigue and an infinite sadness in the veiled blue eyes of this peasant couple. With another prisoner comrade, we were here to replace their two sons.

Their suffering immediately embraced ours.

We arrived at the Goszczynski farm at harvest time. Our first task in our work *kommando* was to mow the fields of oats and wheat. The work was hard and the days grueling. A scythe in hand, we spent entire days mowing the fields around the farm. Under the scorching August sun, Wojtek passed behind us to make sheaves by kneeling on them and tying them with straw ties. We were suffering from the heatwave and hard work, but we were in the open air, without barbed wire and watchtowers, and we could talk freely.

At noon, we returned to the farm where Halina had prepared a lunch that we looked forward to every day. The boss and his wife were very kind and appreciated our help as a gift from heaven, replacing their two missing sons.

Day by day, the fields were being transformed. The gentle waves of ears of wheat undulating in the warm breeze gradually disappeared to give way to bare and rough spaces, bristling with stooks of sheaves proudly pointing their grain towards the sun.

The mowing completed, we carried the sheaves to the farm with the aid of a cart drawn with difficulty by an old horse, stubborn as a mule, aptly named *Uparty* in Polish; ironically, he did not go off so easily when we shouted at him in French his name, *"Hue, Parti!"* meaning "Giddy-up, let's go!" With the help of a wooden fork, we passed the sheaves to Wojtek who was perched on the cart; as we went, the sheaves appeared to be heavier and heavier. We made numerous trips between the fields and the farm because Wojtek could not arrange the load of sheaves too high. But chiefly, he wanted to spare the poor *Uparty* who seemed to look at us miserably begging to let him breathe.

During one of these loads, *Uparty* prematurely decided that the load was largely sufficient and, starting without warning, ejected Wojtek who fell with all his weight out of the cart. For the next few days, he had to stay in bed because of a dislocation of his shoulder.

After a few weeks, the mowing and the transport of the dried sheaves to the farm came to an end. Thereafter, a villager, who had the necessary threshing equipment and rented it from farm to farm, came with four sturdy oxen. These were harnessed and the bovine merry-go-round slowly began to move under repeated lashes. Despite the few pairs of hands that came with the rental of the machine, the threshing was most laborious and grueling. We carried the sheaves with our bare hands to the threshing machine table; Halina cut the ties then spread the sheaf. The thresher and the dryer, driven by the oxen, then separated the grain from the straw.

When the threshing was completed, Wojtek prepared bales of straw that we transported to the attic above the stable. Finally, we took the heavy sacks of grain up to the attic on the top floor of the farm, one by one, climbing a high precarious ladder. The sacks of oats would be used to feed the meager cattle, while the wheat would later be sent to the village mill to make flour. Some of this flour would no doubt help pay for the bread at the village bakery.

During the breaks, Halina would bring us fresh water and sometimes a glass of cider which we particularly cherished. One day, after returning from milking their two cows, Halina sprang a magnificent surprise. She cooked us an omelet with sautéed potatoes for lunch.

I was over the moon! My birthday present had arrived a little late, but it was so welcome.

I admired and then inhaled this omelet that I had dreamed so much about since my failed birthday in the cursed stalag. My fork sliced this savory dish, unctuous to perfection. I closed my eyes and tasted its simple flavor loaded with memories. I saw my mother,

Francine, in her black dress, with a little white lace headdress, cooking my favorite dish for me, her ocean blue eyes expressing her fondness of me. I missed her too. She must, without the shadow of a doubt, be terribly worried about my fate, alone, my father having passed away too soon after falling from a moving train a few years earlier. As I delighted in this succulent omelet, I also thought of Gabrielle. When would we be gathered around the family table once again? I thanked Halina for this delicious meal with repeated *"Danke schön,"* and *"Omelet gut, très gut,"* a little awkwardly, while regretting not to be able to converse with them in any other way than through gesture.

Unfortunately, when the harvest was over, we regretfully had to leave the Goszczynski farm. Our *kommando* was then assigned to finish a beach overlooking Lake Jezioro Bukowiec about three kilometers south of Schivelbein. Every morning, our guards escorted us on foot to the lake where we were then watched by other sentries, bayonets affixed to their rifle barrels. The view of the deep blue lake, surrounded by dense and verdant woods, was splendid. In this end of summer, the laughter of the children who bathed in the lake, accompanied by their mother, made me all the more nostalgic.

The separation and the lack of news tore my heart. Was Gabrielle with Jean-Pierre on a sandy beach too, among the granite rocks, facing the ocean? I imagined them, Jean-Pierre probably now walking on his own and having fun by the water. I hoped Gabrielle could forget the war for a moment by having a memorable time with our little boy. I missed them both so much. Had the news of my capture already reached her? Did she know where I was? The uncertainty was so much harder to live with than reality. The weeks of laying out the beach in this remote place passed with an overwhelming slowness. Except for the threatening sentries who watched us like raptors waiting for the slightest inappropriate movement of their prey to attack and kill them, war seemed so distant.

Then, towards the end of September, we were taken to another small farm with two other comrades to dig up potatoes for three weeks. We were glad that we were no longer under the constant threat of German guns; we again ate satisfying meals. On September 22, 1940, a Sunday of rest, autumn arrived, the landscape suddenly finding itself wrapped in ice. At the other end of the world, the empire of Japan invaded French Indochina without warning. The cold and dreary weather, coinciding with shorter and shorter days, did not bode well for the months to come.

After our potato harvest, the entire *kommando* began to set up wooden barracks for the refugees. Each day our dozen prisoners left the Ritz and walked, often in the pouring rain and freezing cold, to saw, nail, assemble, and set up the barracks, plank by plank. I was a little more in my element and the teamwork brought us enough warmth not to feel the bitter bites of the cold and our deep chapping skin.

In our group, I found myself most often with a young guy from Tours named Gérard Marchand who was cunning as a fox, as well as Father Gythiel, the priest who had saved *in extremis* at Stalag II-D my only valuable possessions, my watch and my Opinel knife. Of course, Jean and Gus were also with us.

"I am starting to get really fed up! It has been almost six months that we walk alternately from the fields to the construction sites and still no news from France."

"Don't worry Gus. I'm sure our families have been notified and one of these mornings we'll finally get some mail," I replied, hoping strongly to myself that I wasn't wrong.

"In any case, I am not expecting anything from anyone," Jean, the eternal bachelor of the gang, replied.

"What should I say, me, a priest? God will not forsake me, but he will certainly not send me any letters or packages."

Father Gythiel was wrong as, a few days later, he was the first in the *kommando* to receive a package, not from his heavenly boss, but from the Red Cross.

"Well Father, it seems your prayers have been answered! A real miracle. Alleluia! Thank Archangel Gabriel, the angelic messenger, who most certainly made sure that your package delivery went smoothly," Jean teased him unmercifully, true to form. "Quick, open these offerings carried by our Teutonic Wise Men to our lares and penates! From today on, I think you should call our guards, Melchior, Caspar, and Balthazar."

"Jean, stop making fun of religion! Remember that Hell does not only exist here on earth! Come rather help me undo this package that a good Samaritan has tied up like a saucisson."

In the hangar, gathered around our central table and heated by a fire that was burning far too quickly in the large barrels that we had to constantly feed with bits of wood that we collected here and there, we held our breaths. All you could hear was the wind howling outside, making the trees quiver, and scattering an icy rain in its path. Despite the few fires, we were all dressed very warmly, the expired steam of our breathing testifying to the freezing ambient temperature.

The priest, helped by Jean, finally opened the prodigal package.

Since we had started building the barracks, our meals had deteriorated significantly. In the morning, only a few bits of dry bread accompanied an ersatz coffee, while the lunch and evening meals were the most monotonous: a soup – a very bad soup – made of water and rare beet leaves, pieces of rutabagas or stinging nettles, seemed to have been gradually diluted with the passage of time. So, when the priest took out of the Red Cross package two dry saucissons, rillettes, raw ham, apples, and chocolate bars, as well as a set of dominoes, we were already delighting in the feasts of the days to come. Our ecstatic applause and whistles, which had nothing to be ashamed of in comparison with the ice storm roaring outside, exploded in our Ritz.

Meanwhile, the harshest winter I had ever known came way before its time.

Mountains of snow added to the freezing cold and stinging winds that had plagued us for weeks. Our days at the construction sites had been considerably reduced, mainly because our guards could endure the extreme temperatures even less than us who were always on the move. As soon as we found ourselves locked up in the Ritz, we huddled, shivering by the fireside, bundled up in our blankets, our hands wrapped in makeshift gloves, strips of fabric found here and there. We had neither warm clothes suitable for our condition, nor good shoes. Our soles had disintegrated over the kilometers of forced marches; we stuffed newspapers in the remains of our clodhoppers to avoid frostbites. Jean hastened to tell us with a mocking air that for once we could trample the press without any risk of retaliation. Of course, Gus added that we finally had the press at our feet!

Time seemed to be frozen too and, to kill it, we would spend hours playing cards or dominoes in frenetic games. We also listened to the stories of our comedy duo, Jean and Gus, our living encyclopedias of humor. Jean started with, "Two French soldiers are on the Maginot line, scanning the horizon. The first soldier asks his comrade, 'Tell me, why did you enlist?' The other responds immediately, 'Because I'm single and I love war, and you?' 'Well, me, because I'm married, and I love peace!'"

Immediately, Gus continued, "During the defense of Dunkirk, a French officer orders a young soldier, a dispatch courier, to bring an urgent message to a lieutenant leading a company. He calls out, 'Hey! *Estafette?*' Immediately the soldier comes to attention and responds quite moved, 'No, my commandant, it's not my name-day, but it's my birthday,' responding to '*Est-ce ta fête?*'"

This firework of jokes and riddles, often off-color, would continue until one of the two threw down the gauntlet, for lack of ammunition, and this time Gus triumphed with his last burst, "Which grannie inspires terror? You give up? Grandma-Chinegun, of course!"

We had received some money for our months of forced labor but, with this meager pittance, we unfortunately could not buy anything. These *Lagergelder*, or camp money, were in fact mainly usable in the stalags to buy tobacco, soap, or other basic products. The morale of our *kommando* was dropping day by day and we dreaded our second frigid Christmas far from our own.

However, our Christmas present arrived to our greatest joy a little early. The day before Christmas, I finally received a letter from Gabrielle and a package. Most of my comrades got lucky enough to also receive long-awaited news and packages from the Red Cross. The letter had been posted months earlier when Gabrielle had learned with anguish of my capture in Dunkirk. The letter was brief, its condition testifying to its repeated reading by French and German censorship. It had been slowly forwarded by the Red Cross which had enclosed a parcel. Gabrielle was terribly worried about my fate and didn't know where I was. She was giving me news of Jean-Pierre and the family; they all wished me courage, hoping that I would return soon to them in good health. They were all waiting for me with concern but also with hope. Gabrielle's words warmed my heart while cruelly exacerbating the pain of my separation.

We finally opened our packages all together with uncontrollable impatience, like the heroes of Robert Louis Stevenson in "Treasure Island" – the young adventurer Jim Hawkins and the wooden-legged pirate, Long John Silver, with his parrot Captain Flint on his shoulder – discovering after a very long journey the coveted treasure chest of Flint's gang.

With unparalleled euphoria, we took stock of the packages to plan our Christmas Eve. Before our amazed eyes were spread out on the altar of our offerings, pâtés, saucissons, rillettes, camembert, jams, chocolate, cookies, raisins, and apples.

Our Christmas Eve that very night was going to be most lavish, considering the circumstances. Gérard Marchand surprised us after the opening of the packages by revealing his hidden treasure; when harvesting potatoes, he had secretly brought one or two potatoes into his pockets every day. Over the weeks, he had piled up a generous jackpot of these tubers so well promoted a few centuries earlier by a famous pharmacist of the French army, Antoine Parmentier. To avoid their unfortunate discovery during the rare searches by our guards, he had carefully introduced them one by one, in rusty pipes of old drains. Those did not draw attention; they piled up helter-skelter with other parts of obsolete machines and miscellaneous bric-a-brac at the back of the hangar.

In the meantime, just before Gérard unveiled his *Parmentières*, our guards had brought us three big round breads and a few bottles of red wine for Christmas Eve, in exchange for most of our collective *Lagergeld* nest egg. We started boiling the potatoes, cut generous slices of bread, and prepared various delicacies. Meanwhile, Jean and Gus tried to give, with the means at hand, a festive air to our sideboard covered with these unexpected dishes. They even prepared a menu formula for our festive and extraordinary feast, thus transcending our generally banal and monotonous meals.

*1940 CHRISTMAS EVE MENU FOR THE SCHIVELBEIN KOMMANDO*

- Treasure of our backyard with its Monsignor Porker fashion show
- Minced Three Little Pigs cooked in their lipids by the Big Bad Wolf from Le Mans
- Unbridled farandole of beautiful Pomeranian buns
- Trou Normand or Minute of Silence
- Belle de Fontenay in heat (thank you Gérard!)
- Master Crow's exquisite prey on his perched tree (thank you La Fontaine)
- Surprises from the Garden of Eden à la Eve
- Fruity snacks
- Sweet treats from South America on old-fashioned cookies
- Sleep conqueror at twilight prelude
- All washed down with a secret fermented in regional cellars: no whine today but wine tonight!

(According to the Gospel of our good Father Gythiel, Christmas is the birth of Christ, our Savior Jesus, who said "Love your enemies!" My doctor also said "Alcohol is your enemy!" Let us follow therefore the recommendations from Jesus and my doctor: Cheers! Merry Christmas, with lots of wine, at the Ritz of Schivelbein!)

~ *Nedeleg Laouen! Glückliche Weihnachten! Wesołych Świąt!* (as they say here) ~

As prescribed by the menu, the Christmas Eve celebration was consequently flooded with wine, as evidenced the next day by all the relics of bottles that had helped us to forget our situation for a few hours. Snuggled up in our blankets on our makeshift mattresses, sated with this unexpected abundance of savors coming from our country, we quickly fell into a phantasmagorical universe where we were free again, entwined with our loves, blissful.

The next day, our jailers let us recover from our excess by staying warm on Christmas day. Our hangovers and severe indigestions appreciated this short respite. At the same time, thousands of miles away, another truce was being observed for two days in the air battle raging between Germany and England.

In the afternoon, I wrote to Gabrielle, looking lovingly at her black and white photo, Jean-Pierre snuggled up in her arms. I had so much to share with her and so little room to express my feelings. Already almost a year and a half that our life had been fractured without warning! I felt so lonely, so incomplete without them. Our life had come to an abrupt halt, ripped apart by our separation, torn by enemy bullets and now under the yoke of our torturers. This war seemed endless, circular, like an ouroboros foreshadowing our inevitable destruction. Nazi Germany kept us hostages, like andrapodons. That ensured the total and unconditional collaboration of the Vichy Regime led by a decrepit old man, the Maréchal Pétain, glorified by his pathetic hymn, *"Maréchal, nous voilà!"*

At the start of 1941, we learned from a misplaced newspaper or from Gus, our spy on duty who was secretly listening to the conversations of our guards, that the English and German troops had started to clash in North Africa. Some of our guards were called to join the German expeditionary force, the Afrika Korps. The Führer's hunger for conquest growing insatiably, the Yugoslav government decided to join Germany. Serbian nationalist officers immediately seized power in a coup; this put Adolf in a dark wrath which drove him to invade Yugoslavia on the spot. In its tracks he also took Greece and Crete.

Over everlasting days, always more monotonous, the year of our capture gave way to another year of captivity and winter gradually dissipated.

# Chapter 12

## *From Rutabagas to Frida*

At the end of May 1941, with eight other comrades of the *kommando*, each less motivated than the other, I found myself on the way to a large farm of several thousand hectares to plant potatoes. The place felt like a factory, with many farm buildings and the most modern machinery. The Goszczynski farm *Uparty* had here given way to several state-of-the-art tractors, pulling various agricultural equipment, such as sowing machines or mower binders. There was also a traditional barnyard, well-stocked with horses, cows, geese, chickens, and pigs.

Muscular and brutal foremen followed us like our shadows, armed with sticks or whips. Constantly humming French songs in the fields, our nonet particularly annoyed these screaming bastards. Fortunately, our stay was extremely short and, to our relief, we were sent back after three days due to the massive arrival of Serbian prisoners who had been captured during the recent invasion of Yugoslavia.

However, we did not return empty-handed from the brief visit to this immense farm. Gérard, as clever as a cartload of monkeys, surprised us that evening by revealing the dead body of a plump hen! In a dark and isolated corner of one of the barns, he had surreptitiously sent it to poultry's heaven. Locked in our Ritz, away from prying eyes and noses, we savored this supreme rotisserie while regretting not having saved a few potatoes for the accompaniment.

While Jean-Pierre had celebrated his second birthday, once again without me, we were individually assigned to various farms in the neighborhood. There was no shortage of work, from picking different fruits and vegetables to spreading manure, from weeding and collecting stones in the meadows to chopping wood into pieces, or from animal husbandry to the various repair and maintenance of the farms.

So, once again, change of scenery!

On June 4, 1941, already one year after having laid down our arms in Dunkirk, the mayor of Schivelbein visited us to announce which farm we should go to the next morning. He accompanied us with two guards to show us the way. On the road, he explained to Gus that we had both been assigned to the worst farms in the village. Our new assignment was not shaping up to be the best. It was with growing apprehension that I headed the next morning to a small farm at the end of a winding dirt road. For the first time, we had been able to walk without an escort from our hangar because the guards now trusted us enough. In fact, they knew very well that without papers, civilian clothes, maps, and any ability to master the language, we would not be able to go very far if any idea of freedom or escape tickled us.

I arrived in the courtyard of a small family farm, dilapidated and grim, with shutters broken or still holding only by miracle on unsealed hinges, with decrepit and cracked walls. A heap of garbage sat in front of a barn older than Methuselah, all imbued with a strong smell of liquid manure. On the doorstep, waiting for me like the Messiah, there was a woman of biblical age. Bent in two and leaning on an old wooden stick, dressed entirely in black, her gray hair unkempt like a Harpy, her skin cracked like an ancient parchment, her gaze cloudy but hateful, she scrutinized me as if I rather embodied Mephistopheles.

I took a step back at her sight, convinced I had met the village witch!

The hideous shrew was accompanied by her daughter in her forties, named Frida Fach. She was hardly more engaging than her Gorgon mother but was by far the better nourished of the two, as evidenced by her generous rotundities. She was decked out in a faded dress, a drab apron that never left her, and a blue and white checkered scarf with blond curls protruding from it. With a rather pleasant visage, eyes as clear as a spring sky, voluptuous lips, high cheekbones, and an aquiline nose, she might have had a certain charm in her youth. But that little phiz was now nothing more than an ancient mirage that was inexorably fading over time.

There was also a young unmarried Pole of barely twenty, Janusz, who had been deported and assigned to this remnant of a farm. The poor man blended perfectly in this picture of phantasmagorical desolation with his club foot and his pronounced gibbosity.

In short, the lame hunchback perfectly embellished that evil place.

As soon as I arrived, the Frida woman sent me out to a field to weed rutabagas and beets. At the sight of the weedy land, I thought to myself that they had certainly all been in cahoots over idly waiting for me; they had left me the pleasure of pulling out the overabundance of weeds that invaded the planks of vegetables without exception. She began to weed about a yard to show me how to do it, while speaking an unknown language. I nodded from time to time, thus pretending to listen to her. Then she indicated to me, with large expressive gestures, that it was now my turn to work.

I took the weeder and began my task. Frida, who had stayed not far from me, came to inspect my work after a few moments to assess my gardening skills. She immediately began to vociferate, flushed with anger. She pushed me and tried to explain that I should only remove the weeds and not the rutabagas. I had indeed taken a malicious pleasure in carefully pulling out the plump roots, leaving intact all the unwanted weeds! Frida, in an endless verbal rage, called me names, which luckily I could not understand. Then she demonstrated again, clearly indicating with movements of her head the beets as *gut* and the weeds as *nicht gut!*

I feigned a revelation worthy of the famous "Eureka" of Archimedes in his bath when he had finally found the solution proving the composition of the crown of the king of Syracuse, Hieron, by immersing it in water, then by weighing it, to compare its density to that of solid gold.

Around noon, as the sun began to beat down with its searing rays, making me sweat profusely, she returned to tell me that lunch was ready. Seeing that I had barely progressed in my task in a few hours, she began to scream like Maritornes and, with a smile on my lips, I hoped that a sudden and thaumaturgic intervention would strike her on the spot with apoplexy.

The Fach Mother had prepared a soup for Janusz and me, accompanied by slices of stale black bread with a few bits of cheese that gave off a mephitic smell. The steaming soup in her cauldron heightened my concerns that the old witch had concocted an elixir of her composition for us. I was not ready to perish under her poisoner's hands, let alone succumb to her charms, totally non-existent, under the spell of a love potion. So, I feigned indisposition from the heat and contented myself with the black bread and a glass of water.

A few days later, Frida asked me to move an imposing pile of old straw to another corner at the back of the barn. No sooner said than done! Of course, when the Fach Mother came to get me for a snack, having finally understood my aversion to her more than doubtful soup, she tried in vain to make me understand that I had moved it to the wrong place. Indeed, I had migrated the pile of straw in front of the large main door of the barn, thus blocking its access. Stubborn like a Breton, I played dumb and continued my work while providing her with lots of *"nie, nie,"* in response to her adamant requests. When Frida returned from the village, she once again entered one of her furies, which had become so familiar. She planted herself in front of me, her hands on her rounded hips, her crimson red face contorted with rage and contrasting with her eternal blue and white kerchief.

Deep inside, I was roaring with laughter, but I was not done yet!

One morning, she asked me to harness the old horse. The poor one-eyed nag only asked to be left in peace. After a life of hard labor in this sinister farm, most often beaten by the two cantankerous women, his only wish was to finally reach in peace the equine Elysian Fields, or any other field for that matter. Each time Frida approached to hand me the harness, I stepped back. She made it clear to me that I was mentally even younger than her six-year-old niece who was there, observing us. But I had no experience with the equine breed, and I didn't want to confront this packhorse whose treacherous only eye looked at me like the eye in the grave had watched mankind's first murderer, Cain.

In desperation, Frida resigned herself to fetch her brother, Hans, a big, bearded, bleak bloke who lived on a nearby farm, to harness her horse. She probably did not hesitate to call me lazy and chicken-hearted but, in the end, I emerged victorious from my deferred struggle with this Cyclopean Helhest.

Barely recovered from these emotions, she then directed me to a stall where an impetuous young horse was blowing loudly through its nostrils and scratching the ground nervously with its hooves. Already apprehensive from my brief encounter with his half-blind patriarch, I followed Frida reluctantly. She asked me to change the straw of the fiery stallion stall. It was far from being a luxury considering Janusz had refused to do so after receiving a stinging kick in the thigh just before I arrived at the farm. I grabbed a pitchfork to remove the old straw and she left me to my chore. Of course, I once again played dumb, pretending not to differentiate between straw, an effective and insulating litter, and hay, a mixture of dried nutritional plants. When she came back and saw the floor of the stall covered exclusively with plentiful and fluffy hay, she almost fainted and had to sit down. Shouting at the top of her lungs, she asked me to immediately replace the hay – which had made the young impulsive horse my new unconditional friend – by straw.

On another sunny but stormy day, after the typical midday meal of black bread and some raw vegetables, the Fach Mother went to take her daily nap. Frida accompanied me behind the farm and showed me a huge pile of wood. She handed me an ax, trying to explain by vivid gestures that I had to chop the wood into pieces; those would feed the old stove and the fireplace during the long freezing days to come. I set to work sluggishly, chopping the pieces of wood at my slowest record pace. Then I nonchalantly piled them up, one after the other, along the farm wall. The house cast salutary shade, shielding me a little from the stifling heat. However, after a while, dripping and panting, I decided to take a well-deserved break. I went to cool off at the secular well that sat near the house.

Passing by the barn, I heard unusual noises, like ethereal whispers. Gradually, sighs rose from the bowels of the barn, almost sounding like groans or moans.

Intrigued, I stealthily approached the barn. I quietly opened a small door to the side. A sort of wail, interspersed with jerky gasps, suddenly grew louder. These seemed to come from behind the two stalls, in the corner of the barn where, after my pranks, I had relocated the immense pile of straw. Quieter than an Apache sneaking up on an encampment of US Army Bluecoats, I approached the source of suspicious noises.

She was there before my astonished eyes, like a Valkyrie riding her wolf to accompany the souls of the fallen warriors to Valhalla; she seemed to have already reached seventh heaven. Her blond hair completely tousled, her scarf lost among the wisps of straw, her skirts rolled up to her waist, she wriggled with all her being and all her weight on the young hunchback who seemed to be dangerously on the verge of asphyxiation and fainting.

Our Quasimodo had finally found his Esmeralda with titanic Teutonic tits!

In a last jolt, the two protagonists exchanged a long groan.

Silence fell on the barn.

Retracing my steps without noise but as quickly as possible towards the exit, so as not to be spotted, I thanked the good Lord for having spared me the advances of Frida the ogress. I refused to think of the unfortunate offspring that could be born of such an encounter with Janusz! I also dared not to think how a military tribunal would judge this prohibited mating of a prisoner with a local woman.

I thus decided to repress these amorous frolics to the bottom of my conscience.

I swore that this banned rendezvous would not set tongues wagging.

However, when I arrived at the Ritz, I could not keep such a secret to myself, and I hastened to declaim, "Guess what happened on the farm today."

"Did you play one of your dirty tricks on them again, Alexandre?"

"No, for once I'm not involved. It is true that I did not put much ardor in chopping wood this afternoon; Frida was once again red with anger to find that I had made a very small pile but along the entire length of the house. Instead, she expected me to pile up high the pieces of wood in an orderly manner. No, today I'm not making the headlines."

"So, you managed to pilfer some food from them too?" Gérard asked me, taking a few fresh eggs and a piece of bacon from his pockets.

"No, you will never guess. Do you remember that the farm also employs a young Polish prisoner, Janusz?"

"Yeah, you already told us that nature had not spoiled him but that he completed the picture very well with the old witch and her harpy daughter."

Taking all my time for the punchline, I replied, "Well, the hunchback has a club foot, but he is not armless! I stumbled upon him on the straw heap with Frida. They were doing a lot more than whispering sweet nothings in each other's ears! Frida is a man-eater under her menacing looks. I hope that after this main course, she will not see me as her French dessert."

"Keep driving her crazy Alex and you will certainly be safe from her fantasies. You definitely hit the jackpot with the Fach's farm!"

Towards the end of June, while I was in the yard filling buckets with water from the well, I had a fleeting glimpse of Frida removing the sprouts from old potatoes, seated on a wooden stool with her legs spread. To my utter stupefaction, I noticed that she was wearing no panties! Ignoring this deplorable sight, I hoped her indecency wasn't a cue that she was trying to make misplaced advances to me. Would she bring me to bay out of the blue in a dark corner of the barn?

I decided to stay further away from her, scared of this maenad. I told Janusz about the inappropriate exposure I had witnessed, hoping he would redouble his attention for his dulcinea. Unfortunately, he hastened to immediately go and tell her the full story without any restraint, which once again put her in a state of uncontrollable frenzy. At least she left me alone. She was no longer talking to me, apart from shouting her usual orders to me.

That evening, I recounted my adventures to the *kommando* gathered around the table for a frugal dinner.

As some of my fellow prisoners had to pass in front of the Fach's farm to go to their daily assignment, the next morning Frida was waiting for them, fit as a fiddle, at the end of the dirt road. They all had a complicit and sly air that spoke volumes about their knowledge of the events of the day before. As they passed, Frida took the hem of her skirt with both hands and proudly lifting it like La Goulue dancing the French can-can at the Moulin Rouge, she said to them in her vitriolic tone, "Look, I indeed have panties on!"

My comrades started to whistle and applauded frantically for her performance!

Taking advantage of her inattention, the very same day I decided to play another of my tricks on her. I visited the henhouse and stole an egg that I secretly brought back to the Ritz. That evening, I boiled it hard; the next day I laid the hard-boiled egg back among the other fresh eggs in the henhouse. I couldn't help laughing when at lunch time I suddenly heard a spine-chilling cry of fright from Fach Mother. Her daughter immediately followed and started to rant. As they were preparing selfishly an omelet for them alone, they had just discovered that an evil spell had been cast on their hens, which were now producing fresh, but hard-boiled eggs!

The last days of June, the work suddenly intensified at the farm. I received the order to spend the nights there to lengthen my work time. Frida gave me a blanket and pointed in the barn to the infamous and dreaded pile of straw, laden with a nightmarish memory. But fortunately, the nights there were uneventful; I even slept quite soundly. One day while changing the rabbit hutches, I forgot, through calculated carelessness, to close the doors of all the cages. I didn't have the satisfaction of seeing Frida's exasperation, nor her frantic searches around the farm to locate the missing happy lagomorphs.

Indeed, at noon, one of the guards arrived at the farm and made me leave it immediately. Happy to leave this cursed place as quickly as possible, I waved them a little "*Adieu*" with a huge smile that said it all. However, I also worried, trying to make sense of this abrupt departure. I wondered if Frida had complained about me to the authorities behind my back to perhaps try to preserve her dangerous liaison with Janusz.

When I arrived at the Ritz, my comrades told me that I had been extremely lucky; the day before, three German officers had reviewed all the prisoners and had asked insistently about me.

They then explained to me the reason for this official visit. Two days earlier, Louis, a shy, skinny, and somewhat effeminate young guy from Burgundy, had suddenly packed his bags without telling anyone.

As usual, he had left the hangar in the morning with the other prisoners, unescorted. He had walked on the road leading to the farm where he worked alone. However, as soon as his comrades were out of sight, he had returned in hiding not far from the Ritz where he had spotted a small boat which anchored on the Rega river. Unbeknownst to the guards, he had shed in a bush his jacket with the compromising letters KG and rolled up his sleeves. He had then begun to row towards the Baltic Sea and a highly coveted freedom. His plan was simple, even perhaps too simplistic: he would approach the coast in this beautiful month of June and try to embark clandestinely on a ship which would take him to a distant destination.

He had formulated his plan on a whim, without preparation, after receiving a letter addressed to him two days earlier. We found this letter on his bed, informing him that his lover, Robert, had recently been deported in France to the Pithiviers camp located in the Loiret. Wild with grief, alone and distraught, Louis had decided then and there to flee to try to get closer to his companion. Gus also informed us that Louis had surprised him the day before his escape by asking him how to write in German, "I am deaf." Louis had found a trivial excuse to justify himself; Gus had written for him, "*Ich bin stumm.*" It was now clear that his rudimentary plan was to produce this paper if anyone called him out, but without any identification papers and laissez-passer his chances of escape were infinitesimal.

His departure forced us all to remain locked up for several days in the overheated hangar, without ventilation. We were choking and sweating profusely, in our underwear all day long, without permission to go out. The air soiled by our odors and by the curls of cigarette smoke quickly became unbreathable. Meanwhile, Gus overheard a few conversations from the soldiers standing guard outside about a recent invasion of the Soviet Union by German troops.

Nothing could stop the delusions of grandeur of the psychopathic dictator!

Indeed, Operation Barbarossa, fomented by Hitler and his generals earlier in the year, had been launched in the hope that it would encourage Japan to attack the United States of America, thus diverting its attention from the events in Europe.

The German plan was evil.

By invading new regions, Germany sought a free and submissive workforce for its forced labor, while seizing the oil reserves of the Caucasus and the agricultural products of certain Russian territories. The ultimate goal was to create an enlarged living space for the new Germany, by hunting, deporting to Siberia, and exterminating Slavs, Jews, Gypsies or any other opponents to the regime of the Third Reich.

Gus also surprised the guards laughing heartily as they discussed recent horrific events. At this end of June 1941, when the Soviet troops were retreating from the temporary capital of Lithuania, Kaunas, the paramilitary troop *"Einsatzgruppe A"* entered the town with its death squads, composed among others of hundreds of SS soldiers and members of the Gestapo. Their sole aim was to exterminate by all possible means, as barbaric as they were hasty, all the alleged opponents of the Nazi regime, in particular the Jews. After having cut their teeth by exterminating Polish executives, Jews, and Gypsies, they were now advancing like a savage tornado towards the Soviet Union. In just a few years of war, these mobile killing squads would relentlessly and mercilessly murder more than a million and a half innocent civilians – women, men, and children of all ages – mainly Jews.

This morning of June 25, 1941, as a sunny day dawned over Kaunas, the commander of the sinister *"Einsatzgruppe A,"* Franz Stahlecker, a Doctor of Law, roamed the streets of the city, megaphone in hand. Driven by his personal chauffeur in an open-top Mercedes convertible, he urged the population to denounce all Jews and hand them over. Sixty-eight Jews thus found themselves captured and transferred to the Lietūkis garage, east of Kaunas. Quickly, a crowd of curious onlookers formed in the garage courtyard. The men, some in suits with soft felt trilby hats, others in short sleeve shirts, the women in summer dresses, all congregated with SS soldiers and Lithuanian nationalists along the inner wall of the garage courtyard. Children in short breeches were perched on their fathers' shoulders to better watch the mournful and morbid spectacle.

In front of these cruel spectators, hungry for blood, facing the cameras of German soldiers and under a blazing sun, the victims had first been cursed, humiliated, repeatedly punched with fists, and kicked with feet.

Unfortunately, this was only the beginning of their suffering.

A high-pressure water hose was then forcibly inserted into their mouths. The unfortunate victims were agonizing under the torture, suffocating, and gradually drowning. The spectators cheered the executioners, clapping with all their might, roaring with laughter, and taking great delight in the sadism of these nationalist assassins.

Then, stimulated by the enthusiasm of this public of all ages, the torturers seized shovels and iron bars.

Itzhak, a frail old man, knelt with great difficulty. He began to pray in Hebrew with the palms of his hands turned to the heavens. A blond fellow in his twenties, in black pants with a big beige belt, clad in a white linen shirt and jacket, shod in leather boots, slammed with a sharp blow his long iron bar down on the head of the patriarchal plumber. The murderer lashed out again and again on the already lifeless body under the excited applause of the crowd.

The purveyor of death of Kaunas had killed its first victim, under the frenzied cheers of his audience.

He was already calling the next one, now coming towards him, shaking all over, terrified. Intoxicated by the smell of blood that spread in filthy puddles in this court of torture, the massacre of these innocent people continued tirelessly, one after the other, without any pity or remorse in the scarlet and savage afternoon.

Skulls exploded. Bones shattered with horrific creaks interspersed with the moans and wails of the dying. Blood and brains mingled together in swelling and loathsome pools that the assassins scrambled to clean up rapidly with the infamous pressurized water hose. Two young students with their father, an ice cream vendor, a musician, a printer, a bookseller, fathers, husbands, brothers, children, all were dying at a frantic rate under the murderous madness of this month of June.

When at last all the souls of the sixty-eight innocents had found an eternal rest, the "butcher of Kaunas" sat down on the heap of entangled and broken bodies. He started playing the Lithuanian national anthem on his accordion, joined in unison by the crowd of onlookers.

History would remember those terrible hours as the Kaunas Pogrom.

Those massacres would sadly recur over and over again in the months and years to come, multiplying exponentially in horror.

In Schivelbein, our movements outside the Ritz had been authorized again, but this time under the bitter control of our guards. Two long weeks had passed since the clandestine escape of Louis. Then, one day, Louis was back, escorted by SS officers.

He was unrecognizable.

His face was swollen and deformed, his lips split and bloody in several places, one of his eyelids closed over a puffy eye, many of his fingernails torn and bloody, burns from cigarette and brands visible on his neck, forearms, and hands. He moved with great difficulty, bent in excruciating pain. Cracked or broken ribs made his breathing difficult and sluggish. Displaying this distressing example of a totally broken man, for love, the SS officers told us bluntly that it was the fate awaiting us if we ever had the madness to attempt or even think of an escape.

A few days later, Louis was accompanied by the guards to the train station for a concentration camp from which he unfortunately never returned.

# Chapter 13

## *From Coal to Confrontation*

After these agricultural chores in which I have to admit I did not excel, as much by inexperience as by malice, I was employed by a hauler in Schivelbein. I would remain there until the end of my captivity.

As 1941 ended, still deprived of my liberty, I received a parcel and a small package, accompanied by a letter from Gabrielle. We could only receive one five-kilogram package every two months as well as two smaller five-hundred-gram packages. We sent labels to our families to make sure, as best as we could, that these precious packages got to us safely. The news was always brief and controlled by censorship. Gabrielle told me that Jean-Pierre was starting to talk more and more; his grandfather had already taught him to count to ten. With tears in my eyes, I learned that he now knew how to say "Papa" well, but I was lucid that I had probably become only a distant memory that would gradually fade away from his mind. She also told me that she missed me every second; I missed them both even more so.

In the large parcel, a new pair of shoes was very welcome, given the state of the vestige of my clodhoppers which had passed away a long time ago. Gabrielle had also knitted for me a gray wool sweater and matching gloves that were going to change my life on the too many frigid days. She also had added noodles and rice which would thicken our meager soups on those long winter days.

In the small package, she had sent me two bars of Marseilles soap that filled the room with a lovely country scent. She had also added some recreations for the long evenings to come – a Grimaud game of fifty-four cards, five playing dice, and a detective story by Agatha Christie, "Murder on the Orient Express." This Machiavellian tale was a masterpiece of imagination, inspired by the appalling kidnapping of Charles Lindbergh's young boy. The death of the wealthy American victim, Sam Ratchett, was most inventive: in the middle of the night, in his first-class cabin, Ratchett's body had been found with twelve stab wounds. Hercule Poirot was going to hold me spellbound, in that snow-covered, immaculate enclosed world. After having untied all the threads of the intrigue, against all expectations the famous Belgian detective would magnanimously leave the crime unpunished. I would reread this masterful book several times as well as, "And Then There Were None," in which the name of the murderer of the many victims isolated on an island was only revealed in the very last word of the story.

A third Christmas away from my family was fast approaching as the Germans now besieged Leningrad. They were advancing rapidly towards Moscow. The news that Gus was able to glean from our guards and from the newspapers found at our forced labor sites narrated that the German offensive on Moscow had been literally frozen in place by extreme polar temperatures.

In Schivelbein, the weather had become one of the most austere and icy at the end of the year. A thick blanket of snow and frost had enveloped the Pomeranian landscape as far as the eye could see, muffling all the usual sounds around. In our miserable Ritz, we shivered from the unbearable cold. Our work was also slowing down with this forced hibernation. We spent most of our time locked up, trying to warm ourselves up as best as we could, while attempting to kill our new enemy – time.

Our Christmas Eve was dull, with fatigue, cold, and loneliness becoming more and more burdensome for everyone. Even the crepes that we had prepared together from buckwheat flour diluted with water and beer, stuffed with various sweets – sugar, jam, chocolate, or honey – did not get the much-deserved success. Indeed, the event that troubled us the most at the end of this year was the incendiary gift delivered by the Japanese at Pearl Harbor. On a paradise island in Hawaii, the surprise and deadly kamikaze air attack of the Japanese air force on the American fleet had just ignited the war in the Pacific. Immediately, in a domino effect, the United States and the United Kingdom had declared war on Japan, while Germany and Italy declared war on the United States.

The war was globalizing worldwide.

Our prospects for the future seemed to be diminishing by the day.

I wondered with growing concern if my fate would henceforth be to remain a sempiternal prisoner in Pomerania.

The work was particularly hard during the first two years with the hauler, Amadeusz, a plump little man with a well-established baldness, displaying the build of a weightlifter with disproportionate biceps; his flat nose, with a pair of round glasses perched on it, testified to his bellicose character but also his weak boxing skills. A short, curved tobacco pipe made of wood permanently sat at the corner of his mouth.

Most often, at the Schivelbein train station, I unloaded thirty tons of coal during the day with another comrade. In the evening, black from head to toe, we dragged ourselves exhausted to the hangar. After a succinct toilet and a frugal meal, we were fit to drop on our cachectic mattresses to rest our muscles and sore joints. Other days we unloaded wagons of potatoes and once a month one or two wagons of sugar. The comings and goings between the cars and the boss's truck broke our backs and shoulders. Like workhorses, we were carrying hundred kilo bags; Gabrielle would certainly have been impressed by my physical condition and my bulging muscles. But my looks didn't impress anyone, not even me when I saw my sad reflection in the window of one of the shops in these streets with unpronounceable names – *Slowiańska, Boleslawa Chrobego, Niedzialkowskiego* – the lack of food making me look emaciated and sickly. Once a week, we received a wagon of miscellaneous items, from cigarettes to various parcels. We then delivered them into town with a comrade and Amadeusz, in his sputtering old banger. It was by far our best day!

The day of the sugar wagons was one of the most difficult. We generally had the reinforcement of other comrades from the *kommando*, including Gérard Marchand. This bachelor from Tours had more than one trick up his sleeve but also in his bag which Father Gythiel had made for him; he always carried it with him. Gérard was a real kleptomaniac, a gentleman burglar, à la Arsène Lupin. In addition to his illustrious shoulder bag, he had sewn in the lining of his coat a few large pockets which were very handy to make disappear, as if by magic, any object or commodity passing within his reach. Gérard was the Ritz superintendent, its grocer, its hardware manager, its main supplier. If we needed anything, all we had to do was ask Gérard and the following days the coveted object appeared as if by magic before our incredulous eyes. Nothing stopped him. He had some of the most ingenious wangles.

One day we were ordered to deliver bags of sugar to the first floor of a warehouse on the outskirts of Schivelbein. We had to climb a long ladder, carrying those damned hundred kilo bags on our shoulders. The work was perilous and broke our backs. So, on the third step of the ladder, I accidentally let go – but in fact quite intentionally – the first bag and the sugar crashed on the ground. The bag tore and exploded under the impact. The sugar scattered around the warehouse in a sweetened whitish cloud. Amadeusz screamed blue murder, but I was jubilant! Taking advantage of this distraction, Gérard had not wasted his time. Always on the alert, he had previously spotted various potential larcenies. His pockets filled quickly. Screwdrivers, candles, cigarettes, matchboxes, pencils, and little packets of sugar piled up at the bottom of his secret caches.

Amadeusz was a good boss even if the workdays of more than twelve hours, six days a week that he imposed on us were very customary. The work was intense and grueling; our muscles and joints regularly begged for a truce. Amadeusz also very easily and frequently burst with brief but terrible anger, most often linked to my pranks. He spoke a little French which suited me well. Over the months, he began to confide a little more, especially when he was behind the wheel of his truck, on his way to deliveries. He then became our main source for the latest world news.

Thus, at the beginning of 1942, shrugging his shoulders, Amadeusz told us, in broken and rather comical French, news from the Russian front, "The Germans need oil and take it from the Caucasus. Still war with the Reds."

We wondered if his support for the *Niemiec* – the Germans – was unconditional or if he perhaps had a penchant for those Reds, the *Rosjanin* – the Russians – but in doubt we remained neutral and silent.

Later in the year, he would tell us about being aware of a massive roundup of Jews in Paris, where women, men, and children were brutally corralled; they were then taken to the Drancy internment camp or other concentration camps. We often wondered if we correctly understood the news that he was telling us; he talked about the place of the roundup in Paris as being in the Val d'If, when we didn't know of any valley in the capital. Much later we would understand that this place was in fact the Vélodrome d'Hiver of Paris, also known as the Vel' d'Hiv!

Despite the regular letters I received from Gabrielle, who was telling me that she waited for me impatiently and tried to give me courage, this interminable separation weighed more and more on me. I had once again missed Jean-Pierre's birthday who, at three years old, was becoming more and more curious. He seemed interested in everything, asking questions over and over again of Gabrielle and his adored grandparents. Gabrielle was also telling me that he looked like me and was a real chatterbox. He could count to twenty, recognized all the letters of the alphabet, and spent most of his time running in the garden; he also enjoyed playing on the swings and riding his tricycle. But one had to be careful with him; he absorbed everything like a sponge and had even beckoned over and called one of the German soldiers, stationed not far from his grandparents' house, a loathsome Squarehead. To avoid censorship, Gabrielle wrote the compromising words in Breton. Fortunately, this German soldier did not understand French and had answered him with a smile, thinking that this sweet little tot was kindly saying hello.

I missed them so much. This life, thousands of kilometers away from them, which had become routine, banal, but so lonely, made us sour and downhearted. Our morale was often very low, but we always had a comrade to encourage us and try to calm our impatience.

Already three years had passed. Three long years!

So many events had changed my life. Would there be an end to my captivity? What was our future? Would we remain slaves at the boot of the German people forever?

After the summer, we learned through Amadeusz of the siege of Stalingrad by German troops. A few months later, as the Germans invaded the so-called free zone in France, the French fleet scuttled at Toulon, preferring to destroy itself rather than to surrender to the enemy.

We also had our Fifth Column. This group, made up of some of the prisoners, did not have the expectation to act in the shadows to overthrow the Nazi party or even undermine the local regime. Led by our comrade Gérard, this Fifth Column was simply intended to steal as much as possible for our well-being as prisoners and to secretly disrupt the local life.

Members of the Fifth Column were asked to reinforce the shopkeepers at busy times. Thus, Gérard and the others ended up at the watchmaker's, the drugstore, or the haberdashery of the village. Most often, their help was required to tidy up, organize, label, or participate in an inventory. They also simply helped clean the premises and cupboards, or even restore and repaint certain stores. Gérard was thus able to get an alarm clock for our Ritz and other prisoners brought back their loot, very precious for the long cold days: pullovers and woolen hats, gloves, and socks. Sometimes the sizes and the colors left something to be desired. Thus, the priest found himself with a pair of yellow gloves which did not go unnoticed; a cap of appropriate color for a demoiselle remained for a long time without an owner.

Gérard continued his theft at the market on Wednesdays, in the main square of Schivelbein, near the Brama Kamienna that we had passed through, escorted by our guards two years earlier. He was so astute that we always looked forward to our improved Wednesday dinner after his help had been requested at the market. Amongst the various stalls, helping the merchants prepare or tidy up their display, Gérard had a field day. His trick pockets and his famous satchel filled up with an abundance of fruits and vegetables, bacon, eggs, cheese, or bread.

Everything was not stolen; the merchants sometimes gave him some unsold products for his services. Thus, we would find ourselves around our table, savoring a wonderful omelet with bacon and potatoes, or a cabbage ragout, or even occasionally a rabbit stew. With our meager salary, we were also sometimes fortunate to supplement these meals with a few bottles of wine.

The Fifth Column also liked to destabilize the lives of certain villagers.

The grocer Kwiatkowski, who did not hide his contempt for the French or his aggravated anti-Semitism, found himself one morning with a flood of Biblical proportion in his store. A Fifth Column prisoner had plugged one of the grocery store's sinks with pieces of cloth and, before leaving the store at the end of the day as the grocer was closing his shop, had turned on the devastating tap. We passed in front of Kwiatkowski's the next day, smiles on our lips, as he worked energetically, swearing at the top of his lungs to whoever wanted to hear him. Armed with his mop and his bucket, he evacuated this tsunami which had suddenly invaded his shop during the night.

The butcher Lieberum, a boor who also openly displayed his aversion to prisoners, had a quick hand when one of us came to help him occasionally. One fine morning, he had the unpleasant surprise to find a few fat rats munching on the meat in the room showcases; roaches swarmed along in a random and disgusting way. Jean had previously noticed that the window of his butcher shop usually remained half-open during the night. He was perhaps attempting to subdue the pungent smell of sliced flesh constantly emanating from his stall. Therefore, to carry out our operation, we only had to capture big fatty rats near the river and move families of cockroaches who had taken refuge as co-tenants in our Ritz. This sudden infestation did the greatest damage to his business. Part of the population of the village even suddenly became vegetarian for a while!

The months, the years, followed one another at the same pace, tirelessly.

Habits had settled in.

Our future was becoming more and more uncertain.

Very early on Christmas Day, the Protestant parish priest, Czeslaw Czacki, brought to the Ritz, with the permission of our guards, some old stained and sagging mattresses. Some generous parishioners wanted to get rid of them, either out of charity to improve their chance of direct access to heaven without an otherwise likely passage to purgatory, or most often quite simply to make room in their home. The old priest Czacki had become friends with Father Gythiel, both celibates and men of faith. He provided him with consecrated hosts for his divine Sunday liturgy at the Ritz or outside in the open during the warm days.

After delivering the mattresses, Father Czacki invited us to come to his church for our fourth Christmas away from ours. We were allowed by our guards to join in the celebration of the Nativity in the church of Schivelbein.

We arrived at the church on Christmas Day 1942 under a snowstorm.

The red brick church with its imposing square bell tower, surmounted by a spire, appeared completely foreign to us as soon as we passed the vaulted entrance. The church seemed to have been stripped of everything. The white and red pillars were bare, as were all the walls. The stained-glass windows were abstract, and no religious paintings or statues were visible.

As soon as we entered this temple, Jean whispered in my ear, "Alex, do you think the Germans stole everything and stripped the church of any decor? It's sinister here. Look at this black and white checkered floor. It gives the impression of moving on a giant chess game!"

"Stop it, Jean. Let's not stand out anymore. It is a Protestant church. We should be happy enough to have been invited. Fortunately, most of the villagers gathered here already know us!"

"Yeah, that's really weird," Gus added. "Look, Jesus has stepped down from the cross! It's empty."

"You are very observant, but in fact Protestants prefer to celebrate the resurrection of Jesus rather than having his martyrdom in front of them all the time. I personally like that, and I find it more optimistic," Father Gythiel retorted.

Then, for our information he added, "Protestants do not believe in the Immaculate Conception either and do not recognize the authority of the Pope. There will be no sign of the cross today and you have probably noticed already the absence of holy water fonts. But at the end of the day, we are all children of God. We all believe in the same God, the same Bible, and a risen Christ."

"Imagine, Father," Jean began mischievously. "If you were a Protestant, you could choose a woman, like Frida from the farm where Alexandre was assigned!"

"Stop your sacrileges, Jean, and let's go join the congregation in celebrating Christmas all together."

After this unorthodox ceremony, we returned to our residence where we spent the afternoon arranging our quarters, clearing all the junk at the back of the hangar, and installing our new mattresses. The large hangar door now remained open, our guards trusting us; they only made a few daily rounds. This new space, cleaned and enlarged, helped us break away from the routine. Our confinement had gradually become our new normal, indeed a bit more comfortable but still as sad and uncertain. We were undeniably lonely men, prisoners of war, and forced laborers.

Time seemed frozen.

Another year had passed, 1943 was looming on the horizon. Would we be free again soon?

The new year arrived, as freezing as the previous months. Work had slowed down. We were still shivering from the cold in our Ritz despite the clothes we had received in our packages or through our Fifth Column. In February, we learned that the Vichy regime had established a forced enlistment of French citizens to work in Germany, the *Service du Travail Obligatoire* or STO. The idea was to compensate for the loss of labor due to the conscription of young Germans who found themselves fighting on the Eastern Front, where they were being massacred.

We wrongly thought that this new "relief," which previously allowed one of us to return home in exchange for three new workers, would allow us to be sent home more rapidly. This new obligation for young French people to come and work for two years in Germany had been the result of nagging and phlegmatic negotiations by Pierre Laval. The new head of the Vichy government sought to buy time, as usual, by all means. The *Service Obligatoire du Travail*, which he had negotiated and took effect in February 1943, changed its name after only a few days. The French people openly mocked its stupid acronym, SOT, which spoke volumes about Laval's negotiating skills.

Many were those who tried at all costs to escape the roundups of the Militia and the French gendarmerie. Hundreds of thousands of men holed up in their basements or got hired on farms to escape the STO. It also was the detonator which triggered many men to join the resistance and the maquis which developed exponentially.

After more than two years spent in captivity in Schivelbein and in particular the long icy days of the last few months, we had somehow become recluses, like members of a new monastic order. Of course, others suffered even more than us in labor or extermination camps. Passing through a gate adorned with the spurious motto, "*Arbeit Macht Frei*," they marched in despondent lines not to the freedom promised in work but rather found in a devious and inescapable death in gas chambers and crematoriums. Millions of innocent people, entire families, were savagely wiped out in these death camps.

Spring finally came back, and we resumed our activities with a vengeance. We were now allowed to walk around town on Sundays, without guards, even on the sidewalks. However, we were forbidden to contact the villagers, for fear that we might find help for an escape attempt. They now knew us quite well because of our deliveries and our occasional help in some of the stores and at the weekly market.

One day in May, as the Warsaw ghetto after its uprising was seeing in reprisal German soldiers and the Gestapo arrest tens of thousands of Jews there, summarily executing them or sending them to death camps, we were getting ready for a merciless fight against our guards. Indeed, we had been painstakingly rehearsing our moves for months and were confident we could beat them. We had formulated a plan that we thought was foolproof. We hoped to emerge victorious from the confrontation. Our guards didn't seem to care a bit and continued their idle and debauched lives.

This Sunday morning, everything was going to be played out around noon.

We took our equipment out of our bags then, in uniform, we did some stretching while reviewing our plan of attack. We had to be ready for this close combat. We would give no quarter to the enemy.

Then, nervous but ready for our mission, we moved quietly to a flat area at the edge of the village. The enemy was already there, in position. Nonchalant.

They too had put their gear on. They were waiting for us firmly, with a dreadful look.

They started to shoot.

The warm-up of their goalkeeper was underway!

Indeed, after watching us play soccer amongst ourselves to relax on several occasions, they had ended up challenging us. We had accepted their dare with an extraordinary impatience, as if the outcome of the war was going to be played out on that field.

The struggle was fierce. We had eleven players and a substitute. The priest was our coach and had no doubt prayed to God *ad nauseam* for a French victory. I was the goalkeeper, not because I was particularly good at that position, but rather because I was less bad than at another position. We had prepared a plan of attack, but our opponents led by two goals at half-time. We had not yet been able to trick their goalkeeper, a German sergeant over two meters in height. Under the jeers of the adversary, we gathered around the priest for his advice.

"Alex, I can see you're doing your best, but we need to seriously strengthen our defenses. The enemy can no longer pass, I want a massive and heroic defense! Gérard, you are the fastest, so you will try to lose your marker by running erratically to divert their attention. When you are ready to receive the ball, you will place yourself on the left side which seems to me to be their weakest point. The objective is simple: you recover the ball, you move up the field as far as possible, then you forward pass quickly to Gérard on the left side; he will be open and waiting for the ball. Then, may God guide you Gérard to their goal and help you score."

"Well guys, we're going to show them that in France we have ideas and that we can adapt a tactic to win," Gérard replied. "Come on, let's believe in it. The battle is not lost! Let's show them that the French are tough and can come back from the dead."

"Amen," replied the priest, exulting like a Trappist monk who had suddenly recovered his voice. Then he proudly added *"Vive la France!"*

The second half hardly started, Gérard received the ball from Jean, dribbled past two defenders and, alone in front of the giant goalkeeper, kicked with all his might a cannon ball which landed in the goal's top right corner. We were jubilant, the strategy already seemed to be working! Our massive defense was holding on firmly; fortunately, I had a lot fewer saves to make. The Germans were blocked; they could no longer pass. A little while later, Gérard found himself face to face with a last defender who brutally tackled him in the penalty box. The mayor of Schivelbein, the match referee with two of his deputies, whistled the foul without hesitation and indicated the penalty kick mark.

The tension was palpable. The spectators who had gathered around the soccer field held their breath. A heavy silence hung over the players. Gérard took his time and, at the whistle of the mayor-referee, stepped forward. He peeked furtively to the right of the goal where the goalkeeper immediately dove and skillfully kicked the ball towards the opposite side at ground level. The ball hit the goal post. For a brief moment, time froze. It began to move in slow motion. After what seemed like an eternity, the ball ended up in the net.

We were now tied!

The last minutes were fierce, brutal, and merciless. I stopped a header from the German center-forward, with some luck or by desperation, then threw the ball as far as I could to the left side. Gérard, unmarked, recovered the ball, and quickly went down the whole field alone to find himself in front of the giant who uttered terrifying screams, like an ogre, to scare him. But it would take a lot more to deter Gérard who dribbled around him and found himself alone in front of the empty goal. With a short kick, taunting the colossus who was desperately coming back towards the goal with long strides, he lodged the ball over the goal line in the back of the net. He thus sealed our victory which we hoped foreshadowed a favorable and rapid outcome of the war. Our guards were magnanimous; they took pictures of our teams and offered us some beer that they had brought with them.

I then thought of Jean-Pierre who had just celebrated his fourth birthday. He would have certainly enjoyed seeing me win this fierce battle against the Germans around a soccer ball. He too was now likely to play ball with his friends and was probably talking like a little man. He must have changed so much over these last three years which had been robbed from me as a prisoner of war. Would I ever see him again? Would I be a complete stranger to him, or would he find this invisible link that united us?

I missed him so much.

I longed for Gabrielle even more.

# Chapter 14

## *From Deliveries to Escape*

At the end of the month, we received a meager pittance in *Lagergeld*, or camp money. In fact, our various employers had to pay our salaries directly to the army of the Third Reich, the *Wehrmacht*, after which we were lucky if we received even half of it. But since these *Lagergelder* could only be used in the camps to buy food or basic products, we could not use them. Therefore, we exchanged them for hard cash with our guards who in the process took advantage, for lack of competition, to make us pay an exorbitant commission and a risk tax. In the end, we very often had to pool our coin of the realm to be able to buy certain foods in local stores to try to ameliorate our dinners together.

At the end of July 1943, under a scorching sun, I was making deliveries with Gus and Amadeusz in his old banger. During a stop, my boss, who had made astonishing progress in French, handed me a heavy crate and said, "Alex, you be a good worker and patient French teacher. Box not to deliver but late for birthday to you weeks ago. After morning deliveries, me give you free afternoon to rest and celebrate."

Amadeusz had become much nicer to me and to the other

comrades who helped unload freight trains and make deliveries with him. He still had an inextricable problem with the conjugation of French verbs, whether regular or irregular, but he made himself understood quite well.

"Thanks, Amadeusz. It is very nice of you. We will share these bottles of wine between us to celebrate my thirty-third birthday," I answered him sincerely, shaking his hand.

Then, in his outpouring of charity, switching from his hesitant and somewhat lame French to German that Gus could translate for me, he passed on freshly gleaned news to us. The Russians had started a counteroffensive and were regaining many towns on the Eastern Front. Allied forces had bombed Rome, captured Sicily, and liberated Corsica. Some of the large German cities had also suffered from Allied air raids; Hamburg had seen a rain of bombs as destructive as the storm of sulfur and fire that God had afflicted Gomorrah according to Genesis.

On Sunday afternoons, we sometimes wandered around the village, where we were now relatively well integrated. Some villagers called out to us, sometimes by our first name, giving us some *"Guten Tag"* or *"Dzień dobry"* or even sometimes venturing a shy *"Bonjour."* The rules of separation between prisoners and the population were not strictly applied in the countryside. We rubbed shoulders with workers, farmers, and shopkeepers every day; we often had our snacks and lunch together. That Sunday of August 1943, as four years had already passed since Ernest the postman had delivered my enlistment order, Schivelbein was celebrating the harvest festival in the central square with the village band. Mingled with the villagers, listening to unknown but catchy tunes from the fanfare, we walked briskly towards one of the refreshment stalls.

Suddenly, I saw her.

She too had come to join the crowd to overcome her isolation and take a break in her routine life.

She strutted with her Quasimodo, however, keeping their distance for fear of reprisals. Her light lavender-colored summer dress, pressed against her body in a gentle breeze, hugged her adipose shapes and hinted at a certain puffiness in her belly: the forbidden fruit of her romantic liaison with Janusz, the Polish prisoner.

Frida was pregnant!

She recognized me but pretended not to have seen me, probably fearing that I would denounce the origin of her carnal sin. I saw her blush, look down, then quickly move away from our little group of comrades to get lost in the crowd.

On this oppressive and muggy day which threatened us with a grandiose thunderstorm, we stopped at a refreshment tent to quench our thirst. We met Amadeusz who seemed to have already taken a head start in his alcohol consumption. He stammered in his approximate French, "Hello, welcome to *Erntefest* in Schivelbein! I, to buy everyone a drink! *Prost!*"

"Thank you, Boss," we replied, only too happy to be able to wet our whistle for free.

A beer stein in hand, we toasted to a near end to this nagging war. Then, Amadeusz asked us, "You, to know Jean Moulin?"

We had to admit that the name was unknown to us. He then launched into a most epic verbal free fall; with the greatest difficulty, given his advanced inebriated state, he attempted to tell us about a few news from France that he had collected on his radio station.

After a fashion, we understood from his story – jumping from a hesitant and often obscure French to a German that Gus translated when he saw our inquisitive glances – that a certain Jean Moulin had died. That resistance leader of the Army of Shadows, nicknamed Max, had died while being transferred by train to a concentration camp on my birthday, July 8.

In fact, about three weeks before my birthday, in a small town near Lyon, René Hardi – known in the resistance as Bardot – an inspector of the *Société Nationale des Chemins de Fer Français* or SNCF, the French national railway company, arrived at a house rented by a doctor Dugoujon. Most of the shutters of the fifteen windows on the sidewall as well as on the main façade of this three-story house were closed. The house appeared to be uninhabited. He crossed an iron gate anchored in a high perimeter wall, took a few steps, then climbed the main stone staircase. He knocked three long knocks on the front door, followed by two shorter ones, the signal agreed upon by the conspirators. The door opened; he entered quickly, without looking back.

Everything was quiet. Too quiet.

Bardot had not been invited to this secret meeting!

As soon as Bardot stepped through the door, the Gestapo and SS soldiers surrounded the house in force. They stormed inside after blowing up the front door. In an instant, they had easily captured all the resistance fighters, including Max. Taking advantage of the ensuing shambles, Bardot – who had curiously not been handcuffed like the other resistance fighters but only had his hands tied with a simple cord – was the only one able to escape his arrest. He vanished by magic like Houdini.

It is true that René had been apprehended by the Gestapo a few days earlier but released quickly. The head of the Gestapo in Lyon, Klaus Barbie, then only had to follow him to the secret rendezvous. Captured, Jean Moulin had first been tortured by the man History would remember as the Butcher of Lyon. Sent to the headquarters of the Gestapo in Paris, he had died of his wounds during his transfer to a camp.

My resistance in captivity was very pale in comparison to that of Jean Moulin and many real resistance fighters who, in the French free or occupied zones, took considerable risks against the invader. I modestly continued to play pranks during the deliveries, and I accompanied the Fifth Column in certain local actions, relatively benign, after dark.

Every day I rubbed shoulders with German workers, two of whom had been prisoners in France during The Great War. Ulrich and Hans, two childhood friends, had been in the front line, holed up in trenches in Verdun. They remembered, with a terror still present in their eyes, the horror they had experienced, curled up in those muddy, pestilential earthy *boyaux*. They had spent weeks in these filthy cesspools, soaked to the bone or shivering under icy snow, waiting for their last hour to arrive. They had been covered in vermin in those filthy dumps, the water trickling down and mixing with the excrements, where rats swarmed in considerable numbers.

The wait was unbearable and the skirmishes, as brief as they were violent, were always the deadliest. During an assault *en masse* of the French enemy, at dusk, they had rubbed shoulders with Death. They still had horrible nightmares to this day, remembering their comrades whose unrecognizable bodies had been torn to pieces under artillery fire. They told me how some of the German soldiers had nevertheless managed to advance to the enemy lines, only to perish with their skulls exploded by bullets fired at close range. Others had found themselves entangled on obstacles of sharp barbed wire, then unable to avoid the thrust of bayonets that ripped them open without the slightest pity in a savage butchery.

Ulrich and Hans were good old fellows, sporting almighty mustaches that made them look good-natured. They bore no resentment within them despite the horror they had witnessed. They described to me how the French soldiers had suffered too, some exposed in the trenches to mustard gas from German shells. This gas quickly attacked the lips and lungs, as well as the eyes, rendering the soldiers blind. Then, extensive blisters developed all over their skin. The soldiers, contaminated and burned by the chemical agent, died within a few hours in horrible sufferings.

When we had the opportunity to drink coffee together, they sometimes shared a shot of schnapps with me which was most welcome, especially when the days got quite rough. They had never married, their fiancées not having waited for their return from captivity. After the armistice, back home, they had lived on the fringes of society for years; the atrocities of the war suddenly appeared without warning in their thoughts and before their eyes at any time of the day and night.

I wondered how my meeting again with Gabrielle and Jean-

Pierre would go. Would they find me changed to the point of no longer recognizing me? Would I be able to rejoin them, or would I end up alone, traumatized like these two nice guys?

Only the future knew what it had in store for us.

Around nine in the morning we had a break, and we grabbed a bite together with other civilians. Once, I told them with evocative gestures, "Hitler, Stalin and Mussolini, get a rope around their neck and throw them into the ocean attached to a heavy stone."

"You're right Alex," Ulrich and Hans replied shyly in chorus.

Later, my comrades told me with a worried look, "You should be more careful, Alex. Your outspokenness will ruin you. Beware of the villagers; some would undoubtedly be ready to denounce you to gain some favors."

"You are right guys. I will try to hold my tongue a little more in the future. However, these three dictators only deserve a tragic and extremely painful death."

A year and a half later, History would finally start making me right!

As a hazy sun slowly rose over the Italian countryside coated with an iridescent fog, a German convoy left Milan for the Swiss border. On this day of April 27, 1945, at the bend of a winding road leading to the village of Dongo on Lake Como, a group of Italian partisans suddenly appeared, weapons in hand. They stopped the convoy and threatened the exhausted and helpless German soldiers with their automatic weapons.

Passing by one of the trucks, Luigi, a young partisan with unkempt black hair, dressed in corduroy pants and a sky-blue shirt with rolled up sleeves, suddenly froze. Was he seeing things? Was it possible? He aimed his gun swiftly at a soldier huddled at the back of the truck in his coat of German air force sergeant. Their eyes met for a brief moment. The soldier immediately looked down and curled up, trying to hide his face.

"*Venite a vedere,*" Luigi trumpeted to his comrades, asking them to come and see his find. Other partisans immediately joined him, roused by his urgent cries.

*"Compagni! Lo riconoscete? Il Duce!"*

Luigi got into the truck and forced the soldier to get out and take off his coat. The founder of fascism, Benito Mussolini – Il Duce – was there in the flesh before his awestruck eyes.

A shrill voice suddenly rose from a car at the rear of the column; a young woman rushed in panic towards the fallen dictator. His mistress Claretta threw herself into his arms as if to protect him from the partisans who had now gathered around him, a dull anger rising in them.

Benito and Claretta were transported by the partisans to the village of Giulino di Mezzegra. A long, restless night ensued, everyone trying to decide the fate of the prisoners. In the middle of the night, British agents alerted to the arrest of the dictator burst in; they retrieved a compromising correspondence with Winston Churchill that Benito carried preciously with him, detailing his secret agreements with the Prime Minister. Before leaving the scene, the British secret service demanded the death of Benito as soon as possible to seal his eternal silence.

Thus, the next day, leaning against a wall, drunken with fatigue and fear, Benito and Claretta stood against each other for an ultimate instant. They stared in terror at the barrel of the automatic weapon aimed at them by Comandante Valerio, the nom de guerre of one of the Communist partisans. The staccato burst of a submachine gun ripped through the silent morning, echoing through the village still asleep. Shards of stone exploded, mingled with the blood of the condemned, as the two bullet-riddled bodies fell to the ground, lifeless.

Il Duce had finally found his place in the depths of Hell.

The bloody dead bodies of the fallen lovers were transported to Milan and hung upside down by their feet in a gas station in Piazzale Loreto square. Quickly, a crowd of raging onlookers, freed from the bloodthirsty dictator, gathered around the hanging corpses, cursing them and spitting on these bodies beaten and disfigured by punches and hammers.

The next day, holed up in his bunker in Berlin for months, Adolf learned the death of Benito and his mistress. As the Russian troops were approaching his dugout closer and closer each day, he began to shake all over. Desperately seeking some comfort, shortly after midnight he married his companion Eva, whom he had kept in his shadow for so many years. He feared that his affair would tarnish his image of a footloose and fancy-free heart to take with young German girls!

After this slapdash wedding in the bowels of the Führerbunker, their fate was sealed. United in death as in life!

Adolf and Eva celebrated their union with a copious breakfast with champagne, then the dictator uttered his last wishes, carefully preparing his departure into the afterlife. He left nothing to chance, going so far as to test the effectiveness of the cyanide capsules on his poor faithful dog, Blondi, a German Shepherd. The Russian clamors echoed at the doors of the bunker on April 30, 1945, when he retired to his apartments with his young bride.

Adolf and Eva sat down on the sofa and, after one last hug, Eva bit into the forbidden capsule. Her agony was short-lived. Folded in on herself, next to the one she had idolized, she took her last breath, her lips cyanotic and enveloped in the characteristic scent of bitter almonds from the poison. Adolf, now alone, took a capsule of hydro-cyanic acid which he swallowed briskly; he then grabbed one of his two pistols. He pressed his Walther PPK to his temple, and his schiz-ophrenic gaze fixed one last time on the wall his portrait, an egotistic megalomaniac dictator.

In a blood-spattered flash, he straightforwardly joined Benito in the underworld.

Eight years later, Iosif Vissarionovich Dzhugashvili, better known under the name of Stalin, a dictator claiming to be a man of steel, would also perish of a slow and painful death. His stay at the Tiflis seminary for several years in his youth had not been enough to atone for his bank robberies, his repeated deportations to and six escapes from Siberia; but mainly nothing could redeem his totalitarian regime and his absolute power accompanied by purges and a radical elimination of all opposition.

This February 28, 1953, late in the evening, Iosif was being driven back to one of his villas in his limousine. Suspicious of everyone, fearing for his life, he had developed the habit of using decoys. Three identical limousines left the Kremlin each day in the direction of three different villas, each time taking different routes. Terrified of being assassinated, he also had all his meals tasted beforehand, fearing fatal poisoning.

As soon as they crossed the heavy access gate, in the impassable surrounding wall, it closed; his limousine took a path in the middle of the woods leading to his dacha in Kuntsevo, near Moscow. Like every day, he joined colleagues and friends in his living room. He took pleasure in prolonging these interminable evenings, most often going to bed at dawn when the Russian people got up to go to work. After many vodkas and other strong alcoholic drinks, the tongues loosened inexorably. He particularly liked it when his guests, steeped in alcohol, became uninhibited. This source of information was invaluable!

As for him, the heart malaises from which he had already suffered several times had forced him to seriously reduce his alcohol consumption in favor of tea. He most often pretended, joining his guests by drinking from his personal carafe of eau-de-vie; however, it was not filled with vodka, as he wanted to make it believed, but simply with water. His poor health had also forced him to severe restrictions on tobacco, although he still took great pleasure in smoking a cigar before retiring to his room.

That evening, Iosif was exhausted. He felt weakened, having become unwell after the intense and heated debates that had lasted all day at the Kremlin. His faithful collaborators had come to keep him company. As usual, he was served tea before retiring to the next floor up of the dacha by his personal elevator. Taking advantage of a moment of inattention, a short man in a black suit, white shirt, and black tie, with a ruthless and murderous gaze piercing behind round glasses, discreetly poured the content of a small flask into the still steaming cup. Vyacheslav Molotov, the same diplomat who had signed the non-aggression pact between Germany and the Soviet Union fourteen years earlier, stealthily replaced the empty flask in his pants pocket.

Later that night, the tea spiked with warfarin, a strong blood thinner, brutally struck Stalin with a cerebral hemorrhage.

For fear of making a bad decision or for fear of saving the dying dictator, his collaborators did not call a doctor until more than twenty-four hours later.

Nothing could save him now.

A few days later, on March 5, 1953, Stalin joined without detour Benito and Adolf who were waiting for him with their feet firmly planted in Hell.

Benito, Adolf and Iosif had undoubtedly found themselves in the depths of Hell. Immersed in a frozen underground lake, the Cocytus, located in the ninth circle at the very bottom of Hell as described by Dante in "The Divine Comedy," the three fallen dictators screamed in terror and pain as Lucifer perpetually devoured them with its three gaping mouths.

The infamous tyrants had not been able to escape divine justice.

By the end of August 1943, we had almost become fully-fledged inhabitants of Schivelbein. Following the home deliveries that we made with Amadeusz and our regular help at the market, the villagers now called us by our first names. Our Ritz was now open to the four winds and our guards, who now slept in the castle, visited us only briefly each day; we were also allowed to go unaccompanied to work.

That morning, as a hot and stormy day was shaping up once again with imposing bluish black clouds, I left the hangar at dawn to go to the bathroom. Indeed, we now benefited from the luxury of a dry latrine, dug in a small wooden hut that we had built by the river.

I was stunned when I discovered the pit latrine fully ablaze.

I ran to warn my comrades immediately, but the fire was already too advanced to save the hut. The thick black smoke that rose and mingled harmoniously with the dark low clouds quickly attracted a few onlookers; we also saw our guards rushing up. They immediately realized that the latrine was indeed irremediably lost. They let the fire take its course.

When the rage of the flames subsided, the planks having been consumed, we discovered among the embers the remains of a charred and smoking body. After having helped the fire give up the ghost with a few buckets of water drawn from the river, we realized with dismay that the shreds of clothing and the beret so characteristic belonged to Gus! We couldn't believe our eyes. Stunned with stupefaction, we were all gathered around the unrecognizable burnt body. We were trying to figure out what could have happened.

We explained to the guards that the pit had not been emptied in ages and that, Gus being an avid smoker, he had perhaps inadvertently set fire to the newspaper sheets hanging on a nail or to the mephitic fumes that escaped from the hole. In addition, we had not taken the time to fix the door which got stuck regularly; it then only opened with extreme difficulty from the inside. Gus ostensibly had not been able to escape the blaze he had inadvertently created. He must have perished in endless excruciating agony while we were all close by.

We all looked totally devastated, so guilty.

The German soldiers ordered us to dig a grave for him near the river. We interred him later for his final rest in the shade of a weeping willow, cradled by the eternal melody of the stream. Father Gythiel celebrated his life simply and spoke hopeful words, wishing Gus a better life, finally freed from the yoke of his captors.

While the priest was uttering his funeral oration, a few kilometers from Schivelbein, a young peasant woman was pedaling nimbly on one of the country roads. She was dressed in an ordinary gray-blue dress and wearing a banal scarf of a similar color. She carried baskets of eggs in the front of her bicycle and on the luggage rack. She was ordinary, not an eye-catcher.

A simple farmer like so many others going to deliver her eggs to farms or to the neighboring town.

But on closer inspection, one could notice that the young peasant was overly muscular, most likely because of her hard labor in the fields. By scrutinizing her even closer, one could distinguish on her face the traces of a very recently shaved beard.

This peasant woman on a bicycle, moving away from Schivelbein with each pedal stroke, was none other than Gus!

A month earlier, Gus had told us of his burning desire to escape. It was relatively easy to escape from a farm but in general freedom was of very short duration with serious consequences; Louis could have testified so. Indeed, as simple prisoners isolated in the countryside, we did not have the critical support that existed in the *Oflags*, the camps for officers. Those took advantage of their long days without work; many specialists forged fake papers and, with the help of detailed maps, meticulously prepared the itineraries that would lead to their freedom after the most daring escapes.

Gus was suffocating in this routine life, far from his own. While we were chatting by the river, he confided to me one evening, "Alex, I can't take this life as a prisoner anymore. I'm going crazy here. I must go home. Three long years already and God knows how long this torment will last. I'm tired of this hard labor for a pittance, and even though you guys are all my best friends, I need to get out of here. I am suffocating! In her last letter, my mother confides to me that she is very ill; I would forever blame myself if I lost her while I languish here without at least trying to see her once again."

"I understand you, Gus, but remember Louis. He was captured so quickly, then beaten up. He's now rotting away in a camp where I can't imagine his condition."

"You're right, Alex, I can't escape without a good plan. Louis had left on a whim and his plan had no chance of success. But I've been going through different scenarios in my head for weeks and I think I've found a way."

He had formulated a daring plan that seemed viable.

"I'm going to cycle to the Baltic Sea; along the way, I'll try to sneak onto a freight train or stow away in a docked boat."

"Gus, instead of Louis' boat, are you going to take a bicycle? Is that your plan? You are sure to get arrested before you even get out of Schivelbein!"

"Look, Alex, this is where my plan is different and can work. To avoid suspicion, I'm going to dress up as a woman, like a local farmer. I'll pretend to go deliver my eggs. I speak German fluently, therefore they will be less suspicious if I am called upon."

"You will need clothes, shoes in your size and papers. But even if you can get hold of all these, the guards will notice your departure and raise the alarm. You risk being spotted very quickly."

The originality of his idea was that the Germans should never be aware of his escape. For this he had devised a most ingenious, but risky, plan.

First, he needed clothes and shoes, as well as a bicycle and eggs. After we were all made aware of his plan and convinced that it could work without any fear of retaliation, we all agreed to help him.

Father Gythiel, who was working on a nearby farm, was there at the right time when the *Oma*, a robust peasant grandmother of medium height, decided to kick the bucket during a summer nap. In extremis, he just had time to give her the extreme unction, then, alone with the dead body, he took the opportunity to go through her things from top to bottom like a vulgar thug. He asked God to look away for a few moments; during this brief instant, he grabbed the papers and the laissez-passer of the deceased who would certainly not need them at heaven's gate. The yellowing, low-quality pictures would make the identity fraud relatively easy.

On his way back from work, Gérard, the foxy one of the gang, stole without any difficulty on laundry lines an ordinary dress and a scarf which he buried in his shoulder bag. Another comrade recovered from a trash can a pair of clodhoppers that must have seen The Great War but, by a heavenly sign, turned out to be Gus' shoe size. The bicycle was another story. We did not want to steal a bicycle for fear of arousing suspicion and raising the alarm. Once again, providence smiled on Gus, the blessed one. During a walk along the river, on the edge of a wood, we discovered a scrap metal dump and other abandoned objects. Under our avid search, a rusty but intact bicycle frame with its wheels emerged from the tools and utensils tangled with fencing wires. Gus, the happy new owner, embarked on his new renovation project for the weeks to come.

The day before his escape, Gus cooked a few dozen hard-boiled eggs to keep them longer during his escape. Most of them had been stolen from the weekly market where some of us sometimes helped out on Wednesdays. He would place a few fresh eggs on top of the basket, covering the hard-boiled eggs, thus providing a more solid alibi.

To hide his departure, I accompanied him to the cemetery, by the light of a red moon. As the bell tower struck the stroke of midnight, we stepped through the cemetery gates, trying not to make any noise. Armed with our shovels, like two thieves of eight or ten-pound corpses for Professor Knox's anatomy lessons in Edinburgh a hundred years ago, we randomly chose an isolated grave, without flowers or decoration; it seemed to have been forgotten from all forever. A simple wooden plaque, fixed askew on a rudimentary cross, indicated the name of the one who would make Gus' escape possible: Józef Przybyszewski.

After having dug and unearthed the corpse of Józef, a poor incarnation of Nosferatu, Gus carried him on his back, skimming the walls to go and drop him off comfortably in the latrine near the Ritz. We placed the remains of the wretched body over the gaping hole of the latrine, and Gus placed his own clothes and his famous beret under the body. Then we went to get a pile of twigs and dead wood, as well as straw. We placed them like an offering at the cadaver's feet in the latrine, ready to be set alight at dawn.

In the first light of day, after having clean-shaved his legs and face, he donned his disguise and placed his egg baskets on his bicycle; he bade us farewell.

"If you weren't leaving so hastily, I surely would have invited you for a dance," Jean called out to him mischievously. "You make a very decent peasant woman next to those I am in close contact with every day. Do not attract attention! Avoid patrols and controls. Take care, Gus."

"Thank you. Jean. We had a good laugh together! Continue to maintain the morale of our comrades with your jokes. I'll miss you. I hope we'll meet again after this bloody war."

"Remember Gus, if at any time you need to escape from a building and all exits are unfortunately well guarded, well ... get out through the entrance!" Jean joked, trying to ease the palpable anguish that reigned around him.

Gus went around the comrades, one by one, with teary eyes but determined to succeed in his escape, at all costs. At last, he took me in his arms and said, "Thanks again Alex for your help last night. I'll owe you that someday. I'm counting on you to light a furnace at the outhouse but give me at least half an hour to get out of town."

"I promise the Germans will see nothing but fire and brimstone," I replied with a wink. "Take care of yourself. Be prudent and enjoy your newfound freedom. See you soon my friend!"

Gus was now pedaling towards freedom, and I prayed that he could reach France safely.

The wheel of time continued to turn, the seasons succeeding one another in a metronomic way.

We learned from our sources that Italy had changed sides and had now declared war on Germany. The Allied bombardments on Berlin had been devastating. At this beginning of December 1943, we regained some hope that the wheel might eventually turn.

As I made a delivery of bags of flour and sugar to the back of a bakery, one of the workers, Hans, a quick-tempered, evil-looking teenager, ordered me to put on an apron. I told him *"Nein"* on the spot, curtly. He approached me and, without warning, slapped me brutally. I grabbed him right away and, in my momentum, we found ourselves on the ground. The buzzard struggled, trying to punch me in the face. I managed to dodge most of his jabs. I tried with all my weight to pin him to the ground and hold both of his arms. After a few moments of fierce struggle, he was pinned to the ground, unable to move. Making sure he had recovered his composure, I released him from my pressure.

Hans left in a pitiful state, but he was soon back with the owner who gave me a reproachful look and questioned, *"Kommunist?"* I was surprised at the query which certainly came from the lie that the young greenhorn had given her as an excuse for the scuffle. I answered her with a big smile and a black eye, *"Jawohl."* She raged and shouted probably numerous insults that I didn't understand, but the matter ended there.

As I returned to the Ritz with my black eye, thousands of kilometers away Roosevelt, Churchill, and Stalin were meeting in Tehran to draft an invasion plan of Europe through Normandy. This was to be decisive in the following year. The Operation Overlord had been agreed upon and was now on the move.

Often, while working, I whistled songs from our country. Although nostalgic, it gave me heart to work. Sometimes too, to annoy those around me, I would start whistling "The Internationale," this revolutionary song to the glory of the workers, born in France under the Commune. Of course, this song of social struggle had also become the anthem of the USSR. The civilians hastened to ask me, *"Bist du ein Kommunist, Alex?"* to which I answered them on purpose in a mocking tone, *"Ja."*

My lie made them angry, but some smiled because they now knew me too well; they understood that I particularly liked to provoke them in spite of the truth.

# "Free"

*The fact that there are so many men still alive in the world shows that
it is based not on the force of arms but on the force of truth or love.
Therefore, the greatest and most unimpeachable evidence of the
success of this force is to be found in the fact that, in spite of the wars of
the world, it still lives on.*
Mahatma Gandhi (1869-1948)

*My son, it is often necessary to know the past, before understanding the
present and facing the future with calm.*
Pearl Buck (1892-1973)

# Chapter 15

## *From Landing to Repression*

At the end of spring, he had left the family ranch near Lake Conroe in Texas.

He had reluctantly left his Quarter Horse Atlantis, a magnificent palomino horse that grazed in endless green fields, colored with carpets of multicolored flowers with evocative names, such as bluebonnet and Indian paintbrush. At the beginning of this month of May 1942, as the windmill was spinning at full speed with a sinister squeak under a wind of terrible force and a threatening stormy sky, his mother Joan had bawled her eyes out when he had left the farm to join his regiment. Benjamin had to avenge some of his friends who had suddenly lost their lives at Pearl Harbor the past December, under the deadly Japanese bombings and suicide missions by kamikazes.

Joan had hugged her only son very tightly, imploring him to stay on the farm. Her pleas remaining unanswered, she had made him swear to come back to her, alive. His father John, a gruff rancher, had not given him the affection he craved during all his youth; for his departure, he had simply shaken his hand in silence. However, Benjamin had detected in his gaze and his handshake that lasted much longer than usual a huge disquietude that he vainly sought to hide from his son.

At twenty, Ben as his friends called him, was a force of nature. For years he had indeed helped with the hard labor at the ranch and, all muscles, he was taller than all his friends by more than a head. With his blond hair cropped very short, eyes as deep green as the lake bordering the ranch, and a face sculpted and tanned to perfection, he attracted all the young girls in the neighborhood like fireflies flitting in the evening around the campfire. He went to dance on Saturday nights at the village saloon, decked out in alligator boots – a gift from his mother for his eighteenth birthday – tight blue jeans with a large shiny belt buckle representing the flag of Texas – the Lone Star State – a black and white plaid shirt, a Navajo bolo tie – a Texan tie adorned with a turquoise stone – and wearing his Stetson, a black cowboy hat that hardly ever left him. His distraught suitors impatiently awaited the moment of a languid dance for two.

Unfortunately, after having continuously danced in line the Cowboy Boogie, the Madison, or the Cha Cha, at the first measures of a dance for couples he took the opportunity to take a break and go have a beer with his friends at the bar. He had therefore remained single, preferring his solo horse rides, to gather the herds or to go hunting game in the woods. Few knew that he had been head over heels in love with Alexis a few years earlier; but she had had to leave Texas in a hurry, heartbroken, to join her father in California where this career officer had just been posted. Ben had been so desperate at the loss of Alexis that he had not wanted to console himself in another girl's arms out of spite.

He had therefore joined his regiment, the Big Red One, sad to leave his family and his friends but motivated to go stamp down this global war that continued to spread like wildfire.

After an intensive training on American soil, he had crossed the ocean for the first time in his life to land in North Africa. There he had received his baptism by fire with the 1$^{st}$ U.S. Infantry Division, fighting bravely in Algeria in late 1942 in Operation Torch. In early

1943, he had fought in Tunisia the dreaded Afrika Korps commanded by the Desert Fox, General Rommel. Lost in the middle of these desert landscapes, he felt a long way from his ranch surrounded by green meadows and woods in Texas. There, in unusual and disconcerting landscapes, he observed unknown peoples, with strange customs and languages.

Then he had once again embarked on a ship to reach Sicily for Operation Husky. The combat had been fierce, and a considerable number of his comrades had perished fighting. He had walked towards the Sicilian mountains, admiring their craggy peaks with typical villages nestled in the heart of forgotten valleys. He had survived and even received a citation for his bravery at the Battle of Troina. Then, at the end of 1943, he had embarked for England. If the language of Shakespeare was more familiar to him, he found it nonetheless most pedantic and precious, even ridiculous. He amused himself imagining how he would keep his saloon fellows in stitches when he returned to Conroe by imitating that aristocratic accent of the pretentious Albion.

The training had resumed, even more intense and arduous. He knew that in the months to come Operation Overlord would be launched to open a front in Western Europe. He prepared himself every day for one of the most intense but hopefully decisive confrontations.

Finally, June 4, 1944, arrived.

Operation Neptune had begun.

The objective was to land a considerable number of Allied troops in Normandy to repel the enemy and win back the occupied territories.

He had embarked at Southampton with his comrades of the 1st Division Big Red One but, after a few miserable hours spent on rough seas, the ships were ordered to return to the English port. He had been happy to have at least been able to fight his seasickness! Considering a number of risks, the General-in-Chief of the Allied forces in Europe, Dwight Eisenhower, nevertheless decided that the landings in Normandy would take place, at all costs, two days later.

In the early hours of Tuesday, June 6, 1944, the historic D-Day, to allow the troops to land on the beaches of Normandy, a deluge of Allied bombs began to rain on the German fortifications and the troops protecting the Atlantic Wall. Soon after, in an incessant ballet, thousands of American and British paratroopers bailed out into a dark and terrifying night behind the German lines to take them from the rear.

Snuggled up against his comrades in a landing craft tossed about on a choppy sea under strong winds, Ben took out a Lucky Strike light-tobacco cigarette from its waterproof case. With a snap of the wrist, he opened his Zippo windproof lighter to light his cigarette and that of his neighbor "Tex Mex" Gabriel, a Texan of Mexican origin.

"Howdy, Gabe. Today is D-Day! We can change the future of the World," Ben yelled at him, trying to make himself heard over the roaring sound of the engines. He was trying his best to reassure Gabriel, who in addition to seasickness was terribly worried about this landing in an unknown territory and in open ground. He reminded him of the importance of this day which could change the course of the world history.

"Thank you, Ben. I'm fixin' to fight the Germans hard, but I don't want to die. I promised my fiancée, Denisse, that I would be back for her soon," Gabe replied. He showed Ben the picture of a petite brunette, in a floral dress with short sleeves buttoned up the front, cinched by a thin white belt, posing with a disarming smile in front of the remains of the Alamo in San Antonio.

"You are lucky Gabe to have a girl waiting for you at home," Ben, who no longer received any news from Alexis, told him.

"Yes, I know. I am going to marry Denisse when I get back home after the war," Gabriel sighed, dreaming of a life filled with happiness with Denisse.

"Well, stay close to me when we land at low tide on the beach. I'll protect you! That will be my wedding gift to you," Ben promised to reassure him, but not really knowing what to expect in the coming hours.

Around Ben and Gabe, an armada of several thousand warships was advancing towards the Normandy coast by the light of the full moon, carrying American, British, Canadian, French, Belgian, and Polish soldiers as well as other nationalities. Nearly two hundred thousand soldiers were preparing for a merciless fight with the sole aim of coming out victorious from the battle.

In the distance, the French coast was approaching rapidly. Everything was still calm under the cover of the night and the prevailing winds. The enemy was not suspicious of the audacity of the Allied troops to cross the Channel on such a rough sea exposed to extremely strong gales.

Ben could now clearly distinguish Omaha Beach, a long sandy beach, several kilometers wide, in the shape of a half moon. The tide was low. It would take about three hundred meters to reach the dunes and storm the blockhouses and other German military installations lined up along the coast.

Ben breathed into his cold hands to warm them up while his comrades cheered the Allied bombings that had just begun. Indeed, warships now continuously bombarded the beaches and the hinterland; they desperately tried to reach the German forces gathered at the top of the dunes. Unfortunately, with low cloudy skies and an impressive barrier of dust rising to the sky from the explosions, the shots were very imprecise. Like the aerial bombardments of the previous hours, they did little damage to the German army.

Their landing craft was rapidly approaching Omaha Beach. Ben and the other soldiers of the $1^{st}$ Division were now standing, ready to attack, their semi-automatic rifles M1 Garand well in hand. Ben smiled at Gabe to cheer him up and called out, "Here we go! Follow me and stay close behind me. Good luck my friend!"

Suddenly the stern of the boat lowered, opening before their eyes, filled with apprehension but also with frenzied determination, a vast expanse of obstacles bristled on the beach. The undependable bombardments from the ships continued and now crossed the repeated fire from enemy cannons and machine guns stationed at the top of the dunes.

Three hundred meters to cover under intense enemy fire, through a course full of traps, each more deadly than the next, before reaching the German lines.

Ben jumped into the shallow waves and quickly strode to the sandy beach, followed like his shadow by Gabe. The shells whistled overhead while bullets peppered the sandy expanse, raising sprays of sand and rocky shards. The first bloody victims were already falling. A slick of dead bodies gradually covered the surface of the ocean, rocked by the rising tide. In this destructive cacophony, they moved forward, running while shooting towards the dunes at random.

To protect themselves from the murderous projectiles, they threw themselves behind the first obstacle they encountered, three metal beams crossed in the middle and anchored in concrete. Ben turned back to encourage Gabe, but his fellow Texan had fallen a few steps back. Eyes wide open with terror, lying on his back, arms outstretched, one could have believed that Gabe, paralyzed with fear, was begging heaven for help. But the gaping red hole in the middle of his forehead, from which flowed a purple stream, left no doubt as to his fate.

Gabriel had kept his promise. He would return to Texas as he had sworn, but in a box adorned with a Stars and Stripes star-spangled banner. Denisse would console herself in the arms of another man, trying to forget the past.

Ahead of him, Ben saw some of his comrades and Engineer soldiers running erratically, zigzagging, desperately hoping to get through the destructive bullet rounds to open the way for the battalions. But the beach was riddled with sanguinary traps. The Germans had placed mines on tree trunks or on stakes, but also in the sand. Bodies exploded here and there, throwing masses of flesh and viscera bathed in blood.

Omaha Beach was gradually being covered with dark spots,

crimson and brown; the air was becoming more and more unbreathable. A curtain of sand in suspension, interspersed with explosives and human fragments, obscured Ben's view along with that of his fellow soldiers, causing them to run blind for some time.

Ben ran past a comrade who was in agony and begging for help, half his body torn off by the explosion of one of the mines. As Ben proceeded towards him, to accompany him in his last moments on earth, a shell from friend or foe fell nearby and interrupted the suffering of the hapless soldier. Stunned and disoriented by the blast of the explosion, Ben resumed his run. He continued to fire relentlessly toward the dune ridge, constantly reloading his semi-automatic rifle with a new eight-round clip.

German troops on the heights had suffered little damage from the imprecise bombardments from the air and from the offshore ships. Consequently, their shooting power, which should have been reduced or even eliminated, was still dominant and deadly. As a result, a terrible chaos hung over this sandy expanse, accompanied by the cries of wounded and dying soldiers, explosions, and unabating gunshots.

Ben had set foot in Hell on Earth!

He arrived halfway at the foot of a sand bank that the Germans had erected and covered with barbed wire. He threw himself to the ground behind the embankment, shielding himself from the increased fire of enemy machine guns. He caught his breath. Ben coordinated an assault with other soldiers, finally able to take shelter from the lethal bullets for a moment.

The soldiers entrenched behind the sand embankment began to fire in unison towards the crest of the dunes as reinforcements arrived. Ben led a small, improvised group on a frantic race towards the dunes.

Still about a hundred meters to go to take shelter below the dunes.

Ben suddenly felt a tear as he neared the goal, but he did not slow down. A bullet had pierced his leg. Safe from gunfire, finally huddled below the beach ridge, he took a bandana from his pocket and tied it over the wound to slow the bleeding.

As the barrage of American gunfire from behind the embankment was increasing exponentially, Ben and the few soldiers who had reached the dune began to search for passageways to climb to the plateau where the opposing forces were concentrated. Crawling up the dune between bushes, like the horned viper he had dreaded so much in North Africa, Ben made his way up slowly but cautiously. He did not appear to have been spotted. He thus quickly crossed the distance which separated him from the enemy.

Prone at the foot of a blockhouse from which machine guns continuously fired streams of bullets at the American soldiers who tried to advance *en masse* towards their position, Ben held his breath. The spasmodic and repeated detonations were deafening. His heart was racing.

He was ready to act.

Now!

He grabbed his first two olive green Mk II grenades, their body pre-fragmented into eight columns in five rows to deliver maximum devastation with their shards. He tore off their pin and, sitting with his back to the blockhouse, threw the two deadly weapons through the opening from which the machine guns pointed. The grenade spoon ejected in flight and the projectiles rolled and exploded on the floor of the blockhouse. He immediately repeated his action and massive explosions ensued inside the fortification, causing a thick dusty smoke to rise through the openings.

Ben stood up and quickly went around the building. The door opened and a seriously wounded soldier came out, gun in hand. Ben did not give him a chance to fire and shot a volley that made him recoil under the impacts. The soldier fell backwards, stone-dead in the smoky opening.

Suddenly, out of the corner of his eye, he caught a movement to his right. A soldier of his age was walking towards him, terrified, holding a Karabiner 98k rifle in aim. Ben did not think twice.

Knowing his own rifle was empty, he rushed over to the stunned soldier, dove and rolled over. He pulled his M3 Trench Knife out of its riveted leather scabbard attached to his calf. Abruptly rising in front of the dumbfounded German soldier, he swiftly stabbed him in the throat with the sharp blade of his knife.

Ben was about to pick up his rifle when a detonation sounded behind him.

The daylight faded a little, as if baleful clouds had suddenly obscured the sun. Twilight was appearing before its time. A bitter taste suddenly poured into his mouth wide open in surprise. He knelt down, arms falling to his sides, hot liquid running profusely down his neck. He saw the ranch of his childhood one last time, Joan and John smiling tenderly at him. Alexis took his head in her hands to place a final loving kiss on his forehead. He mounted his horse Atlantis, commencing a calm walk which transitioned to a frantic gallop. He disappeared forever into the eternal meadows.

Ben had died.

He would rest in the shade of a pine tree in the American cemetery of Colleville-sur-mer. A simple white marble stele lined up with thousands of others, facing Omaha Beach, would remind everyone for eternity of the sacrifices of this courageous soldier from Texas who came to die one day in June 1944 in Normandy to save freedom.

While the last German blockhouse on the coastal plateau along the landing beaches was heroically taken by the Allied forces in the middle of the afternoon of D-Day, Jean-Pierre was playing calmly, carefree in his grandparents' garden. At five years old, this skinny, dreamy little boy with short hair and blue eyes, as tranquil as he was talkative, liked to ride his tricycle in the garden paths; he pretended to be Georges Speicher, the king of Montlhéry, road cycling world champion and three times champion of France. He dreamed of one day winning the *Tour de France* like him.

This little man was the pride of his grandparents and the comfort of his mother who had been alone by now for almost five years, a very long, far too difficult time always filled with anguish. Jean-

Pierre was a born talker. He had to be forbidden to address the German soldiers whom he often crossed paths with in the village. Indeed, his repertoire of nicknames for these invaders was extremely colorful, from Fritz to Jerry. Though they made everyone laugh in private, he had to be reminded to keep these nicknames secret before each outing for fear of reprisals should the name be heard by less amicable ears.

He loved to read stories, sitting on his grandfather's lap. He also spent hours drawing the world around him with crayons and colored pencils. Gabrielle had included one of his drawings in a package recently sent to me in Pomerania. A little boy in shorts, in front of a house lined with multicolored flower beds, held the hand of his mother wearing a blue dress. In the background, much smaller, loomed the colorless, gray silhouette of a man, a rifle over his shoulder.

I had a pang in my heart when I saw my shadow on this child's drawing. I had been relegated to the background, a faceless stranger slowly vanishing from my son's memory. How would our reunion unfold one day, if I had the chance to be released? Would Jean-Pierre be afraid of me? Would he feel an indefinite but indestructible bond deep inside for this stranger who had come back and perturbed his routine? We were not there yet, even though the events seemed to accelerate following the Allied landing in Normandy.

Following D-Day, a rise in civilian massacres would unfortunately bring mourning to France, which was trying to free itself from the Germanic yoke. Stationed near Montauban with its tanks, the 2$^{nd}$ SS armored division *"Das Reich"* had been ordered to punish the strongholds of the maquis to set an example and instill terror.

In Tulle, hundreds of civilians were captured by the SS. In the middle of the city, they hung ropes with a noose from balconies, lampposts, or trees. Dragged along by the soldiers of *"Das Reich,"* ninety-nine innocent people ascended their final ladder before being thrown off balance, hit by rifle buttstocks, their necks strangled by hanging. Their executioners clung to their legs to hasten their demise or executed them with a burst of submachine guns delivering a *coup de grâce.*

At the end of the afternoon, the dead bodies of the tortured swayed slowly under a warm breeze in the heart of the city, like sinister gargoyles. But instead of frightening the resistance members, it reminded them sadly of the evil and vicious spirit of these Germanic persecutors, who had created Hell in the very center of the city which was now in mourning.

The other prisoners who had escaped hanging, only for the lack of ropes, were deported to the Dachau concentration camp. Most never returned.

The next day, about a hundred kilometers away, heading for the Normandy front, the 1st Battalion of the 4th Regiment *"Der Führer,"* who was part of the infamous Division *"Das Reich,"* entered in Oradour-sur-Glane. All these vehicles aroused the curiosity of the villagers. While the pharmacy and other stores lowered their iron curtains, others continued to go about their business while staring suspiciously at the invaders. As the barber's assistant was finishing a client's haircut while the barber had gone to buy tobacco, cries arose.

The SS soldiers were going from door to door, ordering the inhabitants to regroup in the village square with their papers.

Marguerite was in the small village grocery store with one of her daughters when an SS soldier, submachine gun in hand, burst into the store. In bad French, he screamed the order to the grocer and the few customers to come out immediately into the street. They passed Alix, the town-crier, who was going from house to house. He explained that all the villagers had to meet, with their proper papers in due form, in the central square near the church for an identity check. Suddenly, an automobile slowed down next to them. In his Peugeot Model 202 with crates of empty bottles piled up on the gallery, Léon, the wine merchant, was returning from a delivery to a nearby farm. Marguerite quickly informed him about what was happening. He went to park in the village square where everyone was already converging.

The terrible martyrdom was already underway.

This Saturday afternoon, under a hazy sky, the villagers gathered from houses, shops, and neighboring farms congregated in the market square. An interpreter translated the orders which the commander declaimed in a loud and scathing voice. Women and children under the age of fourteen were violently separated from the men. Marguerite sadly left her husband as she and her two daughters were directed to the village church. She wondered what would become of the men and she prayed that she would be reunited with her husband quickly, safe and sound. In dismal silence, the schoolmistress accompanied to the church her young pupils holding hands, in rows two by two. Many women were part of this long and moving elegiac procession. Some carried their children in their arms and others pushed prams where their newborns slept quietly.

Meanwhile, still incredulous, the men wondered what to expect. The interpreter then communicated to them that ammunition had been hidden in the village; the culprits had to come forward immediately. Faced with these fabricated accusations, the men did not react. The commandant turned to the mayor, Doctor Desourteaux, and ordered him to denounce thirty hostages at random. The brave doctor replied calmly that if an example had to be made, he would offer himself with his sons as hostages; but the SS officer had conceived a completely different and most sinister plan.

All the men and boys were placed in groups of three facing the wall of the market square, awaiting with growing concern their last hour.

Endless seconds passed in the gloomy afternoon.

Some prayed, others gently wept for their wives and children, still others, resigned like Alix and Léon, were ready to stoically face their fate.

Facing this stone wall, all expected in silence the bullets that would steal their last breath.

However, the German soldiers did not shoot.

Instead, the villagers were separated into six groups of around thirty men each and escorted to various premises and neighboring barns. The soldiers asked them to sit directly on the ground at the back of the buildings. Everyone was wondering what fate held in store for them, as well as for the women and children, uncertain of the enemy's intentions. Some believed that the soldiers were busy searching the houses, farms, and shops to unearth weapons and ammunition allegedly hidden in the village. They hoped, once the search was over, that the German SS soldiers would realize their mistake and let them return to their homes to reunite with their families and carry on a normal life.

Suddenly, the soldiers received an order and asked the men to stand up. As soon as the villagers stood up, the soldiers abruptly removed a tarp that concealed two machine guns. They began to fire downwards, aiming at the legs of the poor innocent people who were falling, mown down in their tracks. The SS covered the immobilized bodies with bundles of wood and hay, then poured gasoline on the unfortunate men unable to escape. As they left the scene of the massacres, they blocked all the exits. They lit giant infernos that produced agonizing creaking sounds that quickly stifled the cries and lamentations of the tortured men.

While the women and children, locked in the church, were hearing the horrified pleas and cries of the men in the distance, Marguerite eyed suspiciously a crate that had been placed on a chair not far from the main entrance. A few wires escaped from the box and sneaked slyly outward under the double-locked front door. She suddenly realized the likely contents of the box. Before she had a chance to warn those around, the crate exploded with a blasting bang. The church filled with a thick black smoke. In an incendiary tornado, the chairs, the ceiling, and all other flammable parts ignited in an uncontrollable chain reaction.

Panic invaded the sacred space.

The air quickly became unbreathable.

In a flash, the screaming, moaning, crying, and coughing became hysterical.

The SS soldiers indiscriminately machine-gunned those of the nearly four hundred and fifty women and children who desperately tried to escape the infernal blaze through the doors or windows. The cowardly, barbaric butchers continued throwing incendiary grenades relentlessly through the openings to fuel the burning hell.

Marguerite ran with her daughters to take refuge in the sacristy. The thick black smoke blinded them. They struggled to stay together in this horrified crowd moving erratically.

Suddenly, under the intense heat and the weight of the crowd, the sacristy floor broke loose. Marguerite wavered. In this gigantic panic, she let go of one of her daughters' hands as she was leaving with great difficulty the sacristy, now engulfed in flames. Carried away by a human tide, she could no longer turn around.

She had no other choice left.

She had to get out or perish.

She took refuge behind the high altar. She had to act at once as time was running out. After having tenderly kissed her remaining daughter, she lifted and slid her outside through the exploded central stained-glass window, towards a brief freedom. The incessant bursts of submachine guns continued to mingle lugubriously with the wails of agony and the blare of the roaring fire.

In turn, Marguerite stepped through the opening and jumped about three meters down onto a patch of grass. As bullets whistled around her, she saw the bloodied body of her daughter, riddled with bullets, lost forever. She stood up instinctively and, without looking back, ran towards a corner of the church in the direction of the rectory garden. On the road down below, the SS soldiers continued their sordid fusillade of unarmed civilians. Marguerite suddenly felt an intense pain in her shoulder, then her thigh, but her survival instinct carried her to the garden where she laid down among the thick trellises of peas. She then realized that she had been shot five times in both legs as well as in the shoulder blade. Her head buried in her hands, at last weeping for her daughter burnt alive in the sacristy, the other mown down by bullets, and her husband gone, she lost consciousness.

Marguerite did not see the gigantic blaze which devoured all the houses, roaring continuously through the night, lighting the village, forever lost, with an otherworldly glow.

By the time she awoke the next day, an ominously reddish sun barely piercing the dark veil of ashes, six hundred and forty-two innocent lives had been extinguished by Nazi barbarism under the most vile and inhumane conditions.

Meanwhile in Schivelbein, life continued to run its course in a monotonous and depressing manner. We had not seen Gus again and we were wondering if he had succeeded in his escape. We were now relatively well integrated into the local life, and I continued my routine deliveries with Amadeusz.

Our captivity had become our new normal.

The news gleaned at the start of 1944 was encouraging. The siege of Leningrad had finally come to an end after more than two years at the inestimable cost of two million lives. The fierce fighting, famine, and many diseases had resulted in this terrible human toll; but the Russian army had finally kicked the Germans out of the city. The Allied landing in Normandy, which we had also learned about, boosted our morale further.

The course of the war finally seemed on the brink of change.

Although the V-1 flying bombs were beginning to reach London and its surrounding area in retaliation for the Allied landing, their effects were more psychological than devastating. However, they diverted considerable forces to create a relatively effective air defense with numerous cannons, barrage balloons, and fighter planes. Reinvigorated by their victory in Normandy, the Allies then landed successfully in the south of France, between Toulon and Cannes, in Operation Dragoon.

Our hope was growing day by day!

# Chapter 16

## *From Liberation to Transgressions*

On this Sunday of August 1944, we were heading to the harvest festival, *Erntefest*, filled with optimism. While our *kommando* walked the streets of Schivelbein towards the marketplace, General de Gaulle paraded triumphantly in front of an enthusiastic crowd on the Champs-Élysées, in "Paris martyred but Paris liberated!"

On this beautiful sunny afternoon, leaning on the counter of one of the refreshment tents, we were quenching our thirst with a cold and smooth beer. The village band played catchy tunes and couples began to spin around the square. The atmosphere was festive, far from the war and its killings. We toasted to our impending release.

All of a sudden, I saw her pass, pushing an oversized pram.

Seeing her alone, I decided to approach and check on her. I hastened to greet her with a timid hello while leaning over the titanic cradle. Frida had given birth to twins! I watched these Castor and Pollux with attention. They were both sound asleep side by side, two innocent little darlings sharing the same pillow. Fortunately, I detected no apparent deformity that their probable father could have passed on to them.

Then I learned that Janusz had been transferred to a labor camp. Frida had ended up doubly as a single mother. Made evident to all by the arrival of the two Dioscuri, her fantastic rides in the barn must have led to a sneaky denouncement by some neighbors perhaps too virtuous or more likely attracted by the lure of a German reward. In the meantime, Mother Fach had "bought the farm." Frida suddenly found herself alone working on the farm while raising the twins. I sincerely felt sorry for her as I thought about Gabrielle who was also raising our little boy without his father.

On this celebration day, I missed them even more.

A few weeks later, I received a strange letter from Gabrielle. She told me about Jean-Pierre and his progress in reading and writing, but she also passed on a *"Bonjour"* from cousin Gustave who had come to see her. She wrote, "Your cousin Gustave came to visit me unexpectedly. For once, he was clean shaven, and he told me about her incredible adventures."

No matter how hard I racked my brains, I couldn't remember that mystery cousin. My cousin Gustave? I could not recall any cousin by that name. Suddenly, I understood the allusion. The clue was of the most transparent. The grammatical error, "HER adventures," was a code indicating Gustave's erroneous feminine character. Gus, our womanly bicycle escapee, had successfully carried out his plan and had gone to give reassuring news to Gaby!

A year before, Gus had pedaled for hours, avoiding patrols and the gaze of passers-by. In a village north of Schivelbein, he had casually parked his bicycle. Unbeknownst to all, he had managed to slip surreptitiously into a wagon full of various crates. When the train had stopped early in the morning to unload, he had stealthily boarded a wagon in another train, loaded with sacks of grain, bound for Rotterdam in Holland.

A few days later, he had reached his destination. With a stubble beard, he had had to give up his feminine attire and had quickly changed into men's clothes, gleaned in passing on various washing lines. He had then managed to board a boat, as a stowaway, in the direction of England. There he had joined the *Forces Françaises Libres*, the Free French Forces in London. As he spoke German fluently and was a passionate and experienced cruciverbalist, he had quickly gained the attention of the British Intelligence.

On an icy morning in December 1943, he had found himself in front of the famous station X. Blending together the Victorian Gothic, Dutch Baroque, and Tudor styles, this imposing manor with the most original architecture dominated the immense wooded space of Bletchley Park. After a decryption training course, he found himself as a cryptanalyst in one of the adjacent small houses, Hut 8. He decoded and analyzed German messages and those from other enemy countries transmitted mainly by the Lorenz and Enigma encryption machines.

He spent entire days deciphering coded messages with thousands of other servicemen and civilians who worked at the intelligence station. He was passionate about this painstaking work of deduction but often of luck. He had become an important decryption member within the Government Code and Cypher School, known by the acronym GC&CS that some had fun nicknaming Golf, Cheese, and Chess Society!

Most of the four thousand messages analyzed each day at Station X were not only classified as Top Secret but even more strictly as Ultra Secret for the most sensitive ones. They had given the code-name Ultra to this type of information of electromagnetic origin. Therefore, when Gus found himself at a communal table for meals or a cup of tea with other agents, he was strictly forbidden to talk about his activities to anyone else.

It is true that the eminently secret nature of the Ultra program was essential to its success. It had already proven its worth in aiding the Allied victories in the Battle of the Atlantic and the North African campaign. At the start of 1944, Gus had intercepted, decoded, and analyzed the positions of numerous German divisions on the Western Front, thus participating in the Allied victory of the Normandy landings. His superiors had thanked him warmly for his hard work, telling him that the information obtained at the station had undoubtedly helped to shorten the war by a few years.

Gus was proud to have played such an important role during those long months. Mid-September, he learned about the freeing of the port of Brest in Brittany by the Allies. He decided that it was time for him to return home to see his mother who was still unwell. He packed with his luggage a petite, bubbly, red-haired, freckled young girl with rimmed glasses named Peggy. After dropping by to see Gabrielle and give her some news about me, he returned home just in time. His mother had waited impatiently, resigned, dismissing Death with the back of her hand when the latter came too close to her bed of torment.

He introduced Peggy to her, and she smiled, exhausted but content. She wished them both a long life of happiness. Then, happy to know her son was alive and with a soul mate, she passed away peacefully in the night like the flame of a candle burning out, very slowly, without any noise.

He had met Peggy, who spoke French well, at the crossword club in Bletchley Park. They had searched together during long evenings the solutions to many definitions. Peggy's contagious laugh had bewitched him when they had finally found together the five-letter solution of, "as soon as you open your eyes you can't see it," or the six-letter "eye site" or "party song" in fourteen letters. After a while, they had invented a new game of authoring their own crossword definitions. Peggy would challenge him mockingly with her own definition of a "jolly old chap banger eater," and Gus would answer all smiles, "Brit." Then he would take his turn with, "the most beautiful are often virgin." Peggy would declaim "wools" with her irresistible accent, laughing out loud, then ask, "XC Roman generation?" Gus had taken a while to find "nonagenarian," but that evening, carried away by their hilarious verbal duel, they had gradually drawn closer, brushed their hands lightly with their fingertips, and finally kissed tenderly. They had never been without each other afterwards.

Just like the words, their hearts had crossed!

At the end of 1944, events were moving faster. Every day, we saw German civilians pass by with their carts and wheelbarrows, fleeing in front of the Russians or the Allies. The Red Army had now taken up positions in Bulgaria, Romania, Hungary, Yugoslavia, Finland, and Norway and it also controlled the Baltic Sea. In addition, Aachen was the first major city on German soil to fall into the hands of the American army after weeks of ruthless fighting.

In our Ritz, we were preparing for another long and harsh winter, our fifth in captivity. Meanwhile in Moscow, in the presence of General de Gaulle and Stalin, a Franco-Soviet pact was signed by the steadfast Vyacheslav Molotov – who would ironically remain in the annals primarily for the cocktail of the same name – and by Georges Bidault.

Curled up by our makeshift stoves, while a blizzard blew over our hangar and isolated it under a thick blanket of snow, the last major operation of the war was continuing on the Western Front. The Battle of the Bulge, an ultimate megalomaniacal upheaval of the Führer, raged in a Siberian cold. The resistance of the American and British forces, as well as of the French 2nd Parachute Chasseur Regiment, was going to push back the last attempt of German reconquest, but at a price: in Bastogne and other neighboring villages, even more lives than during the landing in Normandy were sacrificed!

The year 1945 was looming on the horizon. We finally hoped for an upcoming and favorable outcome of these interminable years of captivity.

Blocked by the snow and the freezing winter, we were most of the time confined to our quarters. However, every day on short outings, we would meet fleeing civilians and French prisoners on the march, flanked by German guards. They told us that the Russians were not far away. We also learned that a concentration camp in Poland, Auschwitz, had recently been liberated by Soviet troops.

In mid-February 1945, I went to fetch a load of wood with the truck about fifteen kilometers from Schivelbein. As I got out of the vehicle, I suddenly heard cannon fire. Immediately, I turned to my boss, "Listen, Amadeusz, the Russians are coming!"

He turned pale, wondering if Schivelbein would be bruised or worse devastated by this impending arrival of the *Rosjanin*. I reassured him by telling him that the Russian army would not attack civilians.

I didn't know how far from the truth I was.

In the evening, back to the Ritz, I hastened to proudly announce to the *kommando*, "This afternoon, while I was loading the truck with Amadeusz, I clearly heard cannon shots in the distance. The Russians are fast approaching. We will be released shortly!"

"Hopefully, Alex, our guards won't have the crazy idea of getting rid of us before running away from the enemy."

"So few of them are watching us now and they all know us too well. I don't think they would take such an initiative. But, if necessary, we will defend ourselves or we will shut ourselves away in here while waiting to be rescued."

That evening, while singing merrily, we began to put our things away in the expectation of an upcoming release. During the following days, our guards were most anxious and agitated; nothing indicated their intention to eliminate us. After four years in this village, everyone knew us well and appreciated our daily help. We had interacted with our guards without problem day after day and a sort of respect had been established between us. Our guards were on the alert, however, and seemed rather helpless. Fighting echoed around town and seemed to be closing in quickly. They therefore expected at any time to be called back by their command post to rejoin their regiment.

On March 3, 1945, around nine in the morning, our life turned upside down once again.

As the cannons echoed outside the city gates, we heard spasmodic shots and approaching armored vehicles. Our guards burst into our hangar and ushered us into the back of their truck with our bags. Passing through the deserted town, I saw Amadeusz to whom I waved, shouting "*Adieu* Amadeusz. Take care of yourself. *Auf wiedersehen!*" He watched us leave, looking sad and worried. I never saw him again, nor any other villager of Schivelbein.

A few kilometers southwest of the village, the truck left the main road and stopped in a forest track. Our guards ordered us to step down and led us on a snowy path through the forest. We were all terrified that our last hour had come. When we reached a clearing, they ordered us to sit in the thick, sparkling snow. We were shivering, not only from the cold but also from the fear that we were probably living our last moments. My thoughts drifted to Gabrielle and Jean-Pierre, their smiling faces tenderly sketched by the rays of the sun that pierced the undergrowth with a multitude of sparkling lights.

Suddenly our guards raced back on the double to the truck, abandoning Rüdiger, the oldest of the guards who had also fought in The Great War. Limping terribly and seemingly exhausted, he would have been unable to follow them in their unexpected flight.

Rüdi was a good guy with whom we got along well. Alone, distraught, he pointed his gun to a path that twisted through the woods. In silence, still uncertain of our fate, we followed him. After a short walk, we came to a large farm. To our relief, Rüdi ordered the owners to bring us some bread and victuals, as well as wine.

At two o'clock in the afternoon, a few miles away from our now deserted Ritz, we were having some food in the barn, seated on haystacks. Russian soldiers suddenly burst in. Surprised, we raised our arms, but they immediately indicated that we were free. However, Rüdi, who had thrown his rifle to the ground, did not have time to surrender. He was summarily executed in the farm courtyard with a bullet to the back of his neck. Lying face down in the immaculate snow, a scarlet aureole gradually spread around his motionless head.

This detachment of the Red Army of about thirty men included two BA-10 armored vehicles and a ZiS-5 transport truck which had carried the soldiers now standing in front of us.

Their leader, Igor – a muscular fellow with a face carved out of granite, with a crew cut and a piercing sapphire gaze – tried to make us understand by some gesture that we were finally free and that we had nothing to fear from them. It is true that our deplorable outfits, marked with the unmistakable cursed letters KG, and our French accent left no doubt about our condition and origins. They checked our papers anyway to be sure that no German traitors were hiding among us.

We watched these soldiers dressed in their quilted Telogreika uniform, warm khaki jacket and pants, padded with cotton and sewn in stripes, as if they had appeared from another world. Some were wearing Valenki felt boots that looked really comfortable in the snow next to our old worn-out stogies. They all wore a strange fur cap adorned with a red star with a sickle and a hammer in its center – symbolizing the communist union of the peasants and the working-class proletariat – with flaps protecting their ears. These Ushanka hats appeared to be very cozy in the freezing cold of this early March 1945 while we were chilled to the core with our simple caps.

We did not understand a single word of their foreign language, and they appeared so strange to us. Armed with their PPSh-41 submachine guns, known under the name of Papasha that Jean obviously hastened without restraint to nickname "the daddy tomcat," they were terrifying. To break the ice, Igor opened a pocket on the front of his Telogreika jacket and pulled out a pack of Makhorka cigarettes. He offered us a cigarette of this dark tobacco that actually looked like it had been rolled in a piece of newspaper.

After a short break and after having robbed the farm of all food and alcohol with his unit, Igor gestured us to set off. They accompanied us to a hamlet where we arrived in the evening. We were between two fronts, German troops positioned in the west and Soviet forces advancing in the east. Therefore, on that very first night of freedom, huddled together under waterproof canvases to warm us up, we listened with deep concern to the shells hissing incessantly in all directions above our heads.

Three days later, while we were far from Schivelbein, to the south of the city an SS regiment would find itself fully surrounded, then eliminated without any prisoners, by two Russian regiments and a Polish one. After the battle, Soviet troops entered Schivelbein as conquerors, under the frightened gazes of Amadeusz and the other inhabitants.

Russian soldiers discovered our abandoned Ritz; after having informed General Ulyanov, he decided to spend the night there. As the general was going out during the night to relieve himself by the river, a shadow slipped quietly behind him. Hans, the apprentice baker who had concocted a black eye for me, had since been automatically enlisted on his sixteenth birthday in a Pomeranian battalion of the Hitler Youth. He sneaked silently behind the general. In a quick move, he slit his throat. The next day, after the discovery of the body, about twenty men were gathered at random in the marketplace. Helpless, Amadeusz watched the Russian soldiers execute in retaliation the poor innocent villagers. Enraged by revenge and alcohol, the soldiers unfortunately did not stop there; they then went from house to house to rape women and young girls.

The next days, we walked without interruption in bitter cold and heavy snowfall. We understood that the detachment had been ordered to advance towards Berlin. As we passed a large, picturesque red brick farmhouse for horses, we began to comprehend the brutality of the Russian army. Many Russian soldiers belonging to other regiments had already seized dozens of superb stallions grazing peacefully in the surrounding fields and were stealing them with total impunity.

One day at dusk, as we walked down a snow-covered road through a forest of conifers coated with a resplendent frost under the full moon, we saw distant glimmer in the woods. The convoy headed in that direction, and we arrived in front of a set of stone buildings, arranged in a square on one level. I will never know if chance had set this place on our path or if the Russian soldiers had previously devised a plan to stop there.

Igor banged his heavy fist on a wooden double *porte cochère.*

Slow footsteps approached and a judas window opened with a somber creak. A secular, quavering voice asked in German, *"Wer sind Sie?"* Igor explained that his soldiers and freed French prisoners of war wanted to rest for the night away from the raging snowstorm. A key turned in the massive door and a decrepit Catholic nun appeared in the doorway. The Mother Superior of the convent, Sister Katharina, led us through a long cloister which surrounded an interior garden planted with fruit trees and garnished with a vegetable patch. We arrived at an immaculate refectory where we were happy to at last be able to sit down.

Other nuns joined the matriarch who had welcomed us. They were all dressed in long and ample white dresses, draped with a black cape, their foreheads and their cheeks hidden by wimples of white linen covered with long black veils. They carried on their chests simple crosses of black wood and at their belts ebony rosaries. They set the table for us and brought us bread and a steaming cabbage and turnip soup.

While we were feasting on this hot meal, two Russian soldiers left for the kitchen with the nuns. They returned with their arms laden with bottles of wine. These were added to the vodka and other spirits that the soldiers had collected before. Seated all together, we were reassured to have a roof for the night, sheltered from the gusts of wind and snow. We felt safe accompanied by the Russian soldiers who were armed to the teeth. After having enjoyed the applesauce that the nuns had prepared, we laid down directly on the floor. Exhausted from our walk and sated, we fell asleep quickly.

I was suddenly roused from my sleep by the terrified cries of women echoing in the cloister. Without any weapons, helpless under the threatening gazes of some Russian soldiers who were also lying down in the refectory and were telling us not to move, we fell back asleep as the clamor quickly ceased.

The next morning, a Russian soldier named Dmitri approached Father Gythiel and whispered to the Man of Faith, *"Salve pie hominem. Nomen meum Dmitri est."*

Dmitri was a Latin teacher in Leningrad before the war and, having suspected that our parish priest understood Latin, he introduced himself to him this way. None of the Russian soldiers spoke French.

"*Ego sum latinae linguae magister,*" Dmitri explained to him. "*In Leningrad habito et vobis?*"

"*Mihi nomen Pierre est et in Rennes habito,*" Father Gythiel answered in dog Latin, telling him his first name and that he was from Rennes in Brittany.

Worried to know where the cries had come from last night, the parish priest asked, "*Quid egis nocte proxima?*"

"*Puellae stupratae sunt,*" Dmitri whispered, with a lump in his throat.

The priest, dumbfounded, had just learned that women had been abused in the convent the night before.

"*Pulsatus autem sum et ligatus. Neque quidquam facere potui,*" Dmitri explained; he had been knocked unconscious, then tied up, and consequently had remained utterly helpless in the face of the events of the previous night.

Dead drunk, three of his comrades had gone to smoke cigarettes in the inner garden. They had heard whispers coming from a room opposite the refectory at the other end of the cloister. Curious, they had approached the room loudly while staggering, but a nun had coldly barred their way. This had made them even more suspicious. One of the soldiers had drawn his Nagant revolver and, under threat, the sister had taken a key from under her skirts; constrained, she had opened the door to the now silent room.

Nestled in the dark, about twenty young girls, boarders at this Catholic school, stared with wide frightened eyes at these three men who sneered and drooled at the sight of the chaste girls in their white nightgowns backlit by the flickering candles.

One of the soldiers had run immediately to warn Igor and his henchmen who were sleeping in a small chapel. Dmitri had then violently opposed their bestial intentions. Without warning, Igor had unleashed a hard-hitting uppercut which had knocked him out. He had fallen flat on his face under the gaze of a crucified Christ with a helpless gaze. He had not regained consciousness until much later, alone in the silent chapel, his hands and feet tied in front of the altar.

During that time, Igor and the other soldiers had repeatedly and brutally raped several young girls and ten nuns who had tried to intervene. The Mother Superior and two other nuns had been coldly stabbed to death as they tried to escape through a window to seek help.

We had discovered with disgust the hidden horrors of war!

Although free, we felt guilty and ashamed that we had not been able to intervene. We were now suspicious of these soldiers and did not trust them an inch.

When some abused and desperate young girls had begged their torturers to end their agony by killing them, they had replied coldly and cynically, almost as insulted, that Russian soldiers did not shoot at women; only SS soldiers were cowardly enough for such a crime.

Russian officers turned a blind eye to these acts of violence against German women, and tacitly authorized them as a reward for the efforts of the soldiers. Freeing Europe from fascism, the Red Army had in fact convinced itself that these war trophies were not morally reprehensible. Unfortunately, such vile acts would spread throughout Germany with the advance of the Russian troops.

Dmitri was pallid as he recounted the events of the past night. He confessed to Father Gythiel that he had already seen Death up close and that he had lost his father, mother, and brothers.

*"Vidi mortuos and vidi mori in bello. Perdidi patrem meum, et matrem meam et fratres meos,"* Dmitri told him.

*"Barbari estis,"* the priest answered angrily, accusing them all of being barbarians. He asked the reasons for these despicable and condemnable acts, *"Quare? Contemptibile est."*

With tears in his eyes, Dmitri now begged the priest for forgiveness, *"Me paenitet."*

"*Dei iudicium contendam adversum vos,*" the priest added, expressing his confidence in the divine justice.

"*Deum credo, sed etiam in iustitiam,*" Dmitri replied, indicating that he believed in God but also in the righteousness of men!

After learning of the sad plight of the young girls and the nuns, we viewed our liberators in a different light. Even though we were free to move around, these soldiers were in reality our new captors and vile torturers. We hastily left the Catholic boarding school for girls.

In the afternoon, we arrived in a town completely destroyed by the bombardments and fire from the Russian tanks that had preceded us. The specter of the buildings loomed under heavy snowfall. The agonizing silence of the place sent shivers down our spines.

As we were settling in for the night, Dmitri came to inform us that a French woman was in the rubble of a house. I was ordered with the priest to go and help her. After walking through the city in ruins, we came to a roofless, partly demolished house. Among the rubble, in the remnants of a bedroom on the ground floor, we found a young woman in a state of shock, nestled in bed under a thick eiderdown, as snug as a bug in a rug. She had a mysterious beauty in her white lace nightgown, her blonde hair loosened in long curls over her frail shoulders. She was staring at us with a superb green gaze, but devoid of any emotion.

We helped her out of bed and out of the ghost house, then we dragged her on a sled for a few miles in the snow. Father Gythiel tried to comfort her, but she remained silent, her mind seeming to have already wandered to sunnier lands.

When we arrived at a military field hospital, we were asked to put on white gowns and white caps. We looked like anything but genuine nurses in these outfits. The young woman, trembling with fear and cold, was biding her time with us in a small waiting room. The priest finally succeeded in getting her out of her torpor.

"What's your name? What are you doing here? What happened?"

"My name is Marie. I came to work in Germany under the STO two years ago. I have two young boys and a little girl in Paris whom I entrusted to my parents, and I came here to earn a salary."

"But what were you doing alone in the remains of that house?"

"When the bombing started, I was bedridden, very sick; I didn't have the strength to take shelter. Then the Russian tanks and soldiers came. I huddled under my eiderdown, begging to be spared and saved."

We both looked at her in disbelief.

"But why didn't you come out of the rubble to save yourself?"

"I was in shock and couldn't think for myself. Then you arrived. A miracle! I am so grateful to you."

"What were you doing here for the STO? Were you a tenant in this large house?"

"Yes, I rented a small bedroom. I worked in a warehouse assembling shells by hand. A dangerous, delicate, and meticulous work."

I looked at her, not quite understanding why she had left her three children to come to the depths of Germany to earn a meager pittance. I also observed that she was not wearing a wedding ring, but I convinced myself that she probably wanted to have unencumbered hands for her precision work.

Finally, we were taken into an operating room where a Russian military doctor was waiting for us. Marie was agitated. She kept repeating that she was fine, just numbed with cold, and did not need to be auscultated. But the doctor insisted and proceeded with his medical examination. After several long minutes, he turned to us and said in broken and hesitant French, "She is about five months pregnant!"

On the verge of tears, Marie protested vigorously.

"It is not possible. I have lived here alone for two years, and I work all the time. I cannot be pregnant. Tell the doctor he's wrong. I beg you."

But the doctor was adamant. Marie was pregnant, probably from a German. We couldn't help her anymore and we had to leave her in the hands of the Russian soldiers.

As we were taking a step toward the exit, she began to cry bitter tears and hastily sputtered hysterically.

"Don't leave me here alone. I admit, I met a German officer in Paris, and I fell madly in love with him. I left everything for Helmut, even my children, and I followed him here for love. I am expecting his child and his return. Unfortunately, he had to join his regiment to defend Berlin. I found myself alone. I admit that I lied to you. I do not work. The house where you found me is his house where we both lived together."

"Marie, there is nothing more we can do for you. The Russians will decide your fate. They will likely send you soon back to France where you will be reunited with your family."

The priest moved next to her and tried to appease her by praying for her.

"Remember, Marie, the pericope from the Gospel of John. The scribes and Pharisees wanted to stone an adulterous woman. Jesus had told them, 'Let whoever is without sin among you cast the first stone,' and they had all walked away one by one. Then, Jesus had said to the woman, 'I do not condemn you either.' Rest assured, Marie, we are not judging you. God will always be with you. He will protect you and your child. Good luck to you."

We left the room as Marie screamed in despair. She had made a terrible choice in abandoning her children for a man – a German officer moreover – and would have to live with her conscience and the consequences. Before leaving we took off our white outfits and we were each given a loaf of bread. This meager reward brought us a semblance of comfort.

On the way back, Dmitri stopped in front of a tumbledown house which revealed an upright piano among the debris. Dmitri asked us to follow him and sat down in front of the piano. He lifted the cover and with the back of his sleeve wiped a thick layer of dust off the keyboard. He began to play divinely a tune that I did not know; Johann Pachelbel's "Canon in D" immediately won me over and remained in my head for a long time.

# Chapter 17

***From Departure to Arrival***

The next day, after a difficult walk in a violent snowstorm, our convoy finally stopped safely in a small village. Most of the houses had been abandoned by their inhabitants for fear of reprisal from the Red Army. Therefore, we were assigned to one of them, a small, unpretentious hovel at the edge of a forest. Jean and I settled down for the night on an old, decaying leather armchair in the barren and austere kitchen-dining room, near a collapsed fireplace. The other comrades took refuge in the adjacent bedroom or stayed with us, sleeping directly on the floor.

"Alex," Jean whispered to me, as we struggled to warm ourselves under blankets, huddled deep in the armchair, against each other. "I hope our clothes will dry out a bit overnight. The bitter cold permeates all day long through our damp uniforms and our feet are constantly frozen from our forced march in the snow."

"It would be so nice if that fireplace was still drawing. Let's hope our dwelling warms up a bit during the night with all our comrades crammed into these two modest tiny rooms."

"It's sad; we are free, but for the moment our condition is miserable. We have almost nothing to eat since food is as rare as hens'

231

teeth. Most of our "liberators" are brutes without mercy towards the population. They force us to walk in the snow and cold every day towards an uncertain destination and future. For how long is this going to last?"

"Jean, as you say, we are indeed free! The Russian soldiers protect us with their weapons and armored vehicles. Let's hope that before long the war will find a favorable outcome and that we will have the chance to return home."

Pulling up the covers, Jean looked at me sadly and added with a lump in his throat, "You know, Alex, what happened at the Catholic School for Young Girls was revolting. I think about it all the time; it should be exposed. How could these men act like such wild beasts? Are we somehow complicit in these acts that we cannot prevent? Either way, moving forward let's beware of Russian soldiers, even though they are now supposedly on our side."

"You are right, Jean. Alliances are made and broken all the time. Let's remain on our guard! Personally, I can't understand how this poor woman, Marie, could have decided to leave everything behind out of love and make such a terrible choice. I hope that she will get out of this, because she too is a victim of war in a way."

Jean suppressed a shudder and asked me with a mocking air, "Alex, let's change the subject. Since it is so freezing cold here, do you know which travels faster, cold or heat?"

"Jean, you can't help but talk nonsense! I don't know. Tell me, which one?"

"Well, it's obviously heat since you can catch a cold!"

"You're funny! You are always ready for a laugh. It brings us joy."

Then I added jokingly, taking Jean to his game, "Speaking of freezing and wordplay, when you shiver from the cold, you get goose-bumps without turning geese into swans; when you're sick, you also feel like a chicken with a pip. Why do we always pick on these poor innocent gallinaceous animals?"

"Well done, Alex! You are making progress in your joke reper-toire. Well, to tell the truth, I do feel like a lucky duck in this armchair! Speaking of our new Russian allies, do you know why the founder of the Red Army, Bolshevik Lev Davidovich Bronstein, known as Trotsky, always wrote in lower cases? No? Well, he hated Capitalism!"

"Jean, you will always amaze me with your knowledge, futile and often useless, but it's still impressive! Sleep well. The march will surely be long and arduous again tomorrow."

After a few days of marching, we finally stopped for several days in a fortified town, Pyrzyce, south of Stargard. It had already fallen into the hands of the Red Army after being shelled relentlessly by Russian artillery, thus destroying the old town surrounded by ramparts.

Five years earlier, I had dreamed so much of a creamy omelet for my birthday not far from this city, in the Stargard camp, Stalag II-D!

Stargard had suffered from numerous bombardments and had been almost completely destroyed. The people of Stargard had been evacuated; of the forty thousand inhabitants at the start of the war, only about three thousand still resided there. The inhabitants had been forced to leave the city when, in February 1945, the last major offensive, Operation Solstice or *Sonnenwende* had been launched by German troops from this town on the Eastern Front. This last jolt had resulted in a resounding failure for the megalomaniac dictator for whom time was now running out.

Likewise, Pyrzyce was nothing more than a spectral city haunted by the souls of departed soldiers and deserted by its inhabitants. Therefore, we encountered no difficulty in finding vacated bedrooms in the vicinity with, finally, genuinely comfortable beds to accommodate us for several nights.

The Russians now made us work on the abandoned farms between Pyrzyce and Stargard. As food, we had only one bread for ten people a day. This bread contained strands of straw which gave us intestinal aches. Consequently, in three and a half months of semi-liberty, I was on my way to lose thirteen kilos!

One afternoon, we saw a group of Russian soldiers arrive with emaciated prisoners, advancing very painstakingly, looking haggard. These came from the Stalag II-D which had just been liberated. These prisoners, mostly French, joined us; we were now nearly eighty. Before the liberation of the camp, seeing the threatening approach of Russian troops, the Germans had evacuated most of the prisoners of sufficient health for their transport to other camps. At the end of March 1945, a Polish administration finally overthrew the previous German one, and took control of Stargard.

The days passed slowly, occupied with the labor at the farms, while we sometimes heard in the distance muffled bombardments or jerky fire from machine guns. Our condition as "freed" soldiers had in fact changed relatively little compared to our daily life at the Ritz in Schivelbein. We were seriously tired of that interminable wait and our precarious condition.

Mid-April, Igor ordered us to get ready for an advance in Germany. We were all quite excited to get even closer to our country, but at the same time we feared the fierce German resistance that most likely awaited us. Before leaving town, I stopped by an old luthier who had continued his activities with passion, despite unparalleled devastation around his shop. With the little money I had left, I bought a present for Jean-Pierre: a mandolin, used but skillfully decorated with lovely floral motifs.

A beautiful spring day, sunny but cool, accompanied our departure from Pyrzyce. We passed about ten kilometers south of Stettin, a substantial and strategic port opening onto the Baltic Sea, where battles were raging between German and Soviet troops. The Allies supported the fighting by relentlessly bombarding a multitude of strategic positions in and around Stettin. They were aided in the targeting on the ground by the *Armia Krajowa*, or Home Army of the Polish underground resistance movement. Stettin thus found itself with two-thirds of its buildings ravaged, a devastated port as well as the local shipyards and factories completely razed to the ground. During these combats, the population deserted the city and nearly four hundred thousand inhabitants took refuge on the other side of the border.

As these battles raged and resulted in the capture of Stettin by the Allies and Soviet troops, the Battle of Berlin began in a firestorm. Meanwhile, returning from the Yalta conference, the United States President, Franklin D. Roosevelt died suddenly from a cerebral hemorrhage. He was immediately replaced by his vice-president, Harry Truman who, a few months later, unfortunately did not hesitate in authorizing the dropping of two atomic bombs on the innocent towns of Hiroshima and Nagasaki.

At the end of April, we arrived in the immense forest domain of Schorfheide-chorin. The area was dotted with a multitude of lakes, meadows, and fields. Besides the great diversity of animals that were not at all familiar to me, such as beavers, otters, bats, and storks, the Nazi leaders had also introduced elk and bison for their hunting pleasure. Hermann Göring, the commander-in-chief of the Luftwaffe and plunderer-in-chief of the cultural treasures of the invaded countries, had even built his hunting lodge there, adding to its numerous residences and castles.

Our progress through this gigantic forest was slow, interspersed with many stops. After a few days, we were reconnoitering in a dark beech wood when suddenly clamors rang out.

"Alex, do you hear that?" Jean asked me. "The exclamations seem to be coming from the meadow that we can distinguish through the trees. Let's be on our guard!"

I motioned to Jean and Father Gythiel, who were accompanying me, to keep silent and to walk quietly towards the loud shouts and outbursts that we now recognized as orders yelled in German. Igor, Dmitri, and a few other Russian soldiers who were closely following us continued their advance to our left in the direction of the meadow. Before our startled eyes, three young soldiers with the SS insignia on the side of their helmets were pushing with their MP-40 submachine gun four hapless weeping women; they carried infants in their arms, accompanied by young children. A few paces from our position, we suddenly saw an SS-*Totenkopfverbände* officer arrive, dressed to the nines and wearing his cap with its ignominious skull.

He settled into position with his back to us and unsheathed a Luger Parabellum from its holster, pointing it with his outstretched arm at the ground.

A short distance from where we were huddled behind some tree trunks, one of the SS soldiers on our left ordered one of the tearful mothers to drop off her newborn baby and let him walk by himself. The boy, who was four to six months old at most, obviously couldn't yet walk on his own. His mother held him tight to her heart while sobbing and pleading in an insistent and desperate wail. A vicious smile at the corner of his mouth, the soldier then declared, *"Wenn er nicht laufen kann, er wahrscheinlich fliegen kann!"* – "if he can't walk, he can probably fly!"

He then suddenly snatched the infant from the arms of his mother who became hysterical when realizing the soldier's intention.

With unparalleled cruelty and sadism at its height, the SS soldier was about to throw the infant in the direction of the officer, for a macabre skeet shooting where the clay pigeons had been savagely replaced by children.

The soldier grabbed the infant with both hands, took a few steps back, gained momentum, and threw him forcefully into the air towards the officer who immediately aimed with his pistol.

Before he could pull the trigger, Jean, who had stealthily approached him, strangled him from behind, crushing his neck with his left arm; at the same time, he pierced his heart with a long knife in a swift and definitive move. At the same instant, the Russian soldiers, who had taken the SS soldiers from the rear, riddled them with a hail of bullets in their backs, killing them all, and thus saving the mothers and their children.

The infant was now falling in our direction at breakneck speed.

After an acceleration worthy of Jesse Owens, the priest dove desperately at the last second, like the spectacular goalkeeper of the national French soccer team, Julien Darui. *In extremis*, he caught the baby in full flight! He finished his course in a series of somersaults, then got up, the child safe and sound in the crook of his arms. His mother ran to get him back and kissed the priest without restraint, giving him endless thanks.

We learned that the SS had found some Jewish families living in wooden huts in reclusive swamps where they believed they were safe from any persecution. This SS detachment had stumbled upon them by accident as it fled from the Allies. The soldiers had gathered under the threat of their weapons all the men and adolescents. Under the horrified gaze of their families, they had summarily hanged them from the branches of the trees surrounding the houses. They had then forced the terrified women and young children to head for the meadow where luckily our destinies had crossed.

While these Jewish families had narrowly escaped an inevitable massacre in the Schorfheide-chorin forest estate, not far, in Berlin, Russian soldiers had hoisted the red flag over the Reich Chancellery. Dmitri informed us with incomparable joy that the last German soldiers had given themselves up in Berlin.

Scared to death of being captured alive in their underground bunker, Adolf and his Eva joined without delay in unison Benito and Claretta who were impatiently waiting for them, benumbed in the depths of Hell.

On May 8, 1945, Nazi Germany surrendered unconditionally.

The Second World War was well and truly over in Europe!

Now free and without risk of encountering hostile troops, we could finally rest and enjoy our free time while awaiting our repatriation. We had found lodging in deserted houses in a small village in the heart of the estate. We no longer had any obligation to work for our Russian liberators. As we were in a very wooded region, some comrades decided to hunt to supplement our meager meals. First, we had to find weapons; we took possession of the rifles and handguns of the SS killed in the meadow and of other dead soldiers that we discovered at the bend of the paths.

There was no shortage of game, and our meals quickly became

venison feasts where hare, roe deer, wild boar, and fallow deer mingled on our plates. One day, while searching a house with my comrades, Gérard got his hands on a nice piece of fat bacon. That evening, we prepared a colossal shepherd's pie. It was an unparalleled treat. The delicious aroma brought me even closer to home where I would soon be repatriated.

"Gérard, your discovery is very timely. This shepherd's pie is the tastiest," I told him, as we were all seated around a large rustic table in one of the abandoned thatched cottages in the village. *"Bevet ar moc'h!"* – "Long live the pigs!"

Then, dressing my plate with a piece of bread, I added, "I'll always remember the day you revealed your potato stash at the Ritz des Fritz, but this hash beats all records."

"Thank you too, Alex, for your support during all these years of captivity. You were able to keep a cool head and you helped us get through a lot of hardships," Gérard replied.

At that moment, Jean, who was late, entered the room with a big smile on his face.

"Eh! Wait for me for the accolades and to celebrate the victory. I have unearthed something that will make you happy," he told us as he put a crate full of bottles of schnapps on the table.

The dusty bottles filled with a clear brandy seemed to have been produced by hand by the former owners of the house from different fruits as indicated by the handwritten labels.

"And there are still plenty of other crates in the cellar that I accidentally uncovered while rummaging behind a pile of coal."

"Alleluia! God be blessed," Father Gythiel shouted cavernously as he removed the cork from one of the bottles. "Let's drink to victory while remembering all our comrades who did not have the chance to be able to return home safe and sound like us."

"Amen," Jean exclaimed, and we all resumed in unison "Amen!"

We rose to our feet solemnly and, after a brief moment of silence, heads bowed, we raised our glasses. We promptly gulped down the alcohol, so strong that it immediately produced an uncontrollable fit of thunderous coughing.

"Alex, don't go choking so close to going back home," Jean joked. "What would we say to Gaby? Your husband unfortunately died while drinking some *eau*, not just any water, but ironically, some *eau-de-vie!*"

"Anyway, Jean, your jokes will be missed by all of us. They certainly softened the difficult hours of our journey and helped us keep our spirits up. I have no doubt that I will one day see your name top the bill, perhaps as a comic trooper. You could even form an incomparable duo with Gus, our first-time escapee."

"You realize, my friends," Jean added, "we will probably be back home before summer. I can't believe the war is finally over. Almost six years already since Alex and I met on this station platform in Angers with our comrades, some of whom have unfortunately tragically disappeared since."

"Who would have imagined that the war would go on forever? Everything suggested that we would be away from our families for six months, a year at most."

"It's true, we have gone through extremely difficult times, so far away from ours. But we were lucky. We are alive and whole. Soon we will be back with our families and back to civilian life."

Holding up a new glass of schnapps, I said in Breton, "*Yec'hed mat! Hetiñ a ran deoc'h kalz a vloavezhioù all,*" wishing them good health and many years to live.

"*Trugarez. Yec'hed mat!*" my comrades thanked in chorus, followed by a "*Bennozh Doue deoc'h,*" from Father Gythiel, who blessed us all.

After an opulent meal, well washed down with an impressive variety of bottles of schnapps which continued to pile up on our table, our heads were all spinning like weathervanes slapped by a northwesterly wind, and the weight of the last few years evaporated little by little as if by magic. Laughter mingled as we recounted our memories, sometimes interrupted by a few tears. Soon we were singing pre-war songs in unison. Armed with two wooden spoons, a few saucepans, and a chair, Jean improvised on these makeshift drums, while Gérard and I imitated the brass; the priest fancied himself as Django Reinhardt with an invisible guitar. Other comrades joined our improvised orchestra – *sine instrumento musico* – to accompany the songs, "Prosper Yop La Boum," the darling of the ladies, or more precisely their Parisian pimp, and "Ignace," that tiny, charming little name.

The evening continued late into the night to the echoes of "Y'a D'La Joie." Arm in arm, we swayed to the rhythms of "Marinella" or "What Are We Waiting for to Be Happy, What Are We Waiting for to Party?" We most certainly weren't expecting anything more to continue the party that only ended in the early hours of the morning for lack of "combatants" falling asleep one after the other here and there in the most incongruous positions.

Waking up later in the day was challenging; a first-class hangover painfully reminded us of our recent victory. Like Count Dracula, we couldn't stand the slightest light of day, so we spent the rest of the day in the kitchen making a kind of jam from sugar beets that we had found the previous days. This jam helped supplement a meal of crepes in the evening.

Another day, as we were visiting the abandoned farms around, we heard noises coming from a hay barn. Armed with forks, we explored in silence its various corners. I discovered by chance, under a small haystack, a wooden trap door. I grabbed an iron ring and slowly lifted the hatch. At the bottom of a shelter dug out of the earth, two young teenagers with platinum blond hair stared at me with deep blue eyes, huddled together, frail and trembling.

A new Alsatian comrade, Lucien, recently released from the Stargard camp, limped up to join me. He tried to converse with the two children who were staring at us in terror. It turned out that they were siblings and were named Ludwig and Greta. A few weeks earlier, Russian soldiers on their way to Berlin had burst into the fields where their parents worked. They had been captured, tied by their feet to a horse and dragged at full speed on a path bristling with rocks. Meanwhile the soldiers reveled in the spectacle. Then, when their cries of pain had gradually died down, they had been savagely slaughtered, simply because they were born German. At the first crack of the machine guns, Ludwig had hastily dragged Greta into the barn where they had hidden under the hay in the dark and damp shelter. This hiding place had undoubtedly saved Greta from a terrible fate, similar to the young girls of the Catholic boarding school, at the hands of the Russian soldiers. Those spent the night in the farm, some lying on the straw, oblivious to the two children secretly sheltered below them, terrified in the dark.

Lucien informed them that peace accords had been signed but that it would be more prudent for them to hide until our imminent departure with our Russian liberators. At nightfall, under the nose of the Russian soldiers, we came to bring them some provisions to last a few more days in their hiding place.

The next day, after several days in this village, we hit the road again for another destination in Germany, leaving behind the two orphans. We passed north of Berlin through villages decimated by bombardments and cannonades. Landscapes of desolation followed one another. Vestiges of burnt down cars, shredded trucks and tanks reposed in the middle of ruins and spectral dwellings. Apart from a few stray dogs looking for a meager bite among the debris, life had totally disappeared from these villages, where dead bodies littered the streets and the piled-up rubble. The villagers seemed to have fled the suburbs of the city where Adolf had holed up, terrified in his bunker, and had died like a coward.

After nearly a week of walking, we entered a town that had been practically wiped off the map. Only a few rare churches, monuments and houses recalled how Brandenburg, on the banks of the Havel River, had been resplendent before the war. We passed a battered square covered with all kinds of debris; by miracle, a red-brick Gothic-style town hall, nearly half a millennium old, had resisted the intense hostilities.

In the center of the square, civilians waited miserably in an endless and disciplined line for their turn to fill their enameled buckets with a large manual water pump that still seemed in working condition. Most of the civilians bowed their heads, no doubt ashamed of the defeat of their country but above all of the scathing presence of Russian soldiers strutting through the rubble. Some dared to glance at them furtively, with hatred but also with terror. Children in rags perilously ascended collapsed and unstable buildings in a climbing game, imagining themselves for a moment as mountaineers at the top of the Matterhorn; others hoped to find some valuables that they would then trade for food.

A little further on, we stopped in awe of a gigantic statue of an armored knight, several meters tall, proudly wielding a sword in his right hand. Jean approached the medieval representation of the giant to decipher an inscription.

"Alex, look," Jean told me. "You are not going to believe me. It's your ancestor, the knight Roland, the nephew and paladin of Charlemagne!"

"Stop your nonsense Jean, I have no ancestors in Germany!" I replied, offended. "This Roland lost a consonant by protecting France against us, the Bretons. If I remember correctly, it was he who sounded his oliphant at the Roncevaux Pass, before dying, to warn Charlemagne against the Saracens. Absolutely nothing to do with me! Nothing at all!"

"Of course, he was not blowing in a bombard! Anyway, I do love Saracens, especially their wheat flour in savory crepes," Jean laughed heartily. "Hey, guys, did you know it is also this Roland of Roncevaux who tried to break his famous sword, Durandal, on a rock, thus opening a huge breach? Then, the story goes that his sword miraculously flew all the way to Rocamadour! A true magician that Roland!"

"You know a thing or two about this knight, Jean! You will always amaze me with your erudition but once again I think you spend way too much time at the dentist."

As we reached the edge of the vaporized city, we saw the remains of a charred factory. The inscription Arado Flugzeugwerke found on a panel lying on the ground as well as the fuselage carcasses scattered around reminded us that this was where military planes had been mass produced for the Luftwaffe. This strategic target had brought with it the massive destruction of the entire city.

At last, we stopped in a large courtyard, facing a most impressive multi-story building. After asking for information from an inhabitant who was passing on a nearby road, perched on a cart pulled by an old sluggish mule, Lucien told us about this grim-looking building, "It is one of the most modern prisons in the country and apparently it has already had its count of atrocities since it was built ten years ago."

We listened in fascination to Lucien's story as we sat down in the courtyard to finally get some rest.

"During the last few years, some two thousand prisoners have stayed there. Many have been executed without mercy by *Fallbeil*, the Teutonic guillotine, or even sometimes savagely with an ax. But at the beginning of the war, just after having served as a concentration camp for political prisoners, this nightmarish place was the site of a terrifying extermination."

We all looked at each other trembling, in awe of this appalling story and Lucien's storytelling skills.

"This bleak and horrifying place was the setting for the Aktion T4 euthanasia program. Almost ten thousand individuals of all ages, starting with children, found themselves locked up here, declared mentally ill," Lucien explained. "Unfortunately, they were quickly joined by rebellious or marginalized adolescents, with so-called behavioral problems. Carried away by their impetus of cruelty, the Nazis finally also interned physically handicapped people in this place."

"Lucien, I have goosebumps," I replied with a shudder. "What you have shared about this place is grim and abject. What happened to these unfortunate people once they were interned?"

"They were all eliminated. Not a single survivor! Nearly ten thousand souls, dispersed in smoke," Lucien told us, with a lump in his throat.

Pale, his voice broken, Father Gythiel fumed, "But that's not possible, you heard it wrong. Someone must have tried to intervene. The families, the inhabitants, the doctors, the police, or even the priests would have undoubtedly protested this terrible place."

"I don't know how such a horror could have happened in front of everyone's eyes, but they all died in less than two years."

Stunned by this ignominy, Gérard asked in a harsh tone, "But they were Germans. So why these murders? This is insane!"

"The mad dictator just wanted to purge the Aryan race. There was nothing anyone could do to stop this vile and evil megalomaniac."

"Yeah, it's obvious. Adolf surely was the perfect Aryan type with his blond hair and flavescent mustache, his blue eyes and straight nose," Jean burst out in dismay, flushed with anger. "Talk about a good-for-nothing! How could the Germans be so blind?"

From the start of the war, German hospitals and specialized clinics had been emptied of their mentally and physically disabled. The transfer of children, then men and women, from infants to the elderly, to other centers, was a pretext to free up space for war-wounded soldiers. More often than not, the families of these unfortunate victims had not even been informed of their plight. Nearly ten thousand people were thus transferred to the Brandenburg "specialized center" – indeed in euthanasia – in reality a prison for each one of them, condemned to death, without trial, defense or appeal.

These innocent people were to be added to the three hundred thousand victims of Nazi euthanasia during the war.

Lucien now had teary eyes as he told us the horrific details he had learned about the fate of these innocent civilian victims. Some had served as guinea pigs, receiving massive doses of lethal drugs, or being exposed to lethal gases; others had simply been deprived of any food, following the menu E for *Entzug* meaning withdrawal, and had died of hunger. Nazi doctors in white coats, like the Angel of Death, had thus fine-tuned their murderous techniques to then apply them for mass exterminations in concentration camps and for the Final Solution.

Transported in buses with opaque windows, as soon as they arrived, the victims were welcomed by the so-called "medical" staff. Their identity was verified on their file, marked with a death sentence red cross, where the doctors then entered, *a priori*, a potential credible cause of death for their upcoming and false death certificate. This official document would accompany a letter of condolence that would be sent in the following weeks to the families, explaining to them that this death, as unexpected as it was sudden, had in fact been a deliverance for this patient suffering from an incurable and painful disease!

Then, without wasting any time, they were photographed before undressing to join a shower room as a group. As soon as the doors were closed, the assassin doctors opened some valves, not for water but for gas; carbon monoxide gradually replaced their vital air and caused the hopeless people to slowly suffocate. For endless minutes, some screamed in terror while others banged their fists on the doors in an ultimate gasp of agony.

After a few hours, a deadly silence fell over these killing "showers."

After having ventilated the premises, the *Brenners* or burners piled the corpses on carts – not without forgetting first to pull out their gold teeth – and they transported them to the crematorium ovens adjacent to the prison, making any evidence of their assassination disappear forever in smoke.

Little by little we discovered with bewilderment all the other horrors of war that our detention had concealed during our years of isolation. We remained immobile, sitting in the courtyard in front of this infamous building, paralyzed and mute. It was hard to drive away from our thoughts the terrified and pleading looks of these thousands of ghosts who now inexorably haunted this cursed place.

At the end of the afternoon, reinvigorated by a well-deserved nap, we boarded Russian military trucks which had meanwhile arrived in the prison yard. We found ourselves crammed with about forty others in the back of one of the crowded open-air trucks, but we were glad to finally be off our feet. Our morale increased with the passing kilometers that gradually brought us closer to our return home.

The trucks headed west. We drove through a scenery of incredible desolation, testament to the fierce fighting of the previous months. Lines of grieving inhabitants who had escaped the bombardments and recent attacks followed one another on these roads strewn with gaping shell holes. They carried all their precious but most often very modest possessions on carts, wheelbarrows, or bicycles, some dragging their feet with just a suitcase in hand.

After a few hours we arrived in Magdeburg. A spectacular field of ruins lay before us as far as the eye could see. Only specters of dwellings and buildings remained of this once vibrant city, surrounded by mountains of rubble and debris of all kinds. Fragments of cannons, gutted tanks, and butchered military vehicles littered the streets, covered with thick dust, ashes, and stones, or even entire sections of crumbling concrete walls. Rare were the buildings that had escaped this fierce destruction, either by a miracle or by the precision of the Allied bombardments.

The Battle of Magdeburg, which had raged between American infantry divisions and German troops since early April, had resulted in the occupation of the city by Allied troops west of the Elbe River. Sometime later, the Russian forces had conquered the eastern part of the city where we were now heading.

The trucks stopped on abandoned land at the edge of town, and we disembarked one by one. Accompanied by Russian soldiers, we marched in rows of six towards the river. In the distance, we saw a cathedral which seemed to have been relatively untouched, except for some broken stained-glass windows, surrounded on all sides by shattered rubble. Then we walked past a destroyed train station; carcasses of trains were scattered randomly, and fragments of railway tracks contorted like a snakes' nest frozen in time.

A little further on, we passed the remnants of a factory, exhibiting the remains of Tiger I tanks that had not had the opportunity to leave their assembly line; they would never again circulate. We learned that this Krupp factory had fervently embraced the Nazi ideology and had taken advantage of exploiting tens of thousands of Poles, Russians, and prisoners of war as slaves. Nearby, another factory, where enslaved laborers had manufactured the Jumo 211A, an inverted-V twelve-cylinder engine for Junkers planes, had also been pulverized.

Suddenly, an explosion resounded! In a common reflex, we immediately threw ourselves to the ground. In the distance, a thick black smoke rose in foreboding volutes. As we got up, we learned that the Russian soldiers had blown up a gigantic gammadion, or Swastika, which sat atop a sports stadium. All the Nazi vestiges were being removed or destroyed one by one, trying to erase the atrocities of this interminable war as quickly as possible from the collective memory.

As I reached a crossroads, I observed placards posted on the walls with the inscription, "*Achtung! Plünderer werden mit dem Tode bestraft!*" Lucien explained to us that these notices had certainly discouraged many looters from robbing destroyed buildings by warning them that they would inevitably be punished with death!

Finally, we passed a roundabout which led to a large suspension bridge over the Elbe River. In its center, having avoided any damage during the last fierce battles, the former Imperial Chancellor of Germany, Otto von Bismarck, stood proudly, oblivious to the destruction of all the buildings around him. He stood there in all his stoutness – due to many excesses – planted upright in high boots, his uniform covered with a long open coat, wearing a *Pickelhaube* or spiked helmet, his stare shaded by bushy eyebrows, a thick mustache hugging a determined mouth, holding in his right hand a pair of gloves, and resting his other hand on the pommel of his saber.

Lucien pointed to the old Bismarck and anxiously reminded us, "When one thinks that this damned Bismarck had annexed Alsace and Lorraine after the war of 1870 following the capture of Napoleon III. Fortunately, France recovered them both for good after the '14-'18 war, otherwise I might have fought against you as a German citizen. It makes me shiver just thinking about it."

Then, he began to proudly sing a song his father often hummed:

> "You will not have Alsace and Lorraine
> And, in spite of you, we will remain French.
> You were able to Germanize the plain,
> But our heart, you'll never have it!"

We arrived in line in front of the bridge over the Elbe River. The sun was setting slowly and casting orange gleams on the surface of the river. Half-way on the bridge the silhouettes of two sentries stood out against the light, and we guessed they were Russian and American by their appearance.

Igor waved for us to cross the bridge in a line and then bid us adieu with "*Do svidaniya. Udachi Frantsuzi!*" while wishing us good luck.

In a stifling silence, at the end of this day, June 12, 1945, we walked slowly, as in a dream, towards the two sentries. As we passed the American soldier, chewing an unlit cigar at the corner of his mouth, he addressed us with "Welcome!" and a smile of bienvenue.

We continued our passage to the other side of the bridge, mechanically, like automatons. When we arrived at the end of the bridge, where French soldiers were waiting for us, we all heaved a huge sigh of relief.

Our comrades informed us that we would be back home within forty-eight hours, but we still couldn't believe it. After more than one thousand eight hundred days of separation, we could certainly endure two more days of waiting, though they would certainly feel interminable to us.

Accompanied by Allied soldiers, we settled in a large tent where we were served a good meal. We were so happy and finally felt free!

We were going to return to France, to our home, and see our own again! After having dinner and shaving, we took a long, warm, and very relaxing shower.

When we got out of the shower, French soldiers were waiting for us; they escorted us for a medical examination. A military doctor in a white coat proceeded with a quick check-up, one after the other. Curiously, I observed that for one of the cursory exams, the doctor was asking us to raise our arms to the sky.

"Do you see that, Alex? The doctor is still asking us to surrender," Jean snorted at me.

But suddenly, one of the released prisoners refused to raise his arms and tried to escape, pushing the doctor who fell to the ground. He was immediately overtaken with force by two French soldiers who were closely monitoring the medical examination. Surprised, I asked my neighbor, "What's going on? Why is he trying to run away? It's just a simple medical examination!"

He turned to me and replied, "This medical examination is in fact a clever way of recognizing the fake French prisoners of war who are in reality Waffen SS of French origin who fought alongside the Germans."

While the struggling prisoner, screaming like a madman, was forcibly taken away from our group, my neighbor continued, "The SS have the particularity of having their blood type tattooed under their left arm near the armpit. The doctor would have thus discovered that this soldier belonged to the Waffen SS and would have immediately warned the guards. Believe me, he is going to have a rough time and experience a *mauvais quart d'heure*, but he deserves it well. If you fly with the crows, you get shot with the crows. Betraying France and joining the SS torturers! It's immoral and without excuse."

That night, in evacuated Magdeburg, we slept in a comfortable bed, in a house that had been spared. I slept like a log, dreaming of my imminent return, and imagining my little six-year-old boy whom I no longer knew.

At dawn, this morning of June 13, 1945, we took a train to Valenciennes. When the train entered the station after several long hours, we got off on the station platform with a huge crowd of freed prisoners.

We were back in France.

Free!

A chaplain welcomed us on behalf of the Catholic Church. In the hall of the station, he recited a prayer, then said a few words of welcome and comfort, while reminding us of the memory of our fallen comrades. After a minute of silence and reflection, he said into the microphone, "The prisoners of the Morlaix and Saint-Pol-de-Léon region can come and see me."

I went and found another chaplain there, Father Egaret, whom I knew. He asked me my name and where I was from. Immediately, he exclaimed, "What a coincidence! Yesterday, I was at François Pouliquen's in Morlaix where I had lunch with your wife and your son Jean-Pierre! I promised them you would be back home very soon. I will be able to keep my promise as you will get to hold them in your arms in the days to come."

At once, I started to cry of joy.

That evening he sent me and another prisoner from Brest to dine in town at Doctor Rouault's; his wife and his three young children joined us. We arrived in front of an opulent but charming house with a wooden facade, relatively narrow with several floors, adorned with multiple windows and radiant stained glass. Our host described it to us as a medieval Scaldian house typical of the Scheldt basin. Doctor Rouault took us upstairs where he introduced us to his wife, Honorine, an elegant woman with a severe allure, a heavy bun of black hair and a long dark purple dress adding to her austerity. She was surrounded by three young children, a boy and two twin girls, who suddenly brought Frida of Schivelbein back to the surface of my memory.

After introducing ourselves and thanking them warmly for their invitation to dinner, we sat down around a table covered with a beautiful, freshly ironed white tablecloth. The overflow of silver cutlery and crystal glasses was awe-inspiring and a bit confusing after the imposed rigors of our years in captivity. Before starting the meal, the doctor collected himself, welcomed us again to their comfortable abode, and then recited a prayer with his hands clasped, like his wife and children, "Bless us Lord, bless this meal, those who prepared it, and provide bread for those who have none, Amen."

Honorine offered us an aperitif to toast to victory. She had uncorked a bottle of Clacquesin which had escaped the Germans. We gladly accepted this dark alcohol made from various spices and Norwegian pine extracts. The doctor noticed my astonishment when I took the first sip of this medicine-tasting aperitif. He asked his wife to bring slices of lemons, which significantly helped ameliorate the drink.

After a nicely hot vegetable velouté, Honorine brought to the dining room table a dish surrounded by slices of toasted bread, and told us with gratitude, "In your honor, *Messieurs*, to thank you for your sacrifices to save France, I have prepared a novelty from Valenciennes that we recently discovered in a local restaurant. Do you know the Lucullus tongue?"

"I have to confess, *Madame*, that I have never heard of this Lucullus, but it looks really good," I replied politely.

"Come on, call me Honorine, please," the doctor's wife said graciously to me. "I too have to admit that I cheated a bit because it is impossible to find all the ingredients nowadays."

"I'm sure it will be a treat anyway. It looks delicious to me," my comrade added. He was indeed as hungry as I was and would have devoured any kind of food without any distinction or prejudice.

"I simmered this Lucullus of Valenciennes by cooking a smoked beef tongue in court bouillon, then I cut this piece of meat like ham, into very thin slices. For lack of foie gras, I intercalated instead layers of liver pâté mixed with eggs and spices in between the tongue slices," Honorine explained. She was now cutting marbled slices of the dish to eat with the toasts.

We succumbed to the Lucullus which was succulent to perfection. In short, it was a delicacy, and our taste buds were now eager to know the rest of the feast.

Next to our glasses, we had a small cup that seemed to contain water with slices of lemons. Our hosts confirmed that it was indeed lemon water, but they forgot to explain to us that they had provided these finger bowls to rinse our dirty fingers after eating the appetizer. Unfortunately, my comrade and I did not have the slightest idea of their intention, so after the Lucullus we drank this citrus infusion in one go! Only the stifled giggle of the children and the embarrassed smile of our hosts could have let us suspect our awkwardness, but we only understood it much later.

Then, a *coq au vin* topped off the dinner, accompanied by steamed potatoes worthy of Gérard's tuberous treasure at the Ritz. Doctor Rouault then opened a bottle of St-Émilion grand cru 1929 and praised its freshness and elegance, as well as its bouquet and velvety texture. We drank this red wine with the poultry while wondering what made this wine so extraordinary. One must say though that we had not had any serious enological references for ages. For dessert, Honorine surprised us with a delicious, caramelized apple pie and a very black coffee with a strong aroma that contrasted radically from our past daily tasteless *jus*.

During the meal, we made a few allusions to our prison life in Pomerania. We recounted the most picturesque events, such as the escape of Gus, the female cyclist, the panties of Frida, the witch, or our attacks with cockroaches in the butcher's shop, and our spectacular victory in our international soccer match. However, we kept quiet the many sordid and morbid stories, mainly out of respect for the children. In return, the doctor quickly explained the progress of the operations in the Pacific War, which were still ongoing. The Allies, especially the American troops, had faced the Empire of Japan in a merciless warfare for almost four years. He told us that recently the Americans had stormed the Japanese island of Iwo Jima and had emerged victorious after a fight to the death. More than twenty thousand Japanese soldiers had perished, leaving only a handful of survivors, who despite themselves had not been able to commit suicide by *seppuku*. He then showed us the front page of a newspaper with an iconic photograph of some Marines hoisting the American flag on Mount Suribachi on the island of Iwo Jima.

Late in the evening, we took leave of our hosts, thanking them warmly for this very pleasant moment spent in their company. Before letting us leave, Honorine gave us a small packet of candies and said, "These are *sottises* of Valenciennes, mint candies decorated with a ribbon of red sugar. In my opinion, they have nothing to be ashamed of in comparison to the *bêtises* of Cambrai." Then looking at me, she added, "I'm sure your little boy will enjoy these *sottises*. Best wishes to you both as you return to your families. God bless you!"

The next morning, we boarded a train to Rennes. Our impatience was growing with the kilometers that passed outside the windows. The monotonous purring of the train helped us doze a little. We stopped in a plethora of successive train stations where crowds of families and friends were eagerly awaiting the return of the prisoners of war. Those homecomings were most moving, the released prisoners seeing their wives, children, parents, or friends again for the first time in years. But many were those who unfortunately discovered that their fiancées had not waited for them and had tied the knot with someone else, or that a relative or a close friend had passed away before their return. Some found themselves alone, helpless on a deserted platform.

Would Gabrielle and Jean-Pierre be there? Or would I have some bad surprise?

This ultimate wait was becoming so agonizing.

In the middle of the night, the train entered the station in Rennes. I was back in Brittany, gradually approaching our house. This June 15, 1945, as the day rose on the horizon over a countryside shrouded in morning fog, I began to count down the hours.

Six long years had been stolen from me, five as prisoner of war.

Nothing would make up for this lost time, but at least I had the chance to come back safe and sound to my family.

The landscapes were becoming more and more familiar. I recognized in passing some typical church spires and picturesque granite Parish closes. The cars emptied progressively as we reached the different train stations. I embraced my comrades who arrived at their destinations, swearing that these moments lived together would remain forever in my memory and that they could always count on me.

We had become lifelong friends, brothers united in blood and in captivity.

Villages and fields succeeded to green pastures where herds of cows watched, impassive, this convoy pass by, returning from Hell. Heavy horses were resting, lying down on the edge of ridges bordered by chestnut trees, waiting for another day of hard work.

I looked at my watch. In a few minutes it would be nine in the morning and the train would finally stop at Landivisiau station. Minutes then seconds seemed to slow down, the cogs of space-time slowly seizing up.

Time froze inexorably.

Suddenly, a shrill whistle pulled me out of my reverie and with a screeching brake, a platform appeared. A modest crowd had gathered on the platform in front of the station, some waving small French flags. I saw the mayor with his tricolor scarf.

Then I saw them.

Gabrielle was there, in a navy-blue dress with a white collar, holding the hand of a little boy in beige shorts, wearing a sky-blue linen shirt and white sandals. My mother and my in-laws had come too, all now looking for the faces pressed against the windows of the compartments.

The train stopped. Loaded with my bag, I got off the train. My legs were shaking as I stepped onto the platform. I saw her come forward with Jean-Pierre. I dropped my bag on the ground and ran towards them, ignoring the other people who recognized and greeted me.

I looked into Gabrielle's azure eyes that sparkled with endless joy and love. I took her in my arms and kissed her tenderly. Our lips rediscovered one another as during our very first kiss. I felt her heart pounding wildly against mine. I had imagined and replayed this scene so many times in my mind and in my dreams, day after day.

Was I still dreaming?

But suddenly I felt a small hand pulling mine very gently.

Jean-Pierre was looking at me with a big smile that would have melted the eternal snow of Kilimanjaro. I turned to him, that little boy I hadn't known for five interminable years.

I lifted him into my arms and smiled fondly back at him.

He looked at me intently with his deep blue eyes and said, "*Bonjour, Papa*. I was waiting for you. I love you very much!"

After six years, including one of war and five of captivity, what a beautiful day!

# Chapter 18

## *Epilogue*

I slowly open the white shutters in the bedroom, letting in the soft morning light. Outside, nature is still asleep while the sun gradually emerges beyond the hills. I dress simply and go down to the kitchen where I find my wife who has already started to prepare breakfast. While enjoying buttery croissants and a bowl of *café au lait*, I listen to the latest news. They are not reassuring and, as always, a wind of fear and panic has invaded the media and keeps the population on the alert.

After washing up, I put on pants and a short-sleeved shirt, then I go out through the kitchen door into the garden. I sit on a wooden bench to watch the birds flutter around the seed-filled feeders that I have hung at the back of the garden. A family of rosefinches – their heads, throats, and breasts of a bright red – follow one another in an aerial ballet to come in turn to peck their meal. From time to time, other finches or orioles with lemon-yellow feathers join this multicolored whirlwind.

All of a sudden, a pair of majestic royal blue birds land on the edge of one of the birdbaths and one of them begins its morning grooming. I close my eyes and listen to these disparate but harmonious songs which little by little soothe me, announcing a sunny and serene day.

I gaze at the flaming red bougainvilleas, the lemon trees dotted with ripe bright yellow fruits, and the flowering olive trees. Cradled by a choir of windchimes and the monotonous rustle of palm tree leaves swaying with the warm easterly winds, I reflect on these times filled with unforeseen events and worry. The whirring of the miniature wings of a hummingbird with an iridescent breast, curious about my presence and attracted by the bright colors of my shirt, brings me back to reality. I then go home and climb up to the mezzanine to settle at my desk.

Outside, the daily noises slowly awaken. Neighbors walk down the street with their children, accompanied in the distance by the dull hum of vehicles circulating tirelessly.

A new day begins.

Meanwhile in the morning, as I search for documents in one of the cupboards crowded with bric-a-brac, various souvenirs, old schoolbooks, or other publications, I open and rummage through a cardboard box. There I find, under yellowed magazines, a folder that I had forgotten or probably didn't know existed.

Intrigued, I impatiently open the folder and pull out a jumble of black and white photos, an official beige card skillfully written in ink, shiny medals, and a few yellowed pages. In one of these photographs, a group of young people pose in two rows, in soccer player uniforms in front of a goal. In another one, sad and tired soldiers pose without enthusiasm in front of an austere stone wall.

The hourglass of years has continued to trickle, day after day, inexorably ...

Life has followed its twists and turns, bringing joys and sorrows, births and deaths, love and hate.

I stay immobile, watching this slice of elapsed life, with those actors who have either aged or passed away. I begin to browse through the few pages that have yellowed in the darkness of the years too quickly passed. The story is captivating and moving. It puts the recent times in perspective. How can I feel sorry for myself now? How could I forget these long years of absence, of sacrifice, of pain?

A life turned upside down by the madness of conquest and supremacy of a megalomaniac man, of a blind and complacent people.

A life torn apart by a merciless war, with its atrocities, its anonymous deaths forgotten on graves lined up for posterity and on monuments today ignored.

A life interrupted for six long years.

Prisoner in the depths of Pomerania.

A life held up, a heartbreaking separation, a terrifying isolation, but a trusting and ever-growing love!

I now recognize in these photographs this young man who looks like me and stares at me.

My father was twenty-nine when World War II started and thirty-five when he returned from captivity.

A long – a very long – confinement against his will.

My own confinement began a short while ago in California because of the pandemic caused by a virus crowned Covid-19.

My parents had a busy and fulfilling life and, after the war, the family grew over the years – four boys and two girls. My father returned to the carpentry shop with his brother and my mother raised her six children, still in the same town. The children grew up and followed their destiny, all staying in Brittany. I was the exception, setting sail and, after many stopovers, finally casting anchor in California. Children in turn became parents and parents became grandparents.

Life went on, inescapably.

The atrocities of the war and this interminable separation were put away in a closet.

A page of their lives that they tried to forget, memories that they could not erase.

How many sacrifices, tears, sufferings! How could we complain today about our confinement, relatively comfortable, with our families, where the invisible enemy can be fought by simple measures?

How could we not unite and fight against this insidious virus on a planetary scale?

Wars destroy peoples, countries, and families, while this infectious scourge could destroy all life on earth. The defense of individual freedom cannot be done without first considering a global defense. Military and pathogenic assaults require unison for the survival of all. The selfishness of some can have dramatic consequences, endangering an exponential number of people.

One has to learn the lessons of the past.

May the sacrifices of previous generations to save an ideal, a threatened freedom, without worrying about their own well-being, at least not be in vain. Today we owe it to ourselves to follow their example and fight, together, against the world plagues without worrying about our origin and daily comfort.

In this way, we will be able to keep intact the memory of days gone by and proudly pass on a code of honor, integrity, and hope to future generations.

# Alexandre

Sergeant Alexandre Rolland (1910-1995)

*6th Engineer Regiment, 21st Division*